GRAFFITI MY SOUL

Niven Govinden was born in Sussex in 1973 and was educated at Goldsmiths. He used to work in the music industry until pampering pop-star egos lost its allure, and he now writes full time. He is the author of one previous novel, *We Are The New Romantics*.

Visit Niven's myspace page at: www.myspace.com/graffitimysoul

GRAFFITI MY SOUL

Niven Govinden

CANONGATE
Edinburgh · London · New York · Melbourne

First published in Great Britain in 2006 by
Canongate Books Ltd, 14 High Street,
Edinburgh EH1 1TE

This paperback edition first published in 2008 by Canongate Books

1

Copyright © Niven Govinden, 2006

The moral right of the author has been asserted

British Library Cataloguing-in-Publication Data
A catalogue record for this book is available on
request from the British Library

ISBN 978 1 84767 097 7

Typeset by Palimpsest Book Production Ltd,
Grangemouth, Stirlingshire

Printed and bound in Great Britain by Clays Ltd, St Ives plc

www.canongate.net

Part 1

I

My problem is that I can't see myself before the funeral. Really, nothing. Moon's the one who's dead, and I can see her clearly. I thought it was supposed to be the other way round. I've seen those TV shows where a boyfriend or girlfriend kicks it. The one that's left behind bawling alone in their room. How they can't remember their loved one's face and all the rest of it. Even though they've only been cold for about a day. Then they start dragging the pictures out in desperation, or begin to construct their head out of clay. That ain't my style. I was never one for marking every moment with a snap. Never needed to. Moon's got the sort of face that's hard to forget. She's not the one I'm worried about. It's my head that needs moulding.

I know how I looked on the morning of the funeral. Black suit from M&S that isn't one of the old-fashioned ones. Taken-up hems on the trousers, which Mum had stayed up past midnight to do, after she'd finished her paperwork. Two-button jacket that fitted just right across my shoulders. Made me look older than fifteen. Even in that tight moment when I was certain I was feeling nothing, I knew that I was carrying off that suit. I looked tall, and lean, and sharp. If you had been walking down the street that morning, and saw me in that suit, you would have thought I was on my way to a graduation or something. There'd be no chatting about a kid who's off to bury the girl he's just helped to put away.

Moon would have died if she'd seen me in that suit. Bad joke, but I'm too young to be owning this stuff. I should be wearing it when I'm, like, eighteen. I can see it now. A Friday night, me in that suit, her winched out of her jeans and into one of those dresses from Karen Millen that cost too much. We'd go into Kingston, where they'd let us into Oceana without a word. Drinking cocktails and dancing stupid to garage. We could have killed it. Again, bad joke. That's the only thing I seem to be good at right now, cracking the bad ones. (Not even able to crack one off.) Alone in my bedroom. All dressed up and no Moon to see it.

This is the morning after the funeral. I put the suit on again once Mum has left for work. She takes her time, pretending to forget something in the bathroom so that she can pace past my door three or four times. Listening out for signs of life or death. Before Moon started to change things were easy enough and there was none of this pacing. I know Mum's thinking about me, fretting over how things have ended up the way they have, but I haven't got time to worry about her on top of everything else. I just don't.

I can't get myself to look how I looked yesterday. Skin paler, bags under the eyes blacker. Jacket doesn't sit so smart. Pre-pressed trouser seams flap at my bare feet needlessly. Same suit, different look. I don't understand it. But then I think that maybe it's because I'm indoors that I don't feel right.

When I walked to the church yesterday – there was no way I was sharing a car with Moon's parents and Gwyn – it was the first really bright strong day of spring, and the sun was doing its I'm-back-and-bad dance. I took the back roads so that I could walk past the ropey on the way. The original ropey that's in the middle of the wood, not the new one by the church that the younger kids use. It had only rained lightly during the night, so the ground was good to firm. If you looked close enough, because you couldn't catch them from a distance, bare branches were just starting to peep pea-pod green from their tips. Birds were there, but distant, I didn't pay much attention. It was mainly me on that walk, crunching dead wood underfoot, the sun, and the trees with their woosh woosh woosh. Taking my time, because I knew they'd have to wait for me.

Everything in that moment felt good. The sun was teasing the top of my head and I felt that some kind of *thing* was finally going to let itself out. That maybe I'd get through this. I didn't quite

4

manage the sigh, but the feeling that it was coming got me through the day. Even Moon wouldn't have taken the piss out of the effort I was making. I didn't let her down. I delivered.

And I don't use these words lightly. When she was around, we never said these things about each other. Why would we? Why would we even notice them? There's plenty of time to learn these things later. We're fifteen. This life's supposed to be infinite.

So now I'm walking down the street in the suit again. T-shirt instead of a shirt, the first hat I can find, and trainers. It's not quite as yesterday, but it's the best I can manage. Not that it matters particularly; it's a loose experiment. The light's no good down our road. Too many semis on top of each other. It's no wonder I can't get over anything in an environment like this. This place is no Mecca for healing. No comfort to be had in pebble-dashing and crazy paving.

As I turn the corner into Elm Drive, then left into Oakdene, and then into Broadhurst, where the wood lies at its very bottom, I drop the shuffling, and my steps become firmer and faster. By the time I've passed Jason's house – number 32 – I'm breaking into a run. The sun is nowhere near coming out. Everything is flat and grey. Trees look beyond growth. I can't help seeing death in everything. I'm not special in this suit. I look like an idiot who's very much under eighteen, and unsure of himself. A little boy who needs someone to hold his hand. How was it that everyone took me seriously yesterday – looking like this?

Broadhurst is used as a rat-run during rush hour. If you drive all the way down the hill you can cut past the one-way into town, but at this time of the morning it can be deathly quiet. Another bad joke, and an inaccurate one. Everything about Moon's going has taught me that there's nothing quiet about death. Kicking and screaming to the last. Pressing against my ears until all other sounds are shut out. Singularly louder than anything I've ever heard.

There's a car coming now, can't quite make out what, and it slows on my side. Someone with a blocked nose shouting from the window as I carry on running towards the wood. Maybe I was careering into the road, it has been known to happen. I'm moving forward, that's all I know.

'Hey! Hey! Where are you going? Hey!'

52, 54, 56, 58, 60, 62, 64, 66, 68, 70. The road ends at 284. Sun now decides to make an entrance. Coming out from the clouds in full effect, blinding from the right. It's handy. I don't make eye contact with the car. Instead keep running, keep focusing on the numbers. You hear about all kinds of nutters these days, accosting kids.

'Come back! I just want to know where you're going!'

The car isn't leaving. I should have brought my bike. They wouldn't have seen me for dust then.

'I don't want an argument,' calls the blocked nose again, loud enough so all of Broadhurst can hear how odd they are.

I think about heading back to Jason's house. He smoked his way back to reality after his sister was in a hit and run. Twenty blunts a day at the worst point. Once the front door opens and he comes staggering out, I wouldn't be bothered then. But the wood appears as the street dips into the hill, and the whoosh whoosh hits the back of my ears. A final incentive. I pick up a gear, and break into an all-out sprint. I'm the fastest at school. 100, 200 or 400m, take your pick. There's not one fucker who can touch me. Lynford Paki they call me when I'm on one. 132, 136, 144. I reckon I'm at touchdown in about thirty seconds. Ain't no one going to be bothering me then.

'Veerapen! Veerapen, stop! Stop, will you?'

It's not the name that registers, but the voice. Mum. It's enough to make me stop dead in my tracks. Maybe I am losing it, if I can't even recognise when my own mum is speaking to me. I turn at last and realise. She's in her silver Astra and nurse's uniform. Breaking the rules and wearing her hair down because she got the curls straightened for the funeral and is making the most of it. Fucking roving district nurses. Always on the snoop. She gives me the Florence Nightingale face. Arms are back on the wheel in a flash, fresh from brushing away tears. She thinks that I didn't see them.

'I thought you were sleeping,' she calls, because although I've stopped running, I won't go near the car.

'I heard you crying,' she says, when that doesn't get a response. As if blabbing about my crying to the whole street is going to get me to open up. Aren't nurses supposed to keep things confidential, like priests?

'I'm going for a walk,' I say, 'to the rope . . . to the wood.' Still hopping left to right because I don't want to stop moving – if I do, you can probably tell that I'm shaking.

It's freaking me out to see her so upset, and trying to hide it so badly. Maybe it's easier to see once you're out of the house. My head still feels muddled but the fresh air definitely seems to be doing something. That I'm even noticing it is a start.

'Why don't you come back with me, eh? I bet you haven't had any breakfast.'

'Not hungry,' I say.

We both look at our watches and see it's close to midday anyway.

'OK,' she says slowly, taking a breath, the way I've seen her do on difficult home visits, when some old codger refuses to have his bag changed. 'Why are you wearing your suit, sweetheart? You'll get it filthy if you walk through the wood again.'

There had been no mention of my muddied hems yesterday, when I'd arrived at the church, an hour later than I should've. I think she was just relieved that I'd showed up.

'Got no other clothes. You can't be bothered to do any washing. Too busy larging it with your new boyfriend.'

She pretends to ignore that, even though I can see her eyebrows arching back and forth. It's the first time I've opened my mouth on that particular subject so harshly. I'm usually much more easy going. Moon being buried six feet deep has given everyone some extra time.

'It's going to rain in a minute. Let me give you a lift home.'

'I'm walking,' I repeat, 'to the wood.'

'Sweetheart,' she says again, holding her hand out, fluttering her fingers like I'm a little bird that might swoop for some bread. She's

7

spent so much time with pensioners, she's pretty much taken to speaking with me as she does them; cajoling one minute, brisk and no-nonsense the next. It makes you wonder whether she means any of it, if she's simply on autopilot.

'I just don't think it's a good idea for you to go running off on your own at the moment . . .'

But I'm off before she has the chance to say anything else.

The wood smells better than it did yesterday. Damp, soft. Good enough to bury myself. Even as I slow the run into a walk, I can still hear Mum shouting after me.

'Veerapen, I'm not nagging, love. I'm worried about you! Come back! At least take my hat off. What are you doing wearing my hat?'

2

There's no point in people asking me a barrel-load of questions at the moment, not when I'm barely capable of remembering my own name. I'm upset.

But until a month ago I was the captain of the school Challenge team. Mum calls me the brainiac when she remembers. Usually when she's cooking dinner with some quiz TV on in the background, and I'm getting all the answers right.

Challenge is a lame version of University Challenge that the council set up. It's designed for kids, meaning that they're obliged to drop in the odd question about Fiddy Cent in between posers about the lunar landscape and the name of a combustible metal that appears on the Periodic Table as Mg.

American high schools have these quiz decathlons that are way more glamorous. They have their own unique branding and their special dedicated coaches and some big-time prizes. You can actually go to a better university just by winning one of those things.

In our lame-ass equivalent no one is impressed by intellectual triumph over adversity. You can come from a less modest background and wipe the floor with one of the better schools; you can whip their ass and be applauded, but under no circumstances can you let it go to your head. That would be way too American for anyone.

I won't lie and say that I don't like it, because I do. I'm into it. But I won't show any more enthusiasm than that. No one wants to listen to a bunch of geeks congratulating each other. It's unattractive. And I'm not a science geek, or any other kind of geek. Just clever. Can't do anything about it. And Challenge gets you out of school one afternoon every three weeks, as the team gets to bus it into various Surrey shit-holes to take part in the regional heats. Combined with the odd days I have to take off for my running events, I'm virtually a part-timer at that place.

So I can understand why it's my brain that goes first. It's obvious. This is what I mean when I say that I can't see myself. Moon's death has turned me into some kind of spastic overnight. Maybe I should start calling myself Dr Mental or something. Or whatever is the Anglo Indian Yid flid equivalent.

I'm a mess. Take music, for example. Not that I'm particularly interested in music right now, but nonetheless . . . Maybe a month ago, if you'd have brought up Jay Z and tried comparing the Black Album with Dangermouse's Grey Album, I probably would have taken you out. Offered a commentary of such length you could've transcribed it into an essay and published the fucker. (I'm not showing off here, I just know a lot about hip hop. Everyone knows it, like they know about the running, Moon, and everything else.) On mornings like this, ask about Jay Z, and I'll say Jay who? I couldn't give a shit about this rhyme or that. All I want is my Moony Suzuki back.

3

I'm walking to the furthest edge of the wood. A hop and a skip and you're on the bypass. Every car that drives past feels like it's going to mow you down. Each whoosh like a mini-hurricane. My flares flap like bunting. I find myself heading to our spot. Dr Mental autopilot again. Jason is already there, burning some stuff, and bashing the shit out of his phone. Doesn't mention the hat. Neither of us says anything.

4

We're in Tesco with Mum after school. This is at the start of the year, when things made a bit more sense.

No one goes shopping with his or her mum after school anymore, not unless they're sad or God Squad. We're tagging along, because Tesco means a lift into town, and the buses round here are wack. Moon wants to get the new NERD album, and I need some trainer laces. Not that it really matters what's on our shopping list. An hour or two in the mall is better than a kick in the teeth on a Monday afternoon. Way better.

The downside is that we have to help Mum push the trolley around Tesco, but that only takes half an hour, so no biggie. She's not one of those clingy women you see out with their kids. Mum likes me to help out, pull my weight. If we're lucky, we can just about scoot around the aisles without anyone from school seeing us. Mum's cool and every-thing, but I don't want people thinking I'm from one of those 'multicultural' families that has a hundred relatives and needs to do everything together. Just the thought of that kind of set-up is excruciating.

We end up riding the lifts, pissing about like a couple of ten-year-olds. They're see-through and small, like coffins, running at two miles an hour, but still manage to get us excited. Mum looks disappointed when we meet her outside Tesco empty-handed. She likes her routine, and keeps Wednesdays for the supermarket run, but pushed it forward because we were making such a big deal of hitting the mall to get our stuff.

'That CD's not out yet. I got the dates wrong,' Moon goes.

Mum nods like she doesn't believe a word, but doesn't ask me about my laces, in case I give an even more useless lie than Moon.

She's more than made up for our lack of purchases though, with enough House of Fraser bags to fill two cars.

'From the sales, OK?' she goes, before I can get a word in.

People love shopping in this town. You never see anyone on the high street or leaving the mall without a carrier bag. I'm not as fussed. As long as I get some new CDs every couple of weeks (the ones that I can't download for free that is), and a new hoodie or a pair of trainers once in a while, I'm happy. Can think of several hundred things that are more important than money and the things that it can buy you. Don't understand everyone's preoccupation with it.

I don't lay any of this on Mum, though. I'm not a name-and-blame person. She works hard for the things she shops for. Deserves to buy what she wants. One of the benefits of no longer having Dad around is that Mum doesn't have to hide her shopping in the garage, eking everything out a couple of days at a time. It almost makes up for the fact that he was such a bastard.

In Tesco, Jason is stacking shelves in the Tastes of Italy aisle, which makes Moon's day. She's had the hots for him since last Tuesday, when he smacked Dan Pearson one for saying that Lizzie Jennings is a fat twat. Every girl in that classroom was in his thrall after that. Even I have to admit, there was a certain grace about my mate Jase as he cut Pearson's nose open. The way the blood hit the floor in one thick spurt, like the cold tap on max, was pure poetry.

He sees us first from behind his boxes of imported pasta.

We break into a round of hugs. Hugging is the new thing — everyone has to hug everyone else. Hello mate, hello geezer, hello darlin'. It's bollocks, but I have to do it too, whenever I'm with any of that crowd. With Moon it's a given, and if I'm not showing willing, she gives me a prod, and if that doesn't work, a punch. Funny, isn't it, I can't remember the last time I gave my mum a peck on the cheek, and here I am in aisle 33, passing the love like a fuckwit. At school it's worse, half the people you hug in the canteen you fucking hate. Girls hugging girls. Boys hugging boys. No one believes you when you tell them how tough it is to be a teenager.

'What you two doing here? Come to see how I line up the vermicelli next to the rigatoni?'

'Always wanted to know how they do that.'

'Heard it was a new Olympic sport.'

'Mentalists. If I wasn't working, I'd be having a cheeky spliff before dinner, not poncing about here.'

This one has smoking on the brain. He probably still hasn't registered that I never touch the stuff. Don't see the point. Jason is madder than the rest of us, but to most people at school, he'll always be known as the guy whose sister was killed in that hit and run. There's no getting away from it.

Aside from me and Moony Suzuki. We're not into labels and all that shit. At least that's what we're currently telling ourselves.

Moon giggles at the first mention of nutters, and its accompanying floorful of dropped Ts. She's become like that whenever she's around Jason.

'We've been hanging round the mall,' I say, 'looking for evidence.' By which I mean, hoping to find a couple of God-Squadders out with their embarrassing parents. Digging for dirt. Everyone is looking to have one up on someone at that school.

'Come round later, if you're knocking off any time soon,' I

continue, knowing that Moon will have to owe me one if he does turn up.

'Uh huh, uh huh,' he goes, kinda interested, kinda not, his eye on the pasta he's stacking. They drum it hard into those boys, these supermarket managers; Jason takes his job very seriously. He can't rest until all the boxes are lined dead straight.

'TV and shit, easy for a Monday. They're showing *Barbershop* on Sky, around eight, I think,' she says, knowing it.

'Cool,' he says, 'I'm there.'

Whilst Mum is at the checkout, Moon drags me back across the mall to the kiosk where they turn a blind eye, buys twenty Benson, and a packet of king-size R. She's got some gear in a tin under the carpet tiles in her wardrobe and she's planning on bringing it over.

'Gotta make our guest feel at home,' she goes later, when it makes an appearance in my room. She's always so sure about everything. Knows that he's going to show. And who would turn Moon down? She's not popular but she's perfect. Works out. Isn't a shortie. Long layered mud-coloured hair, which she swishes to her advantage. Clear skin that's never seen a spot. This open face that says to potential suitors, mould me, whilst her brain says the opposite. A great rack. Half the school is after her.

She's wearing her new Nike-girl hoodie, baby pink to match her top braces, with only her push-up bra underneath. It's an outfit designed for easy access. Luckily I haven't seen *Barbershop*, so I'll be able to keep my eyes on the screen no problem once she and Jason get down to business. Almost.

He turns up on the dot, wearing one of the Triple 5 Soul shirts with only three buttons. They don't even make it past the titles. Someone should make me a saint, the crazy shit I have to put up with.

5

The price for not looking whilst Moon is getting touched up is three Benson and a whole tube of Pringles. Both banned substances on my new diet sheet, one stuck on the fridge door, the other above my bed. Multiple fags may sound excessive for a near non-smoker, but *Barbershop* is a long film. My chest feels it in the morning. There may as well be two Sumos sitting on top of me. At training, I'm coughing up all kinds of shit. Casey isn't impressed.

'Cigarettes are a one-way ticket to an early grave,' he goes, as I hack my way around the track.

He looks at the state of me and prescribes a 1200m warm-up, followed by a series of 200m sprints, because I was choosy about telling him who I was smoking with.

'Don't be doing with the bad crowds, V-pen. They aren't with you when you're on the track. I'm only interested in one winner, V-pen. The finishing line is only concerned with one winner, V-pen.'

He's been calling me V-pen ever since I started with him last autumn. Nothing I can do about it.

I trained with the Harriers all through primary school, up until the end of the last summer holidays, when we had a disagreement about me training there after hours. They didn't like it that when the place was shut, I'd bring Moon, Jase, a couple of others, and a few bottles of sauce. Fences around the place are babyishly short. Even Moon in a skirt finds it an easy proposition. I admit I was mullered on my alcopops by the time we left there, usually no earlier than ten-thirty, but technically I had still been running. I told Mum that I'd reached the top age limit and had to look for training elsewhere. She was too busy to follow it through, so took my word for it.

Casey had been a regional Harriers trainer, one of the local hot shots, but then he disappeared for a while, after some boy started blabbing about being touched up. Bad news for the Surrey Harriers. They were licked at most of their meetings after that. They had replacements obviously, but no one who employed the same technique. The new guys were all about encouragement and nurturing. They worried about self-esteem and hurt feelings. Casey's the other way. He doesn't believe in hand-holding. More an all-out bastard who demands you hand over your life. Expects total dedication, and very rarely gives his charges a second chance. Show your fallibility and you're out of there. The centre, in their panic, forgot all about this, and the sagging silver shelf that he had helped them to accumulate. They lost a good 'un. But fantastic for me. I hired him on the spot.

That makes it sound more glamorous than it actually was. We met in an out-of-the-way Starbucks in Walton, where we both begged each other like a pair of faggots. His begging was more hysterical and outdid mine. He's still the best trainer in the county. No one can touch him. You can't accuse me of not giving anyone a second chance.

Also, I know he's not interested in me. I did my homework. Twelve-year-olds are more his thing. I could whop it in his face and he wouldn't so much as flinch.

Obviously I didn't tell Mum about Casey, because the mere mention of his name would give her a stroke on the spot. The charges had been dropped, but the alleged incident at the Harriers had been splashed across all the local papers, and had even made an edition of *London Tonight*. Surrey's first paedo scandal. Past achievements aside, it made him our newest celebrity.

'Gimmie a break,' I say, when I'm near to passing out, after a fresh round of sprint hurdles, and he's getting all Saddam with the stopwatch.

'It was only three Benson, for fuck's sake. It's not like I was smoking crack or anything.'

We have to train on the public track in the park, because the Harriers won't let us anywhere near their precious facilities. Yes, there are two tracks in the same town. Welcome to Surrey, where you get double everything on a plate. At this time in the morning, six on the dot, it's perfect. The place becomes my own personal training space. I don't get psyched out, having to look at the other kids who may be better than I am. Out here, like this morning when there's only one man and his dog, and Mr Paedo PE, I'm all calm and focus.

Rep hurdles are a bastard to do. We call them hurdles, but they're mini-hurdles, more like steps. You could replace them with tyres or beer cans if you wanted to, the principle's the same. Any old object to jump over. Casey is being a tosser with the reps. Won't listen when I say I can't do them. I jump twenty of the steps, twenty seconds' rest, then jump another twenty, then another rest, then forty, and a rest of ten. I've done three of these circuits and feel worn out.

Casey doesn't look worried, or bothered. He's standing inside track, stopwatch dangling onto his chest like some medallion man, and idly glancing at the *Sun's* back pages.

'No slacking, V-pen!' he shouts every so often with a quick glance up.

This is a harder job for him than it looks, considering how quick the reps are. If I were one of those twelve-year-olds he liked so much, I'd probably fall for it. As it is, the way his eyes flick back and forth indicates that, for this morning at least, he feels as un-focused as me. Someone of Casey's calibre doesn't do laid-back, unless there's a lesson in it somewhere.

As I'm jumping, I wonder if his lack of attention has anything to do with his fear of being outed as the local child catcher. Most of the locals think that he left the area late last summer; totally unconnected to the mysterious fire which burnt his bungalow to the ground the day after the *Post* stupidly printed his address. Not even I know where he's living at the moment, but my guess is that it's still somewhere along Parkside. The dew on his car windscreen is never quite dry when he pulls up to meet me in the car park every morning.

I suppose I could find out if I wanted, get all *X Files* on him, but I never ask. Somehow I think it's his business.

I can understand how having your home unexpectedly going up in smoke can make you nervous. As far as he's concerned he doesn't show it, not to me, a kid, when he's shouting the orders on the track, swearing at me for fucking up the last 50m like I always do on a distance run, and getting all preachy during the cool-down on why I should stop eating so much junk. It's an act you can almost believe. But when I'm running, always when I'm running, when he thinks that I can't see him, I notice the way he looks over his shoulder nervously, all the time shouting at me that I'm a slow spazzy fuck-up.

Then again, it's just as likely to be a picture of an Under 21s Premiership player that's distracting him. They're anyone's at the first sign of flesh, these PPPs (Paedos in Public Positions).

Casey's kind of negligence is like a red rag to me. Sure, I could take it easy, especially now I'm warmed-up, but I'm not like that. It makes me want to kill the speed on those reps. I'm getting through them faster and faster, until the ten-second rest stop becomes this inconvenience I want exterminating.

At Harriers these days, they just teach you to run towards your goal, nothing more complicated. It's only since I've taken on Casey that I've been introduced to visualisation. Casey is a firm believer in seeing what lies at the finish line. Thinks it makes you a better runner.

I'm at the early stages here, so everything I picture is pretty obvious. In recent competitions, particularly the 100m, where any advantage on the opposition is welcome, I've used the image of a girl waiting at the finishing line; hot pants, baseball cap, bare tits, and holding a can of ice-cold Pepsi. It sounds cheesy, but she's won me two races. Depending on how the run is going, who the actual woman is can vary, from Carmen Electra, to Mrs Maude, the geriatric who runs the library. Also, this morning, I seem to be visualising the whole of Moon's left tit — the only one I managed to clock last night (Jason's mouth was pretty much clamped on the other).

On the longer runs, and also in training, I'm a lion, breaking the leash and roaring to victory, to devour my bareback girl. I know that there are faster cats that I could visualise, but it's the lion I like. Hair wild and rangy, something like mine (can't work out whether that's the Tamil gene, or the Jew gene). A fierce, fast, ferocious hunter, capable of giving any opponent a good mauling.

Casey calls a take-five, must have done, as he's now lying on his back with the paper. I'm still proving my point with the reps. I do that sometimes when I'm running, zone out. Really believe in my ability to kick ass.

'Come on, you young Turk,' he goes. I've told him before I'm Indian, not Turkish, but he never seems to remember.

'It's seven-thirty. Cigarette punishment is over. Say ten Hail Marys, and make a promise to Jesus, or whomever you pray to, that you'll never touch the weed again. Not if you're serious about your sport, that is.'

'I am serious, you fruit,' I laugh, as we head towards the car park.

He lets me call him a fruit from time to time, so long as I make it sound jokey and not malicious.

'Want a ride home?'

He asks me this at the end of every session. Today, his tone suggests that his heart is in it more than usual. Normally, he makes it sound desperate. This time, it looks like he means it, really needs to have me in the car.

'No thanks, Casey. I'm best walking.'

'OK, young Turk.' He turns quickly to the car, a solitary hand held behind. Useless at hiding his disappointment.

Casey's feelings fly over my head once we are off the track. I'm not stupid. I know you can only trust a fruit so far. By the time I reach the park gates, and Casey has got into his Clio, I've already forgotten about him.

6

Everyone calls me Veerapen. It's a family name, that's why I've got it. Veerapen Prendrapen. Some bright idea of Dad's. Had a heritage bee in his bonnet. Name your son after your grandfather, and then bugger off. How's that for motivation? Mum, who's from Bexhill, and very much not a Tamil, wanted to call me Ari, or Alexander. Thought they were classier. She lost the fight on the first name, possibly because Dad went to register my birth on his own, when he told her he was going out to get a nappy bin. As consolation, he went with her choice of middle name, Isaac. You get me? I'm a VIP. The only kosher Tamil in Surrey.

I don't have an abbreviation, a nickname. I could use the VIP, but would have to let on about the Isaac. I only let Casey call me V-pen because I feel sorry for him; because possibly I'm the only friend he's got. Anyone else is having a laugh if they think they can short-change Veerapen into an acceptable variant. I had all the V-is-for-Vera bullshit when I was at primary school, and Vera Duckworth, and V-for-vagina. I had to kick it all out of them. Veerswamy, Vondripen, Very Pen, Pig Pen, Cow Pen, Play Pen. Kind of enjoyed it. Really got a buzz when some kid thought they had a bright idea. Every booting got me higher up the ladder.

Vera will crop up every now and again, usually when some new tosser tries to become popular with the group by trying to pick on the Paki. But he gets the wrong Paki. I'm six foot, so you shouldn't mess with me unless you really think you can have a go. When you hear 'Oi, Vera' bellowed down the corridor, it's like a siren telling you to run for cover. Anyone who's in the way is just as likely to get thumped. I had to prove a point fairly similar to this about a week ago. You should have seen the tumbleweed once I'd clocked the guy who'd spat it. It was like some *Matrix* shit, the way I was flying about.

Luckily, Jase is around to back me. This guy's brought two mates with him, one of them being Dan Pearson. Bust lips, dented egos, chipped tooth, broken finger, and a kick in the head. My favourite moment is when Jase holds the guy down, and I stamp on his face. We are all fight, us kids.

7

Moon's in my room, testing me on questions that may come up on a forthcoming High School Challenge. Mum should be doing it, but has been called out because some old biddy has fallen down the toilet pan or something. I'm lucky to still be on the team after what happened to that guy's face, but the semis were coming up and they needed me. There wasn't enough of a talent pool in that school for a sub. I was let off with a warning. Two of the guys, who were caught putting the wrong boot in at the wrong time, were suspended. Pearson and Jase got the same deal as me: nag fucking nag. As usual, I kept it all from Mum.

'What's the capital of Australia?'

'Is that the hardest question you got? This is supposed to be the semis.'

'Stop stalling, idiot, you either know it or you don't. What's the capital of Australia?'

She's in a bad mood because she missed the fight, and also because there's been no text from Jase since he had a nibble on her nipple.

'Darwin.'

'Ha! Canberra.'

'Fuck! Like they're going to ask me that anyway.'

'Don't get all sniffy, thick boy. Remember how that African kid

20

from Hampton Wick didn't know the new name for Bombay? Lost them the comp. He looked like he was going to top himself when we saw them in the car park afterwards, remember?'

'We were pelting their bus with stones, Moon, that may explain his petrified look.'

'Possibly. But you obviously need a few more hours with an atlas, and less time cleaning up the school corridors.'

Her annoyance at not being called to watch the fight was, again, noted.

'Any chance I can come to training tomorrow?'

'At six a.m.? You're having a laugh, aren't you? Not even the rapists are out at that time of the morning.'

'Don't be stupid. I'll be making an entrance, well after six-thirty. Just thought you might need some encouragement. And I haven't seen you run for a while.'

'And this has nothing to do with you wanting to get up close and personal with the town kiddie fiddler?'

More to do with Jase being there. I'd mentioned he might be popping down earlier.

'It's been bugging me. I want to see what he looks like.'

'You've seen the papers, you know what he looks like.'

'Not in the flesh. I want to see how he acts around you and every-thing. I may spot something you don't . . . and I've got my new camera phone. Might be worth a couple of quid.'

'No one's interested in a picture of Casey.'

'I reckon your mum might be.'

'Moon, he's a good trainer. I don't need you baiting him.'

'Duh! Like I'm that thick. I'll take the dog out with me. He's never seen us together, right? What could be more natural – girl taking her dog out for a shit first-thing?'

I'm about to spam Moon with my mouse-mat for lowering the tone of the conversation, but Mum pops her head round, fresh from the pensioner crisis. It had been a fairly serious stroke, and nothing to do with the toilet. She has the polite face she reserves for visitors, even though it's only Moon, who doesn't count. Holds a smile that's attentive but slightly sad. Means that the guy who had the stroke probably died.

She holds a bag of Chinese.

'Dinner for three,' she says. 'Don't worry, Moon, I've just seen your mum. It's fine. How are the questions going?'

The whiff from the noodles gives me instant memory loss. We virtually bulldoze her to the plates downstairs and polish off the lot. I don't remember to ask Mum how she's doing.

8

'Shall I give her one?' asks Jase. 'Something's telling me she's up for it.'

We're having an impromptu rest from technology. Options are limited so we're taking refuge down the ropey. Mum's got the afternoon off and is pampering herself with smelly shit. His mum has agoraphobia brought on from his sister and the hit and run, and never leaves the house. It's cold but at least we can piss about without getting shouted at. I don't like busting lessons, what with me being on a short lease after the fight and all, but Jason's in a good mood and talks me into it.

'I've got an iPod, what more can they teach me about technology,' he goes, as we brazen it out of the gates. Praying that the cameras aren't switched on. It's all about the frontin'. (They usually switch them off during lesson-time to save money. It's common knowledge amongst the dealers.)

Jason has a fuzzy skinhead, like playdough that has gone black and started to leach out, and is lanky lanky lanky. You can get away with calling him lurch if you're a mate, otherwise expect a blow to the balls. Like I've said, I'm six foot, give or take, and he's already towering way over me. Makes you wonder why anyone would want to have a go – but they still want to try it. The Goliath principle, I presume. Everyone wants to tackle the monster.

He's a funny boy, is Jase, but what I like the most about him, aside from the fact that he's so dumb with his goofy jokes and shit, is that he has this energy that is mad unpredictable and comes out of nowhere. There's a charge that comes out of him that can give anyone standing near an electric shock. Moves like a very tall featherweight. I've had it a couple of times, so I know what I'm talking about. One minute you're outside the offie and talking to people and everything's all easy, the next he's over in a corner without his legs even moving, and he's got the guy by the phonebox in a headlock, and all without a word; bish bash, nice to meet ya, crack. I'm never bored when he's around.

I'm a good boy really, but I won't lie about it; I like the street violence around here. It's probably one of the reasons I'll never move out of Surrey.

Today he's carrying, so we're smoking a couple. You kind of have to if you're out with Jason, that's the rules. I'm having one puff out of every five, doing a Bill Clinton with the inhalations. Ever so gently, since my lower lip is still the size of a fish slice after last week's Vera-baiting. I'm not a wuss. I just have a race in two days' time, and want to win. Jason's guzzling enough for both of us anyway. He barely notices what I'm doing – and what I'm not.

'Should I give her one?' he repeats.

'Why?'

'Why not? She's hot. V, you've been busy lately with your running and that nerd stuff. You're not paying attention to what's going on. You should see how she looks at me.'

He's the only person I let call me V.

'And how does she look at you?'

'Like she wants to eat my dick.'

We laugh like a pair of duffuses.

'Well,' I go, in my posh voice, 'speaking as someone who's already sampled the goods, I'd say she's well worth boning.'

23

'Are you saying you've done her? And not told me?'

'It was the Christmas holidays. She was bored. I was bored . . .'

I'm more stoned than I realise. Moon is going to kill me.

'What do you make of this?' I'm saying quickly, pulling a letter from my bag, realising that I don't really want to get into what I got up to with Moon. Also, trying to play it cool, because the last thing I want is him getting any further than her tits.

Jason does a double take and starts chanting, pulling out a similar letter from his jacket.

'Who's bad? Who's bad? Who's bad? Who's bad? Shit, I knew there was something I wanted to tell you.'

The letters are from the school to our parents, telling them that their children are shit.

'We're in for it, aren't we?' he goes, after scanning my letter.

They are the same word for word, even down to the spelling mistakes — an extra c in fracas, and one n too many in unprovoked. The Year Head is requesting a meeting at our parents' earliest convenience. We don't see either of them being free for that meeting. Ever.

Jase hands over his letter and I stuff both of them in the tree. Push them as far down as I can manage, grazing my fingers as I pull them out. We could have started a nice little bonfire instead, but Jase hasn't got much lighter fuel left and is being stingy. The tree is hollow at a certain point of entry, round halfway up. The only way you'd find it is by climbing the thing. And there's little chance of that round here. Most of the guys at our school are happy to stand outside the offie and get pissed. No one is interested in climbing a fucking tree. Not unless you're using it as practice to get up drainpipes.

'Teachers are always busy,' I go, once I'm back on my feet and dusting down.

'You think?'

'Chances are, they'll be too stressed with the key stage tests to worry about us. Anyway, who's going to remember a small scuffle when Lucy Gilbert has just been knocked up?'

'You're funny, d'you know that, V?'

Jason is so far gone now, he's grinning like one of those kids who's been shot-up with too much Ritalin. I might as well be talking to myself.

9

This is how we have our fun: Friday night, cold and clear. Riding our bikes from Broadhurst to Auriol. A two-mile circuit that takes in the best of our area: video shops, kebab shops, offies, pubs, posh coffee bars, and more old people's hairdressers than there are old people. None of these interest us. We've already had a drink, and we don't want to have our hair done. Our rule is that we'll lap and lap until we find someone to have fun with. This will normally be in Auriol, where it's more densely wooded than Broadhurst, and is less hardcore with the street lighting.

Like fruit pickers, we're seasonal. Summer is no good for our fun. We work better in the darkness of winter. One kid's terrifying gloom is another kid's safety net.

We trawl until we come across a suitable player. If it's someone from school, great. Someone from the upper years, even better; usually a Year 12 muppet who still hasn't passed their driving test, and is too much of a dork to go out drinking.

Tonight is a night like any other. It's seven-thirty. We've been on the road for twenty minutes and haven't passed anyone of value. A man with a briefcase who's on his way home from the station; an old woman who looks like she's heading for the bus stop at the top of Auriol. Neither of them are right.

We can lap four or five times until we find what we are looking for. We're pros. We're fussy about our playmate. We could go onto the high street, where there is guaranteed to be all-night action, but we prefer it here, on these streets. Catching people only yards from their houses only adds to the fun. Another bonus point if we can get them under a Neighbourhood Watch sign. There is minimal over-eighteen activity round here after dusk. Adults with any sense know that they need to drive everywhere, even if it's just down to the Tesco Metro at the bottom of the street for a pint of milk. The muppet kids don't have that luxury, and this is when we strike.

There's no one in our houses to give a shit where we are. Mum is on another block of late shifts, this week it's been seven out of seven, and Jase's mum has gone to her group meeting where she talks to other depressives who've lost children and eat too much cake to get over it. Jase says it's a kind of AA for grievers. Apparently they know everything about each other except their real names. I tell Jase that people have to give a name for everything these days, that they won't be happy until every aspect of human nature has been labelled or explained; that soon there'll be a support group for people who still can't come to terms with the end of the *Lord of the Rings* trilogy or something, but he's cycled so far ahead I don't know whether he heard me. Racing off and ploughing up the hill that leads into Auriol at the first mention of his mum and her group.

This kind of picking on people comes naturally to us. If I didn't run, and Jase didn't smoke all the time, I guess this could be our second careers.

Jase is on his way back down. He's almost flying down the hill, hand off brakes, feet elevated from pedals, but even at those speeds the prospect of take-off isn't pleasing him. I suddenly think that if a car pulled out of one of these side roads any moment now, Jase would go the way of his sister. I feel like the biggest loser to be thinking it, but can't help it. That thought, that death, is always there.

He's already back in my face before I stopped thinking my horrible thoughts, luxuriously picking the scab. Looks pissed off.

'This is stupid. There's no one about.'

'Give it some time, eh? There'll probably be some action after eight.'

26

We always make sure we have our fun before ten-thirty. Any play-fulness that coincides with closing time can lead to situations with older kids that are out of our depth. I speak from experience.

'Fuck that. It's too cold tonight. Let's go back to that commuter, and then we can go indoors.'

Jase is the only person I know who calls home 'indoors'. His family aren't even cockneys. We're all pretending to be something round here.

I agree that this commuter's our boy, and we black up: caps on, hoodies up, scarves wrapped tight around our faces, so that all you can see are the eyes. I make sure mine is pulled so tight that it feels like its been stitched into my head. It wouldn't take the police five minutes to knock on our door if the scarf fell and the commuter got a full-frontal mugshot of a local Paki wearing Nike. There's only about five of us in this town. Finding the right teenage darkie is no needle-in-a-haystack exercise.

Jase is on fist duty tonight, we take it in turns, leaving me to be the cameraman. He leads, a head-start set at a standard thirty seconds. Means potential playmates let down their guard as they see the lone cyclist riding past, until, that is, he does the sharpest of U-ies, arriving at a point too close to their personal space for comfort. (Early on we made a decision not to go after the girls, unless we chanced across one of the school bitches who needed to be taught a lesson. Bad karma otherwise.)

This commuter, who's walked up and down the hill, and now onto Lower Park Road proper, sings like the rest of them. He's early fifties, and kinda fit looking, but doesn't put up any kind of fight. Must be down to the surprise element, I suppose. Textbook scenario.

I normally have a moment on the pause button once I've done the U-ie with a playmate and got into their space. Probably my favourite part of the job. When you suddenly crash into their universe, become a part of their history. A second or so is all you need. Taking that time to register their face, and to clock their brains working overtime: eyes invariably widened, forehead and brows wriggling in fear like a can of worms. Looking for information that I am regrettably obliged to give.

Jase takes his spectator moment after. He says it's because he likes to see their distress once they've realised that they've been punked. So there's no time for niceties with the commuter, or intimate eye contact; once he's headed in their direction, he's strictly business. Makes out he's grabbing the briefcase, but gets the guy on the ground, classic trip-style. Gives a push, just one, when the commuter makes his only attempt at a struggle. All this without a word being said. (Another reason why it's better to leave out girls. They normally want to have a fucking conversation with you as you're trying to go about your business.)

At this point, I'm in the area, phone ready on camera option. Jase holds him down – the classic foot-on-the-gas pose – and I click: one, two, one more for luck. Done.

He's still not making a sound, this commuter. We're all three of us united by our heavy breathing, but that's about it. With blokes this age and build, you have to be in and out like a dynamo, before they regain their senses and start acting the hero. This one guy chased us all the way to the bypass. He only stopped because he was winded or was having a heart attack or something (couldn't have been anything major, because we never saw it in the local paper).

He's still on the floor as Jase gets back on his bike. I've stayed on mine the whole time. It's all about the preparation. I'm silky smooth when we're on operations. We pedal off and he doesn't move an inch, just flat on his back with the heavy breathing. Briefcase held tight to his chest.

'Quiet bugger, wasn't he?' I go, once we're over the bypass and back in our area, where there are cars driving past and busybody neighbours who can vouch for us should a shadow of suspicion be cast.

'Did he say anything? Before I turned up?' I go again, because Jase has caught the commuter bug and isn't saying anything either.

'How brilliant was that?' he goes. 'I didn't think I was in the mood, but once I'd got down the hill and saw him poncing about with his briefcase, walking so fucking slowly like some old fool, I knew I was going to have him.'

'That hill at Auriol is steep. You wouldn't be walking quickly either after getting up that.'

I get this knot in my stomach that lasts about a second. Something to do with the guy being older than my dad and not walking very fast. I don't get knots like this when we punk the dweebs and the dorks. The one time we did a woman, I got the knots about a thousand times worse. They're unexpected, and momentary; when they go, it's like you almost imagined them. But an essence of them always lingers, like a niggle. No one wants to feel a niggle rising from their belly to the back of their throat when they're meant to be grinning from ear to ear, trying to be as high as a kite.

'Did you think he looked familiar? Like someone's dad?' I go, jumping up and down like we do after a hit, but still bowing to the niggle.

'This is Surrey, mate. They're all someone's dad around here.'

'You didn't tell me if he said anything.'

'It all happened so quick. He started some bollocks about "What the hell are you doing", but once I had him on the ground, he shut his trap.'

We're both marginally disappointed that he didn't give us a 'Don't hurt me.' They're always a good ego boost when you're feeling despondent and insecure about yourself. Another souvenir you can replay in your head again and again. The antidote to a persistent niggle.

'I think we've seen him before.'

'Bollocks, have we!'

Jase's showers half a gallon of spit across my cheek, he's so fucking excited. Spits even more when he sees the pictures: three close-ups that I like to call 'Man On Ground In Misery'. I should be an artist, or a proper professional photographer, the way I capture the human spirit.

And fear. You could be distracted by a couple of wet leaves that have fallen across his face, but the eyes of the man are pure fear.

That moment when you realise that you are no longer in control of your own trajectory. That you are old or frail or cowardly. Or maybe just the moment when you realise that there are people more powerful than you are. That when it comes down to it, it's all about the power of the muscle over the intellect.

'That, mate, is genius. Fucking genius! How good is that? That's great!'

Jase never speaks faster than ten words a minute unless he's really excited. And the excitement to word-speed ratio is at it's most extreme, akin to Paris Hilton teleporting out of nowhere and fucking him on the spot.

Less to be proud of, however, when I show Moon the pics the next day. She says that the eyes of 'Man On Ground In Misery' belong to someone who resembles Pearson's dad.

10

Evidence, good photographic evidence that you can carry around on your phone, is the new Top Trumps. Everyone's doing it. The first to complete the set rules the school. What exactly constitutes a full set is yet to be defined. We pretty much make up the rules as we go along.

This is our arithmetic: a fight is worth two slaps. Getting something out of a shop is worth two fights. Hassling commuters at the train station is worth half a slap. Steaming a train, as the kids from the Rose estate do during half term, is the equivalent of ten fights.

It all has to come from your own hand, and you have to have a strong stomach for it. Making sure you've got at least a few of these on your phone for emergencies – i.e.: when a gang of five are about to knock a couple of strips off your awkwardly pretty face, you can show them a photo of you doing the exact same thing to a twelve-year-old and get off the hook. I'm no coward, so I don't have to stoop so low, but it does happen. Yellow-belly kids all over this town are kicking the living shit out of the poor bastards the next rung down on the food chain, just so they won't get mashed. We all know that it's a sickness, but we can't help ourselves. (Think it all started when a group of Year 12s became hung up on Darwinism in A Level Biology around the same time they started getting camera phones.)

And when you see a really good photo, you have to cough up for the privilege. (For Year 8s and below, this simply means they won't get beaten up. For anyone my age, photo exhibition demands re-numeration. Niggas gotta show me the money!)

Happened to me last week when I had to buy Moon this CD by some old woman called Julie London. She scored with a filmed piece of a bus driver losing control of his vehicle and crashing into the greengrocer's on the Broadway. She wanted it for this song called 'Fly Me To The Moon', which she thought was really funny. Shelling out the twelve quid was worth it.

'Are you being ironic?' I asked.

'No,' she said. 'I'm being pedantic.'

We played her camerawork back again and again: bus swerving and ploughing into store front, melon after melon rolling towards the road. Such a procession of melons, like Jase could only dream of. People screaming like idiots. Her battery ran out before she could see what happened to the driver. Moon would be unbearable if she had got that.

There was a nasty rumour going round last term that one of the South Efrikan supply teachers was confiscating the worst evidence he could find. Rather than taking it to Year Head or whoever, he was flogging downloads onto some bogus website he'd set up. A kind of lucrative cyber-looting. We all do a bit of swopping on MSN from time to time, but it's harmless stuff. A fiver here and there, or some Smirnoff miniatures if that's your poison. Not PayPal.

Old Mandela milked the Year 12 punks. Bled every violent experience from them until they were weak and white. And being the first, they were the best of the bunch. They were dedicated to the cause, merciless and without fear. You could almost feel for those unrelenting bastards, until you remember that none of them had any heart to begin with. He only got found out when some other teacher, a non-supply, non-South Efrikan, was 'browsing' the web and came across them, which is suspicious in itself. How does someone browse a child-slapping site innocently? Only Year Head knows the answer to that one. The South Efrikan was shipped out before the end of term. Deported, we'd heard. Back to J'burg or whatever fucking township he came from. The creepier browser stayed on, but only to teach those over sixteen. Hmm . . .

This is Surrey, where nothing bad ever happens.

II

Moon wears five hundred bracelets under her school cardigan. Rolls up the sleeves at breaktimes to give everyone a flash of quartz and rubber. She isn't bothered about having skirts that are short or shoes that are high. Says it's a waste of time, another uniform.

'I'm not interested in turning up to school looking like one of Charlie's Angels,' she goes. 'I've come to school 'cos I wanna learn stuff. Looking like a slapper is bollocks.'

She can afford to say this because everything about her face is nearly perfect. She doesn't need to draw shit on to create cheekbones or eyes or lips. No craters to cover or clumsily bleached taches to hide.

(It's only after she's gone that Gwyn, the evil sister, blows her cover. Tells me about something called sheer make-up.)

Moon is always looking in the direction of the louder girls when she says this stuff. Girls like Kelly Button and Lizzie Jennings, who wear too-tight jumpers and a market-stall weight in gold jewellery. Especially Kelly Button. Making out like Kelly's the ringleader. Of the dress-like-a-slapper movement. If their eyes meet, Moon will stare and Kelly will scowl. Neither is a fan of the other's work.

Moon is the least popular girl in our year. Aside from the library crew, and her sister's friends, most of the bitches won't speak to her. It also doesn't help her popularity that she isn't a fatty. Fat girls with make-up have herds of friends. They stake their claim on various parts of the playground like competitive buffalos. It can feel like living on a ranch some days.

Things would be different if she wore shorter skirts or played a little sport. As things stand, she's like the girl from the Fantastic Four; invisible for the most part, until one of the eligible boys clocks that she's looking pretty fine, and then every girl in class will have her on their radar. Willing her to suddenly disappear into whatever's this week's equivalent of the Bermuda triangle.

'So how come you can say all those things, and still wear those?' I go, bringing it back to the bangles and crystals that smother her pulse points. She's never without these, or the plastic handbag with the flowers on it, picked up from Cancer Research. She thinks she's like the girl in that eighties film who always wore pink.

She laughs and gives me the W. *Whatever*.

'Because I'm vain. And I'm a girl. I never said anything about not looking pretty.'

12

Can't sleep, and not just because of the niggle after slapping the commuter who could be Pearson's dad. Toss and turn like a maniac. It's better being out of bed, better still to be out of the house, so I get to the park at five-thirty and start warming up. The park-keeper looks at me like I'm a nutter when he arrives at the gates to open up. If I was, say, twenty years older, closer to Casey's age, he'd take one look at me and call the local constabulary.

It's six years today since Dad ran off to Germany with the woman

33

who was supposed to be his optician. It's the anniversary we pretend we never remember. Mum cried in her room last night when she thought I was watching *EastEnders*. Not because she misses him, but more to do with the shock. She stills feel the shock. Wash away the make-up, toss the new clothes into the laundry, and it's still as fresh as anything. And it's been hard for us. He doesn't have a clue, with his emails that act like nothing ever happened, and those fucking cheques, which we have to take because nurses get paid shit. This is why I don't return his calls. Because he's a selfish bastard.

Casey turns up at six on the dot. He strides onto the track, gives a 'Howdy, Mr V-pen, sir', but still has a shaky look about him. He's wearing the same orange and navy tracksuit and white vest he had on at training yesterday. Same Nike cap, same trainers. This is definitely a sign that something's up. Casey wears his track-suits in strict rotation. He's a stickler for routine. If I have five-day training, which is where I'm at currently, I never see the same ensemble. Green and red Mondays, blue and white Tuesdays, orange and navy Wednesdays, baby blue and black Thursdays, red and white Fridays. Today is Thursday. I shouldn't be seeing the orange for another week.

'What's with the Tango-man tracksuit?' I go, as soon as he gets within shouting distance. 'I thought you like to, uh, rotate the looks.'

'Washing machine's broken,' he says, and starts bitching about me doing a slack-handed warm-up because I thought no one was watching.

'God's always watching, and don't you forget it,' he goes.

'I think you forgot to have a shower, when God was off watching *Queer Eye*,' I mutter under my breath after I've got a honk under my nose. It isn't just the washing machine that's busted. He reeks.

'What's that?'

Luckily he doesn't hear, otherwise I'd be doing an extra five laps for cheek.

Casey has an Irish body. Tall and built; strawberry white skin, brown gold crop growing out into a sulky skullcap of curls, a once-trim body which, thanks to worry and drink, is now slowly turning to fat. And old, around thirty-five. If you passed him in the street you'd think he was a butcher or a builder. He didn't look like this a year ago, and this is the worst thing, I think. That a lifetime of fine-tuning his body, of exercising self-discipline, to the cost of everything else, so that he was as close to a panther as you can become in human form, was all lost. It's like getting a Lotus and leaving it to rust in the yard. The biggest waste.

I would never tell Casey this as he might get excited, get a stiffy at the thought of me studying him physically, but I have so much respect for him and what he's done. I wouldn't be working with him otherwise. Olympic squad at nineteen, try touching that. I often think about him and his body — because even now any athlete can still see what an awesome machine it was. You only have to look at the way he walks — and wonder about the pivotal moment over those few weeks last summer that made him decide to let his body go.

There's not time for too much funny business. The race is tomorrow. North East Surrey Under 16s. I'm competing in the 400 and 1200m. How's that for versatility? My timings are all out this morning, though. 1200 is the worst, running it like it's the marathon. I can't get my head together. Must have something to do with thinking about Dad, and the unexpected reappearance of You've Been Tangoed. My left shoulder and upper arm are still hurting from where the guy at school booted me. No signs of bruising left, but it hurts like hell. I keep this from Casey too, before he offers to lay hands. He's very eager that way.

'Where is your fucking head today, boy? God pardon my language,' Casey's saying in my ear, after I mess up another 1200.

'I'm trying the visualising, and it's not working.'

Like I'm going to tell him about Dad. I'm lying on my back, out of breath, because he's made me do fifty push-ups for messing up, followed by squat thrusts. With the shoulder, it's agony. I'm almost crying.

'Do your Hail Marys and quit moaning,' he says whilst I'm huffing and puffing like some out-of-shape fatty.

I'm hoping to get on with the next run. Skip the lecture.

'Don't blame the technique, V-pen. That's bullshit. It's not working because your heart's not in it. Blaming the technique. Sign of a bad athlete.'

That's enough to get me on my feet. Hopping about like Ali.

'What kind of motivation is this? Aren't you supposed to say how great I'm going to be tomorrow, instead of this fruity telling-off?'

'Hey! What have I told you about calling me that?'

We're both pissed off, and skulk to our respective areas. Him to trackside, by the long jump, where his trainer marks have already given him a ready-made grave; me back to the starting line. During the next 1200 I visualise being chased by a naked Casey. He's got an acorn, and is screaming after me like a girl, 'Want a lift? Want a lift?' It seems to do the trick. I break my previous best. A couple more of those and everyone's happy. Now, when I'm on my back again, top off, doing some quick chest curls, he lies down beside me and tells me how great I'm going to be tomorrow.

'I know,' I say, getting up, only after I've finished my reps. Making no effort to put my top back on. I like how my pecs look at the moment; it'll take more than Casey to get me to hide them. The trick with PPPs is to give them eye contact the whole time, especially when they start doing things like lying down next to you. They're quick to wheedle once they see the first sign of hesitation.

I'm back on my feet and start on the cool-down within a minute. I don't like the attention as much as I think.

13

Moon catches up with me at lunchtime. We're in different sets, so half a day can go by when I barely see her. I'm walking quickly down the corridor because I've been told to avoid trouble. I need to avoid trouble. The school letter proves it. She catches me up, finally, and pins me against a locker. Legs all up my back like we're a couple — which I love, as it winds everyone up — and clutching her phone like it's an Oscar.

'You're not the only one who's been busy with the pictures. Just so you know, I got mine.'

'Of what?'

'Of you, stupid . . . and your PPP.'

'Fuck! When?'

'This morning. I told you I was going to do it.'

Moon now has a smug look, like she just ate shit. Everyone is giving us the eye, though that's more due to the leg action and the fact that my hands are now cupping her tits.

She runs her hands through my hair, taking locks through her fingers, and gives a firm pull. It hurts like hell, feels like someone's stabbing me in the head with a handful of pins, but of course, I'm turned on by it. Have to turn in towards her so that no one can see how physically turned on I am, especially as it's in public, and implies an intimacy most of them are still dreaming about.

It's always the same with every girl I've been with. They always go for the hair; they can't get enough of it. Thick and black, curls stubbornly upright, stiff like a cherub who wants to get it on, framing my face like the centre of a lightbulb, and finished off with pearly whites that know how to grin. That's the cherry on top, my cheek. If I'm frozen out by the hair snobs, I'm all theirs for the cheek.

Like I say, I don't know whether it's the Tamil in me or the Jew in me, but I've got to give thanks to someone for pulling that off, the hair, when I was bubbling in the gene pool. It's a calling card I'm happy to have.

Kelly Button, still unsuitable but very tasty, is one of the crowd in the corridor. I think she's interested. She has this look on her face that suggests she wants to take Moon out. Pull her hair and stamp her sovereign rings into her eye sockets. It's a good job Moon's talking in my ear or she'd be dead meat.

Moon flicks through her photo file and pulls it up. Me on the floor with my vest off and nips out. Casey almost on top of me. His mouth is millimetres away. It's a post-snog-that-never-happened kind of photo.

'How come I didn't see you?'

'Because I was undercover, dufus.'

I start to panic because I look like the biggest faggot. If this fell into anyone's hands, say Pearson's for example, I might as well move schools.

'Fuck! What are you going to do with it? Moon, don't even think about sending this to Mum.'

'Course not, VP,' (I let her call me VP occasionally), 'it's going nowhere. You were taking the piss out of me the other day. I just wanted to prove to you that I could do it. Think of it as evidence.'

I'm very cool before I say this. Don't want to give her the wrong idea, that I'm bothered about any of it.

'But we're mates, Moon. Why would you need evidence?'

She thinks for a moment before replying, 'I don't know, VP. I just do.'

14

I should have had her surveillance work deleted on the spot, but I didn't. Too much of a softie. I'm like a giant Mr Whippy, all floaty and genial. I was feeling it all the more too, because I remembered the extra warm glow I had after we did it at Christmas. It was spilling it to Jason that did it, made me forget to watch my back. I'm a foot and a smudge taller than her, and carry enough muscle. I could have had that phone out of her hand in a flash. File deleted before she even noticed. All just by holding my hand above my head. But I don't. At that point, her having that picture didn't seem to be a problem.

I'm too busy worrying about my own evidence. It's tough trying to be hard, when you've got this conscience-thing pricking into you the whole time. If our latest slap turns out to be Pearson's dad, then we've got problems. Moon is convinced that it is. Parents' evening last term, when she was serving the coffee and spilt half a cup on his trousers because she has poor hand-to-eye coordination, and was completely the wrong person to be asked to walk round with a tray of drinks. She says the look in the eyes was something similar. Also, the half-bald head is something of a giveaway. She promises to keep her mouth shut, even from Jason. Takes a bag of Maltesers and some micro cardigan from H&M before I'm completely sure.

I don't know what I'm worrying about. There's no way this would get back to Pearson. The man looked so old he'd have trouble recognising us anyway. We were wrapped and Nike'd up like all the other kids who live round here. Needle in a haystack. Also, it was very dark, which helps. Thank God for conservation areas and low-level lighting. Local heritage is a slapper's best friend. It nixes modern security techniques. And even if Pearson did get hold of the slap somehow, there's very little to trace it back to us. Unless, of course, Pearson's dad knows anything about bikes, in which case Jase's Mountie Series 5, polished titanium and very specalised, leaves us wide open. But, like, he's going to know anything about bikes!

It's a niggle larger than the last. Stays for days.

15

Mum and me are having celebratory KFC in the car on the way back from the races. I trounced the 400 and the 1200m. I'd like to say the wins were down to the lion, but they had more to do with Casey chasing me naked. It was a last-minute decision, the only image I came up with that would stick. I may have to shag Moon again just to make sure that Casey and his acorn don't come back next meeting.

You don't get two minutes to yourself when you've won a race. Because the organisation was cack-handed, people are everywhere once I've cleaned the 400, all vying to give me a pat on the back. All aside from my trainer, who's been told to keep well away. I give him the results by text. Today, however, this includes a pat on the back from the Harriers, which is the best of all, because you can see it's choking them.

'Congratulations, lad. Those were excellent runs, really excellent,' goes Brendan Dean, the slug who got me thrown out of Harriers in the first place. He always calls me lad because he can never pronounce my name. He runs the Harriers deal across Surrey and Kent, rarely seen but often heard. Very creepy guy, like the Childcatcher, only uglier. And he has the driest skin in the world. When I shake his hand I literally feel a layer of skin coming away. Makes Freddie Kruger look moisturised.

'You are doing magnificently this season. Our guys will have to watch out for you in the finals!'

'They'll have to watch the smoke from my trainers as I leave them behind.'

I was expecting him to say something else entirely, because I know he's been keeping a close eye on my progress since I left, but the unexpected courtesy doesn't throw me. I'm not bothered about being a gracious winner.

'And you're still training alone, I hear?'

'Yep. Nothing anyone can teach me. I'm a natural.'

'Well . . .' he claps his hands together and you can see about a pound of skin flakes falling to the floor.

I'm glugging my energy drink and almost throw it back up.

'. . . I know we've had some differences, but if you'd like to return to the centre . . .'

'Piss off.'

'You'd be more than welcome. Although I can see your manners are as elusive as ever. Goodbye.'

Two reasons for ending the conversation: Casey, whom no one over the age of fifteen knows about, and I see Mum coming over (ref: reason number one).

'What did he want?'

She thrusts a KitKat in my hand and throws daggers at Brendan's under-moisturised back. She's about as keen on him as I am.

'Nothing. Just wanted to know my secrets.'

'I hope you kept them to yourself! Bloody hypocrite. If he was that interested in the first place, he should have made an exception and kept you on. Those stupid rules about age restriction. You're only fifteen, for Christ's sake.'

Her eyes start popping out, the way they do when she's on a roll. She only shuts up when I give her three bars of the KitKat.

Moon says hi and then disappears. She's being elusive. I haven't seen her since she showed me the picture yesterday. She's with her bitch sister, who hates me; I could hear her booing as I passed her in the 400. They're off to see Incubus at Wembley and now things are wrapped up, are making their haste to leave known.

'Congratulations, great run,' spits the bitch sister.

She's standing at least five feet away, as if coming anywhere near me is cutting into her time with precious Incubus. Mum is right next to me, so I'm forced to acknowledge the bitch sister as Gwyn Jones. If she wasn't, I probably would have ripped into her saggy Welsh arse. Great tits, though. Make Moon's look like lemon slices.

The Jones girls are local landmarks. Everyone knows them, even if you don't go to our school. Moon has the looks, Gwyn has the tits. Both have the milk white skin, which, in Gwyn's case, does her plenty of favours. Without that complexion she'd look like Quasimodo. Although Jason is interested in Moon, like we all are, he's always saying how he'd take Gwyn's tits anytime. Says they're wank tits.

Moon waves from Gwyn's car and says she'll call me. She throws daggers at Kelly Button, who's been shivering in her tiny skirt, and making eyes at me for the past hour. Like I don't know what she wants.

The KFC in the car tastes like heaven. It's a rarity. Mum usually insists on the house being a fast-food-free zone, claiming that there are more chemicals in those things than there are in an E.

'When you're out with your friends, there's nothing I can do about it. But when you're at home, I'm not giving you any of that junk.'

On the days before a race I stick to the pasta, chicken, fruit. I'm not Lynford yet, but I am taking it as seriously as I can.

Mum hadn't been to one of my races for a while. Too busy working. Has to take my word about how good I am. Gets verification whenever she catches my mug in the papers. Normally after a race we'd have a laugh about things, take the piss out of the other runners, especially the ones who dribble, or start praying before the whistle. Today she's seriously evangelical, going on about how this could really open doors for me if I stick at it, and how we really need to find a trainer to give me the one-on-one attention I'm entitled to.

My mobile goes. It's Casey. I flick it off straightaway.

'Who was that?' she asks.

'Wrong number,' I say.

She's not listening, though, still too het-up about my chances.

'These bloody Harriers are taking the piss if they can't see what's in front of their noses. You were the best thing to ever happen to that centre, and they just let you walk away. I'm going to have it out with Brendan if he doesn't set you up with a trainer. I'll take it all the way to the top, if I have to.'

I drop the drumstick, and start telling her how I'm happier training on my own. Inwardly I'm shitting it, because I know that this is the moment when I should tell her about Casey, but luckily it starts raining as we turn into Broadhurst. Chucking it down. Rain hitting the windscreen so fast and so thick you can't see shit.

Mum drives around Surrey most of the day because of work, but isn't the most confident at the wheel. Her trick is to over-compensate a lack of bottle with speed. Many a time we've come within inches of a parked car, a wall, or various cyclists. The only time she takes it to snail trail is when the elements hit, like they are now. She's stopped going on about my running, and jumps off the gas, so we're rolling at about 10 mph. The wipers are flapping across the screen at max but doing fuck all.

'Shit,' she goes.

She literally only ever swears in the car.

'Relax, we're on Broadhurst. We'll be home in a couple of minutes.'

In her mind it's half a mile of potential hazards.

Jason is on the street getting soaked. Must have finished a shift at Tesco. Looks like he's spent his wages there too. Carrying more bags than Pauline Fowler.

Mum's going so slowly she doesn't even have to stop for Jase. I flip open the door and he throws the bags in, followed by himself.

'Hello.'

'Hello.'

'Hello, Mrs Prendrapen.'

'Don't be so formal, Jason. Vivienne, remember?'

'OK. Hello, Vivienne, lovely to see you.'

He drops it so smoothly, it's enough to make Mum blush. He's a right charmer, is Jase.

'Have some chicken,' I tell him. 'It's the shizzle.'

'Fo' shizzle, m'nizzle,' he goes, which makes me break out into giggles like some girl.

'Can you speak proper English whilst you're in the car?' says Mum, smiling, but with eyebrows raised. 'I might not be able to make out every word, but I know swearing when I hear it.'

There's enough time to exchange pleasantries in the minute it takes to reach his house. I have a quick glance at the bags as he's shaking the rain out of his brittle skinhead turning to fuzz and onto Mum's back seat. Three of them are filled with ready-meal crap; the others are crammed with boxes of Matchmakers. His mum, as well as being an agoraphobic, is a bulimic, also brought on by the hit and run. This would be funny if you didn't know her, and hadn't heard about how she feeds almost solely on Matchmakers (and when they're in season, Easter eggs). But we know Jason, so it isn't a laughing matter. His dad ended up leaving because of it — but he still sees him, so at least he doesn't hate his as much as I do mine. Mum knows the situation inside out, and has tried to help her several times, but Billie — Jase's mum — won't listen to anyone. Each visit is a failure.

Mum stops the car outside Jason's. The car stinks of damp and stale chicken. The rain was a five-minute wonder. Now it's non-existent. She laughs girlishly at her panic, because we have company, like it's me making all the fuss.

You know when Jason's mum is having a bad day, as the curtains will be drawn. One of those days when the pain of her daughter's death becomes too great. Opens a wound so wide, she needs to fill it with all the refined sugar she can fit inside her gullet. A day when the son that didn't die can do nothing for her, aside from bring the chocolate. And plenty of it. We all look up as Jason gets out of the car. The curtains are pulled tightly shut.

16

We get into another fight. This one's after school so there's no worry about letters turning up unexpectedly in the fallout. At least that's what we think. Me, Jason and Moon are minding our own business when we walk into the new cunt who started all the Paki trouble up the week before. He wants a settler, didn't like being made a fool of. Brings the same two jokers who tried to see us off in the corridor. That means Pearson, who's looking even more vicious than before. Me and Jase are well up for it. We're anyone's, if it means proving a point.

We are all fight. It's what we want plastered above our graves.

We throw down on a patch of grass opposite the school. The council gateway we call it, as behind us lies the Rose estate. Once the jackets are on the ground, ties stuffed into bags, we are officially not in uniform, so let rip. I'm worried about Moon being there. Chivalry isn't dead in my house, and she gets that this might be time to keep her distance. She takes the gear and stands on the corner.

A crowd quickly gathers. It's two hours 'til there's decent TV, and too early to get goggle-eyed in front of MSN. The people need entertaining. We also know that some do-gooder teacher will catch sight of our goings-on from the car park within the first five minutes. It'll probably be a more litigation-weary member of the species who'll need to go and confer with some other teacher friends before stepping in. There's little time for ceremony or name-calling, just boots and fists.

Jason has an aunt staying with them at the moment; come down to look after his mum. She's in the room next door to his – not his dead sister's room – which has put a hold on him wanking himself raw of an evening. It comes across in his fighting. He takes the two jokers and kicks them to shit. I'm still giving the eye to Moon and already he's at it. Once he's got them on the ground he has no use for his hands, the boots do the talking one kick at a time. He's going at it so quick, it's almost a garage rhythm he's knocking against their ribs. The sound of bones being broken.

One week has passed since the last fight. Scars have barely healed. From outside the circle we probably look like a bunch of old-timers. Scabbed fists punching scabbed-over faces. Sore, weeping eyes washing over freshly blackened skin.

The kids around us are all shouting like they're at Old Trafford. Jason's trying to tell me something but I can't hear a word. I still find time, however, a nanosecond, to spot Kelly Button standing with a group of girls to my left. Eyes going flutter flutter flutter.

This leaves me with the new boy. Not quite alone. Moon appears from her corner and throws a book at his head. Combined science, a heavy hardback with lethal corners that could rip skin to shreds. He turns at her, pissed at the intervention of a girl, giving me a window to jump on his back. He's heavier, but I'm taller. The surprise is enough to floor the bastard. Then I do a bit of Jason with the kicking.

New cunt doesn't stay on the floor for long. He's up and ready. Uses all his trademark moves, mainly the groin and the shoulder kick. He really knows how to use the shoulder kick. Gets me right where the last one left its mark, top left shoulder between blade and back. I never worry about being vocal at these things. When he gets me on the shoulder for the second time, I let out something gutteral that sounds like a roar because it really fucking hurt.

He sees the weak spot and goes for a replay, but doesn't quite manage it. Jason, who's now on the floor with the other two idiots, wriggles our way at speed and grabs his skanky ankle. New cunt is taken by surprise, jigging about one-legged, like some German beer-drinking circus freak. Furious because everyone's laughing like fuck. Laughing even more as he tries to shake Jason off.

Then a bottle catches the back of Jason's neck the moment he's on his feet. One of new cunt's friends trying to be clever, the one who isn't Pearson. It's a small bottle and doesn't quite hit the mark, most of the impact missing the neck entirely and swallowed up by air. Spastics. Aside from Pearson, none of them do any sports, so it's no wonder.

Everyone gasps, loud, like how you get in a pantomime, as the arrival of a bottle always marks something new — the disappearance of good clean fun. They have left some kind of result, however, a small nick at the right side of Jason's neck. He's been wearing a Man-U scarf all winter, so his neck is very smooth and white. Blood trickles slowly downward in a thin stream, a drop at a time; making his neck and the nick look like a freshly squeezed McFlurry.

They think that means the fight's over. It ain't.

Moon drops bags and coats, and joins us for the final stretch. They're in a gaggle, still laughing about the cut. Think we're coming over to shake hands. As if.

There's the three of us, and the three of them. They're on the floor; we're making sure they stay there. Six-boot chorus. The kids are going wild. Which is when the committee of teachers, a thin procession of one timid four-eyes after another, finally turns up.

In the Year Head's office we're made to stand through the suspension dance. Moon is told to wait outside, so it's just us boys. Year Head seems oblivious to the fact that Jason is dripping blood all over her kingfisher-blue carpet tiles. From a slow trickle it has now increased to a steady drip drip drip. Blood trail criss-crossing his neck like graffiti.

I have it all my own way. Say it's racially motivated, which it is. Enough witnesses come forward to confirm that several 'Pakis' were uttered. They don't mention that most of these came from my mouth when I was slamming the cunt. It's not enough, though. New cunt is refused the luxury of mellowing into an old cunt, and is excluded, permanently. I'm excluded for the rest of the week. Jason too. Today is Thursday. Means I can write it off with Mum as an INSET day. The exclusion means fuck all. The school secretary has gone home, so the corresponding letter won't even arrive home 'til Tuesday. Discipline in this place is a joke.

Disappointingly, none of the boys have broken anything. Pisses us both off. We thought that was one of our better performances. Still, it did get me top prize, Kelly Button's hand down my trousers at the ropey the following afternoon. She thought I'd been fantastic.

Moon's meeting with Year Head is way shorter and limited to shouting or finger-wagging. Something to do with Gwyn being head girl and putting in a good word. Her parents do the grounded thing, but unlike most, because they're older and don't have a life, make sure she adheres to it.

Moon lives across the road. It's impossible to avoid each other, but somehow, with her pushy parents' help, she finds a way. I don't hear from her for over a week.

17

Moon's death has pushed everyone who's left living into an alternative universe. We don't talk to each other; we all float around like helpless fatties bobbing randomly in this sea of significant glances. Mum's been doing it so much lately she's starting to look mental. If you stuck your head through our window of an evening, you'd think we were a family of autistics – me with my arms folded across my chest, sat watching the TV and letting the dinner on my tray grow cold; her sitting on the sofa opposite, watching me watch the TV. Sound up so loud you can hear it from Broadhurst. Our house has become Loony Tunes, but you can't diss – it's Mum we're talking about. She's so worried, she's *this* close to giving me my computer back.

Gwyn isn't so kind. She is hurting more than I can imagine, but that shouldn't mean that what I had with Moon should be brushed off as insignificant. She talked to me more than she did her family. Man, we were tight. Her parents realise it, so why doesn't she? How is it that Gwyn can walk past me in town one day without a word?

It's mid-morning, and there's next to no one in the mall. I'm in town purely for something to do. Mum's given me a shopping list and thirty quid. Figures it's as good a first step as any.

Pushing the trolley is satisfying, and I tell Mum this later. Mentally ticking each item off the list, bagging them up at the till, picking a ripe avocado for Mum as a surprise treat, makes me feel like I'm doing something. First time since . . .

I'm struggling with the shopping as I walk out of Tesco and spot the bitch sister. Gwyn knows how to play it. She isn't worried about hiding or sparing anyone's feelings. There is no diving behind the flower stand, or disappearing into Oasis as soon as she clocks me.

Instead, eyes fixed firmly in the distance, probably as far as Starbucks, at the mall's furthermost entrance, she flicks the volume on her iPod and walks past me.

Only the fact that we're within touching distance gives it away. Closer than touching distance. The fibres from our coats are virtually frotting. Her tidy pace means nothing. You don't walk that close to anyone by accident.

It makes me even more confused. Two nights before the funeral we're crying down the phone at each other. Expressing all kinds of regret that we've been unable to spill before our parents. Then, at the wake, when I thought things were getting friendly, we nearly get into a fight. I was going upstairs for a slash, and tried to peek into Moon's room. She jumped on me like some shemale from WWF. Dropped the lady-like act. Approaching sounds on the stairs cut her short. And now I'm being treated like a ghost. This grief is a funny thing. I don't know what to think.

I watch her as she bobs past the flower stand and the Body Shop, following as she curves down the final stretch, and losing her at Starbucks where she drowns in a splurge of freshly latte'd pensioners. She looks as immaculate as ever. One of those girls who've come straight out of the catalogue. She may be into all things rock, but Gwyn never looked like a teenager in her life. She never saw the point. When Moon dyed her hair red, she was a bitch for days about it. Not even the parents were as bothered.

The moment is so quick as to be unbelievable. It's only when I see her pace quicken as she reaches the mall doors, a slight skip breaking into a run. Some silly old church-goer dithering with her M&S bags gets in her way and is almost pushed aside. I realise that I didn't imagine it. This is the silent treatment. She acts like she knows.

All the way home, I'm still shivering from that brief moment of contact. Temperature dropping, like my circulation's gone haywire. It's a feeling similar to when Moon used to touch me. Especially on those nights after she disappeared from her boyfriend, when our meetings

49

had to be brief. Those hour-long meetings, sometimes shorter than that, were all about news, and food, and touch. Not sex, nothing like that, more a sense of confirmation. We couldn't keep our hands or lips off each other. A touch that jump-starts my circuits. A touch that makes me feel. Don't ask me to explain how a static touch from Gwyn gives me exactly the same feelings. It just does.

18

Pearson's face is a picture. Skin the colour of a tomato that's been kicked down several flights of stairs. Nose flat like a pancake because I've almost broken it. Looks like he's been slapped in the face with a giant fly swatter, or as if he's the last one squeezed into the tube carriage as the doors slide shut. It's a result.

In my mind, his looks have been permanently busted. The pretty-boy thing he does with those caterpillar eyebrows that gets the girls all wobbly, even the sensible ones, is gone for good. Except, the ladies don't seem to see it that way. Think his squished-out nose makes him look sexier, more of a bruiser. I couldn't do anything about messing up the puppy-dog eyes, that was my mistake. Injured boat with eyes like that is always going to win the girls round. Combined with the thick lips, it's an unbeatable killer combo. Enough to make you sick.

And boy, does he milk it. For the next few days, once the suspension nonsense is over with, he's with a different girl at every break, giving them the inside story on his physical discomfort. Working the lie that he's holding back tears, the fucker.

Get a girl on her own, buy her a pizza slice and a drink, get some sob story going, and it's pretty much in the bag. If me and Jase didn't have a reputation for being so difficult, we'd probably be acting exactly the same. There are at least three girls that we've heard of in the last week that hung out with him in the sports hall changing rooms after school. And 'hanging out' figures are like icebergs – we all reckon the real figure is much higher. Way higher.

Pearson's good fortune nags at me until it becomes torture, and for two reasons. The fact that he's getting more than he deserves, and the fact that it's all down to me. I meant to disfigure the bastard, and now it looks like I've done him a favour. And while I'm sat home stewing after school, he's seeing all the tit he can down the sports hall, and all because I gave him a pasting. It sucks.

19

'I'm being sued. That's why I'm late.'

It's raining, really belting, so I'm forced to take up Casey's offer of a lift home from training. Mum is on early shift, so won't see when he drops me door to door.

'Who would want to sue you? Some geezer offended by your new choice of trackie?'

The Clio smells of kebabs and booze. I inhale like it's an essential oil or something, unless I want to open the window and get completely soaked.

We're not even driving anywhere, it's raining so hard. Sat in the car park, until Casey gets better road vision – he only has one wiper that works. It's a traditional English still life that some old artist or other forgot to paint: ex-pervert and future athletics star getting cosy in Clio at dawn. They should put it on plates.

Casey is on overdrive with his clearing-the-throat action. If you closed your eyes you'd think he was starting a tractor. Several football pitch areas of forest are cleared before he can get the words out.

'My favourite family from last year. Claiming emotional damage.'

His tone is all over the shop. Was trying to be flippant, but his voice goes too high. Makes him sound like he's going to start crying or something.

I can't deal with this: men showing emotion in public so early in the morning, and then the smell. It's enough to make me leg it. Better a chest cold than all this blubbing and rank stinkiness.

But I don't go anywhere. We've never spoken about that family before. Never. Unspoken rule number 4578. Drafted via psychic powers during our first meeting at the now-legendary out-of-the-way Starbucks. People will pay pilgrimage to that fucking Starbucks in Walton after I've become famous and told Trevor McDonald the secrets of my life.

'I don't understand the greed of these people. I'm an innocent man, but they are not happy until they have stripped every single thing from me.'

'Tell them to fuck off. You're the one who had his house burned down and everything.'

Casey laughs the dry, brittle laugh which adults are so good at when they are trying to show you the weight of experience they carry on their broken shoulders.

'You've got a lot to learn, Mr V-pen. Damaged kids, whether the cause is real or imaginary, is the Holy Grail when it comes to compensation claims. Me and my shabby lot don't even come close.'

'Ask me and I'll do it. Just say the word. Me and Jase can go round and rough the kid up a little. Persuade him to change his mind.'

'It's not about him, young Turk. It's about the parents. That kid's no better off than I am. We're both cash cows as far as they're concerned.'

At race meets, I do remember the kid's mother being a little on the showy side. She was always wearing hats.

'I'm sure they've got the best intentions,' I say stupidly, only because I can't think of anything better to say.

Better this, than lamely trying to convince him that everything will be all right if he leaves it to the proper channels, because we all know that it won't. Once your card has been marked as a PPP, there's no going back. It's over. You may as well kill yourself.

Casey doesn't answer. Just opens the door and runs out. Crumbles under the pressure of trying to be brave. Shoulders heave a great deal, up and down until they're like jelly. I turn on the radio and pretend that I don't see it.

20

Moon and Gwyn are the girls that we are all looking for. Even saying their name together over and over makes them sound like thirteenth-century princesses.

Moonandgywnmoonandgwynmoonandgywn.

Magical. If there was any justice or romance left in this world, they should be riding white horses and wearing wimpoles. We're doing medieval at the moment. Like most of the girls around them, even the ones they're not friendly with, or hate even, these are sisters who know their own minds. No insecurity here – or none they'll show to boys, anyway. Also, they are straight-edged all the way – which, for anyone over thirty, means that they're alcohol-, nicotine- and narcotic-free zones. Moon keeps a bit of gear under her bed, but like me never touches the stuff. Uses it for – how does she put it? – 'man magnetism hahaha'. The irony being that those girls don't need a cheeba wand to get any boy hooked. They are beguiling enough. Look at me and Jase. Caught.

21

Pearson's success with the ladies post-fight makes me feel a whole load of things, like a sick stew. I don't like to feel uncertain about anything. On the way home from school I shag Kelly Button under the ropey. It's too muddy for us to do it properly. We wriggle in the mud like a couple of rugby players. It's Kelly's fault for being up for anything. Our route home through the park takes in a clutch of bushes, where we try again, this time with her mouth. Just to make sure.

22

Moon decides to reappear for the next Challenge session. Nothing to do with having the afternoon off school or anything. As the team's official bag carrier/supporter, she's allowed. Everyone else has to pull a sickie or grovel.

This is a week since the so-called exclusion. I'm pissed at her and she knows it. She sits next to me on the minibus all the same, but we say nothing until we're almost past Chessington, en route to Godalming.

'I know you've been coming round every day after school,' she goes. 'I could hear you from my room. It's been a bitch. But when my parents say grounded, they mean it.'

'Moon, it ain't that hard. Haven't you heard of MSN, slipping a note through the door late night, coming down to training with the dog?'

I knew not to txt after being gloated at by Gwyn outside the newsagent's, whilst Jason was arguing with the woman inside over why a packet of Benson Silver should pass across the counter.

'They've taken her phone off her, troublemaking boy, so don't waste your precious 5ps with your texts.'

Gwyn was known as the only girl in the upper school who didn't own a mobile as a point of principle. She thought it made her cool.

'There was life before mobile phones,' she'd more than once said. 'They're worse than TVs for vegetising the brain.'

The three of us thought she was sad.

'It's lucky she doesn't have a phone,' goes Jason, when he finally comes out of the newsagent, fagless, "cos she doesn't have any friends to call on it. Just a smokescreen, innit?'

Moon doesn't mention the txt thing either. Too embarrassed probably, but still manages to look affronted the way that only girls can do when they're in the wrong.

'I was grounded. That means being a good girl and listening to her mummy and daddy.'

'Like you didn't manage to sneak off all those times before? You'll need a better excuse than that.'

Aside from this, I cannot get any more from her on how she's spent the last seven days.

She uses the journey to focus solely on the team. Like me, she takes her position seriously. Getting Mr Morgan to crank up the stereo whenever a good tune comes on, doing her impression of every saddo boy band all rolled into one after a horrific car accident; it's all geared to make the four of us in the bus laugh our arses off. Even Peter Kei, aka Chinese Peter (like Gwyn, a reluctant teenager, who is so serious that he never laughs at anything), broke a smile at Moon's seated moonwalk for paraplegics.

I love it that she can make a dry old nerdy bus wet their pants. Love that she tells the jokes that I've already heard in private. The ones we made up lying on our backs watching MTV Base, and pissing about in my room, waiting for Mum to come home with the dinner. When Moon is on form, when she's got the charm offensive in her head, she can light up anywhere. And I love it, that everyone loves her silliness the way I do. It's a proud moment.

By rights Mr Morgan should be slapping her down for most of the things coming out of her mouth. She's distracting his driving for a start, but he's in a good mood today; for the same reason, we're all feeling great, out of the school for the afternoon, and he laughs just as hard as the rest of us.

I take a swig from the Evian bottle the moment after she does. It's the most intimate erotic thing you can do whilst you're sat beside of a group of nerds. Normally, this is the kind of stuff she notices. Today she doesn't.

Moon hugs me at Godalming's gates. Another love-you-mate, love-you-darlin' hug. Throws the body in, tight squeeze, small pat on the back, very egalitarian. The whole team gets them. I wait in line for my hug — I'm at the end of the queue — and console myself that this is the best I'm going to get. For the last half hour of the drive, after the toilet stop, she moved to the front next to Morgan, giving him the one to one, ignoring everyone else. Txts on her phone like a maniac. We're all over the place with each other today, not acting right. It's only the small peck on the cheek that indicates any recall of past conquests. Feels nostalgic. I want to tell her that she's special, but Morgan's nagging us to hurry up so I don't get the chance.

Godalming's team are killer. They should be, considering the school. The three on the team, two boys and a girl, are friendly enough. Surprisingly non-nerdish. The first to come over and shake hands, confident and chummy, showing us up somewhat as we were good and ready for our usual tactic — to avoid all prior contact by throwing evils and bitching in a corner.

We're all presentable enough, but they're more evolved, closer to mini-adults with the odd patter of teen talk thrown in. There are the smallest of looks on their part, reassuring, expected, when they see our uniforms, a defiant paean to man-made fibres, all shiny and static. They, smug in their grey wool blazers that seem to fit just so, as opposed to ours, which just 'fit', are the perfect hosts.

I've got all my rings on for this very reason, big chunky bastards. Put them on in the bus when Mr Morgan was concentrating rather too much on Moon's homage to all things rock. He has yet to notice that I'm wearing nearly all of them. When he retires to the back of the hall, I'll slip on the daddy, the knuckleduster, which Jason attempted to buy from a Goth shop in Guildford, and when that didn't work, stole. I don't know much about woollen jackets, but who needs wool when this little beauty gives you the edge?

Usually before a match the teams will crack open a Diet Coke and chat about skate parks, whilst the teachers talk about the drive and make some vague allusion to the tension of the forthcoming head to head. The world-famous knife-edge. There is plenty of this here at Godalming. We each sit in our corners in the teachers' lounge and talk rubbish. Means that boys bands and film crap are mentioned from our camp more than once. They're happy to sit there and let us do the talking, more interested in their own reflections. We can talk about East Coast/West Coast and the traffic until we're blue in the face. Doesn't mean shit. The general expectation by all in the room is that they will win.

But here's the thing; we manage to hold our own until the final round, brilliance that surprises everyone. The reflexes of my eggheads, Peter and Charlotte, are ridiculously slow. Neither of them do any sports so I shouldn't be expecting miracles. Get them in front of a Playstation or a textbook and they're fine. Give them a buzzer, a light, and a room full of judgmental girls, and they've got problems. The guys on the other team are protean all-rounders and don't seem to have this problem. They look like they wouldn't be rubbish at anything — except perhaps rapping. Normally we can polish off the quick-fire, but today it virtually finishes us off.

Up until this point tension has steadily mounted, apart from Moon, who's too relaxed. There hasn't been a dry seat in the house. I look up from the quizmaster occasionally and see teachers from both sides cacking it. Now that we're starting to lag behind, however, everyone relaxes.

I press the buzzer on every question, regardless of whether I can take a punt or not. You have to be in it to win it.

'In politics: which act passed in 1984 made it illegal for companies to subjectively discriminate against employees purely on colour, creed, or sexual orientation?'

I buzz.

'The Equal Opportunities Act?'

'Correct.'

'In history: which monarch's accession ended the wars of the Roses?'

I buzz.

'Edward II?'

'Incorrect. Godalming?'

'Henry VII.'

'Correct.'

The Godalming squad gleam modestly at my fuck-up.

Chinese Peter wakes up and gets in on the act, now beating me with the fastest finger. I catch his glance, realising that he's fuming over that crowing look from across the competing table. Gives me and Charlotte the nod that we're going to have it.

He aces some background on the Geneva Convention, and correctly names the infamous early Picasso painting that got everyone in Paris wetting their pants. Godalming get the year the Titanic sunk. Charlotte dredges up the first lesbo who flew across the Atlantic single-handed and gets sloppy seconds on the nationality of Marie Curie when the wool blazers fuck up by saying she's Swiss.

The Godalming vibe is now not so friendly. The friends of the wool blazing three, and there are plenty of them, are throwing evils the size of rocks. The smiles from the teachers as we just inch past them on points become tighter and more fixed. The only love we have in the room comes from Morgan. Moon is so relaxed she's virtually tranquillised. In previous matches, she's on her feet shouting abuse at this point. Heckling the opposing team whenever they get a wrong answer. Barking like Snoop when we scoop points at their expense. Even Morgan comes to expect it.

Today there's none of this. She's barely paying attention. I make for eye contact between questions, not because I need to be worshipped from my podium, but because I need help. I'm saying it silently, final call, team mascot, to no response. All she's concerned with is her txting. The girl with no friends sending and receiving like a maniac. Doesn't look up once.

Chinese Peter can't stop beaming. Our successes, the ruction they've caused the opposition, colour his face and cloud his judgement. He buzzes in on naming all three members of Busted and cocks it up. Says James, Charlie and Ed. Everyone laughs like cackling witches. The Godalming captain throws me this smug look which may as well be a red rag. Arrogant bastard. I finger the knuckleduster decisively, twisting fingers back and forth, like I'm ready to use it. At this point, with only a minute or two left, all fronts are well and truly dropped; no one is interested in being polite.

I give Peter the *Whyyy?* look, so does Morgan and even Charlotte, who never appears unhappy with anything. It's always been our unspoken rule: I answer the music questions. Chinese Peter for science and equations, and Charlotte for everything else.

Now Moon decides to join in and gives the captain of the Godalming the finger. Too little too late, darling. He looks straight past her. Thanks to Peter's over-eager finger, they have now officially caught up. This pissing about takes another thirty off the clock. My stomach is turning over like a car engine. The question master seems in no hurry to resume play. Looks like he wants to laugh like the rest of them. Probably plays golf with half their parents. Get on with the questions, dammit! Some of us want to win.

Last twenty on the clock.

'What is the capital . . . Prendrapen . . . of Australia?'

Shit. That night in my room, and now my mind goes blank.

I look up for Moon. She's still txting and doesn't register. In a world of her own. I'm looking and looking. Nothing. It's the longest five seconds of my life. Worse than any run. Not that the answer's eluding me, there is that, but that Moon is somewhere else when she's supposed to be here for me. Doesn't she even feel the change in the atmosphere? I don't understand it.

Charlotte breaks into a nervous cough.

'I'll have to hurry you,' says the question master irritably. You know he's itching to give the point to the other side. It's written all over his face.

I give Moon one last chance, but she's still staring at her phone. I don't wait, I can't.

'Adelaide.'

'Incorrect. Godalming?'

'The capital of Australia is Canberra.'

'Correct.'

'Fuck.'

Ding! Match ends. We're slaughtered.

It's a miserable ride home. Morgan thinks the radio will do the trick to cheer everyone up, but none of us are having it. Dizzee Rascal never sounded so lifeless. I make a point of sitting with Charlotte, taking the back left window – the furthest seat possible from Moon. Try my hardest not to stare at her, but can't help it. She's talking to Morgan, looking confused. How do you think I feel, babe? I want to shout. I'm the confused party here. What have you been playing at?

At the petrol stop I break into her bag, fish the phone. I have to see what the big attraction was. Hope it's worth the price of me now blanking her. She's saved her recent history, silly girl. The whole story is there for me on a plate, complete picture, no join-the-dots. I catch the txt volley to and from the one particular person who's captured her attention when she should have been concentrating on the match, and saving me from a thrashing.

A new boyfriend. Pearson.

PART 2

23

I have the same dream every night, where Moon has her hands around my throat and is strangling the life out of me. At the point before I lose consciousness, Moon's hands become Casey's, and he's stroking my face as much as he's throttling me. This is when I wake up, heart beating faster than if I'd done the 100m, sweating like a P.I.G.

The dreams started before Moon died and they still keep coming. I'm the King of Repetitive Strangulation. It doesn't scare me. It should, but it doesn't. Anything to keep me closer to her, that's why.

24

Part two in the rehabilitation programme: Mum takes me to dinner round Jason's. She notices the slight change in me and pounces on it. Thinks it might do me some good to be with guys who have been through a similar experience, that a bit of soul-searching activity with different people might gee me up. Moon wasn't killed in a hit and run, and she isn't my sister. OK, both deaths were unexpected, like a fish falling out of the sky and slapping you on the head. An unknown hand flicking the inner switch that shuts off your feelings, mine at least, but I don't see any other similarity. I sulk for a day, but end up going, more for her sake than mine. She's been going stir crazy staring at my expressionless mug every night. New boyfriend keeping a low profile out of respect. This is her way of opening us up, by visiting all the best folks our town has to offer. Means I can find myself on any number of sofas.

Part Three, the final stage of the programme, grieving spring semester, is dinner with Moon's parents and Gwyn, though none of us are ready yet for that particular evening. We have a long way to go before that invitation appears.

I do see Mum's point, I do. There has to be a point when you think, fuck it, and you stop wallowing in this dull ache that seems to be consuming you. But I just don't know how ready I am to cut my losses. I'm still hoping that maybe there's something in this pain worth holding out for.

Mum brings wine, for obvious reasons. Me and Jase even get a glass, which turns into two, and then three. That's how I know how messed up these women are.

Jase's mum, Billie, has made a roast, and makes a big fuss about us eating everything up. There's enough food for ten people. She makes do with a chicken wing, two potatoes, and a vat of buttered carrots. The three of us take it in turns to watch her eat. Billie, normally sensitive about dinner with company (i.e.: she never invites anyone round, ever), relaxes with us, secure in her new role as counsellor rather than counselled.

I'm expecting Billie to give a sermon any minute, but there isn't one. Instead we talk about how Chelsea is slaughtering just about everybody, and whether Catherine Zeta has had any work done. It's only when we're all clearing plates that she makes sure we lag behind the others, and whispers in my ear.

'It gets better, Veerapen. It gets better. I know it doesn't seem like that at the moment, but it does, I promise you.'

Her hand squeezes my shoulder. It's the most reassuring touch I've had in days.

The food is good, not like anything Mum makes, who's all about steam cuisine, and not a fan of standing over a stove for longer than fifteen minutes. I'm used to watching my carb intake over protein, can't get out of the habit, but since I've no use for that regime any more, I keep quiet when Billie piles the roasties on my plate, scoffing everything put in front of me.

I'm starting to notice what I eat. Feeling the muscles in my legs and belly grow slack from no track work, feel the extra weight when I walk, but no guilt. Different month, different body. Nobody can expect me to go back to how I was before.

There's ice cream for desert, not chocolate. No Matchmakers. I expect she's keeping them for herself when we've gone; gonna rip open those boxes and stuff herself silly. I'm a malicious bastard. A big one. Billie's a lovely woman, why do I have to ruin everything good by thinking this junk?

As the evening progresses, it's clear the dinner is all about the mothers. Another bottle comes out, followed by the Baileys. Finally, they want to open up. Stuff they've been keeping from each other over the past few weeks. Itching to compare notes. Me and Jase are only getting in their way. We go and hide in his room after the ice cream. He's downloaded this new Dizzee remix, which is heavy, and plays it on loop for about an hour.

'What's been happening?' I go, meaning school.

'Not much. There's flowers everywhere. Head's been going round, offering counselling to anyone who was in the corridor when it happened. Lizzie Jennings missed the science test because she said she was too upset. Sat in her office from third period through lunch.'

'Lizzie Jennings skipped lunch? Shit, she must be *really* upset.'

It's the first time we've laughed since it happened.

'They say Year Head's gonna lose her job over it. What with her being there at the time and not . . .'

'Don't wanna talk about it,' I go, feeling the proper dinner about to rise out of my stomach, ''cos there's not a lot we can do to help her, is there? My head's too mashed to make sense of it.'

'I've got some knowledge for you, V.'

'Appreciate it. I'm so fucking dumb right now.'

'Check it, there's nothing you can tell me about death,' he goes, looking down into his lap, rolling one out without a care. Billie turns a blind eye apparently. Payback for the chocolate.

'The only thing you need to understand, yeah, is that the luck-iest person is the one who kicks it. For them, it's all over. Done.

They're the ones who don't have comeback. Not like the rest of us.'

Jason missed Moon's death by about a minute. He still looks like he wished he could have been there. I'm glad he wasn't. It's not the sort of thing you want your mates to see.

I wasn't sure whether he was talking about emotional fallout from his sister and the car, the latest buzzword on Mum's radar, or if he was specifically referring to my situation. Since the funeral and that moment in the wood, we haven't seen each other. Steered clear. Thinking it was maybe better that way. Not much fun in mute chatting to mute. Dinner has been good, but the two of us here now, alone now on his bed, is uncomfortable. I'd rather be with Gwyn. We both feel it, though the spliff does something to take some of that unease away, at least for him. Dizzee rattles in my head with the smoke and neither of us say much else after that. Smoking buddies, nothing more.

25

Moon's not going to make me look like a pussy in public. She's not the only one who can get themselves attached. Kelly Button blows out Lizzie Jennings and takes me to see Britney. Her and Lizzie had been planning this trip for months, but what with us getting together, old tatty ginger is left out in the cold.

She tells us she's fine about it, 'I'm not bothered. Not bothered,' she goes at every lesson and every break, meaning she's as mad as fuck and probably suicidal. Lizzie has plenty of friends, but isn't as tight with anyone like she is with Kelly, so she takes this kind of stuff seriously. Kelly tells me she's not bothered either. Wants to take her boyfriend and that's that. Shit, Lizzie would drop Kelly like a stone if by freak chance she managed to get a bloke of her own (one with a guide dog). Also, Kelly's dad got the tickets so it's pretty much her shout who comes with her. End of.

Britney is the first proper date, the official one you tell your mates about, but in keeping with how the girls run things these days, we have a pre-date a couple of days before, which consists of riding the bus into town after school and eschewing Starbucks for Café Nero. Here she makes plans on where we're going to meet, the best kind of clothes to wear, and how we're going to get home. All I need to is prop my elbow on the table and take it all in.

Kel manages to snack and organise at the same time.

At the point when our plans have been formalised – that's to say, that she's happy with them, and she's going on for the hundredth time about how excited she is, and saying that even though Britney is getting kinda lame these days, that it'll still be an amazing show which'll put all those lapdancers in the shade – my plate of food is still untouched.

Her eyes shark about my chips.

'You're either not hungry,' she goes, 'or you're incredibly nervous. One of the two.'

I could have told her about how gluten is the biggest *verboten* on my diet sheet, and how a chunk of ciabatta would slug me up and turn my running a notch down, making my steps lumpy rather than sleek. But it's easier this way, keeping my mouth shut, staying silent and mysterious, so that she's always wondering but never completely pinpointing. The truth, that I'm really fucking nervous on my debut pre-date, and that I'm a Nazi about food, isn't what a girl needs to hear.

Britney mimes throughout the show like the lazy whore she is. It's only the costumes that keep me awake, all see-through body stockings and slivers of g-string. Without these brief flashes of titty and camel toe, beds appearing out of nowhere, and girl dancers snogging each other for the hell of it, I'd be falling asleep. Everyone else around me is hysterical with joy, making me feel like the world's biggest party pooper.

About halfway, when she's getting all serious and true to her artistic self, the on-stage confessional, my phone goes. It's Jason. He always knows when to call at the most inappropriate moments. Last week it was when Kelly and me were getting comfortable round my house, now it's Britney. I can barely hear him and shout down the phone like a twat. 'What? I'm at a concert. Britney. BRITNEY SPEARS! BRITNEY!' etc. Everyone around us shoots me like I'm the biggest piece of shit. I could have left the call but knew that if I made a big deal with Jason it would get back to Moon. Kelly gives me the smallest of nudges but keeps her eyes fixed on the stage – we've all been waiting for Britney to make some reference to her mismatched marriages and this feels like it could be the moment. We are sat in an area teaming with homosexuals. I don't know whether they want to thump me or do me. I'm wearing my new Nike vest top and my Jesus Is My Homeboy cap so I figure it's maybe a little of both.

On the way home we act like one of those couples that's been together years; we don't speak to each other. Kelly's pissed about the call. She's at her most dressed up tonight, Von Dutch from head to toe, ironed mouse hair cascading from her flat cap, giant gold hoops that are more high street than hip hop, and isn't happy with anything that makes her look immature. Giving off the vibe that I'm the most childish accessory she's got. Also, she's annoyed because I wouldn't get out of my seat to dance to 'Toxic'. The only time I did move was when one of the friendlier-looking homosexuals went out for a slash, chasing him up the concourse and persuading him to get a couple of extra beers for two children in need. I thought I'd got a result, because I felt her displeasure fairly early on, but even half a cup of Carling, as warm and as yellow as one of the samples in Mum's car boot, wouldn't placate her. She didn't touch it.

Kelly dances like she doesn't care. Come the Madonna duet it's my turn to keep my eyes on the stage, on the audience below, anywhere but on her. Kel relies on the homosexuals around her to complete the routine when she sees that I'm a hopeless case; she is Britney, they are Madonna. I can't help it. I'm a runner not a dancer. We play about in her room all the time, but I've never seen her dance like this before, like when you're really caught up in the music and the spectacle; vocal and abandoned. I learn more about what's going in Kel's head in those three minutes than I have done in the past two weeks. Her moves are all passion, and they are solely for her. I'm well aware that this isn't a seduction dance. Her eyes would be open otherwise.

Watching her from the corner of my eye, all I see is her profile, button nose, skinny slug lips, the eyelashes of a cow; cheekbones as high and contoured and shiny as an Audi panel. She spray-tanned the night before, giving her skin the colour of over-done toast, something close to mine. From this angle I don't recognise her. It's like looking at someone else. Honest moments like this always make me nervous, that's why I'm happier nodding my head, hands in pockets, wondering when Brit's now fully-clothed prancing will stop. I don't do emotional exchanges through dance or otherwise.

The tube is so noisy there isn't any need to add to it; our silent state is approved. Carriages crammed with more sportswear than JD, including what looks like an orange and black trackie, similar to Casey's; some dad out with his kid. You get a better class of person in Wembley. More homosexuals clapping their hands and waxing lyrical on how 'Slave 4 U' compared to the MTV version, and some drab pasty woman over thirty with a big red mouth looking like a sore vagina harping on to her equally ugly friend about Steve from head office who wasn't responding to any of her advances. Poor bastard, whoever he is, having to look at that every day. I try and make eye contact with Kel, and when that doesn't work, knock her knee in the direction of the drab women, as if to say look at those spinster freaks, but she doesn't see the joke and shoots me the look she's picked up from the homosexuals.

'I should have known better than to bring a bloke. At least Lizzie would have danced with me.'

'I *was* dancing.'

'Veep, slouching around with your hands in your pockets isn't dancing.'

'Tell that to Michael Jackson.'

Britney being the diva bitch monster down to the last single molecule took to the stage over a half hour late, meaning by the time we push through the cheap trackie bottoms and the *Sex and the City* cast-offs, and finally reach Waterloo, we miss the last train by two minutes.

'Disaster, mate,' goes Kel. 'Bloody disaster.'

She's always calling me mate when she's not using Veep. Her family are traders so everything's all cor blimey guvnor, strike a light. It's not what I'm used to.

Kel calls her mum, who panics and duly dispatches her dad up the A3 pronto.

'Listen to me, Kel. Stay where there's plenty of people, and don't talk to anyone,' she goes, the quivering modulations of a normally hardy woman who has been floored by sitting through too many evenings of *Crimewatch*.

She calls back five minutes later.

'Better still, stay near the security cameras. It's the safest place to be.'

It makes you want to disappear for an hour or two just to shit her up.

We pool the last of our cash and set up camp on the Burger King balcony. Fags for Kelly, a milkshake each, and a jumbo box of nuggets for me. A feast. This was exactly the reason I'd endured ninety minutes of Britney's cod artistry and an hour of Kelly's wrath — for this late-night one to one with my beautiful girlfriend.

Kel isn't like Moon, so everything is easy. I don't have to try so hard. Her eyes soften after a sip or two of milkshake, curled lips shift from down to up. We snog in Burger King for what feels like an hour. Her lips are the tenderest I've ever felt, her tongue the longest, her breath the sweetest.

There's this sign tattooed to my forehead that says I'm hookable. She hands over the snogs, knowing this.

Now that we're going out officially, Kel is holding back on the sex. Wants us to talk more, hang. Since my treat in the park, we've only done it once — on my sofa when Mum went for Chinese. A fifteen-minute wonder. She still flirts like a mother whether we're alone or not, but unlike Moon none of it's for show. When we talk, she only ever has eyes for me, there's none of this looking over my shoulder to check who's around, grass-is-greener bollocks.

After the Pearson business, Kel's honesty comes as a welcome relief; feels like a holiday away from female madness. I'm not as bothered about the sex as I thought I would be. Sometimes just being with her is enough. I'm shooting them off every night obviously – I am fifteen – but I ain't worried. Sooner or later she'll get so hot and crack, and then the curtains will part, haha.

Jase thinks she wants me to respect her. Read it in *Cosmo* when he was stacking the magazines at work. I do respect her, I tell him. I buy her bus ticket, drop in a ten pack of Benson when I can get served, spend Saturday afternoons down the mall, take her nan to the park. If that isn't respect, I don't know what is. Jase looks at me like a retard.

'Mate, that's not even the start of it. If you want to get into her pants, you're going to have to do better than that.'

Like he knows anything. Jase shags one of the part-timers, a Micra-driving housewife, in the stockroom once every three weeks if he's lucky, but he's never had a proper girlfriend in his life. A casual grope with Lizzie Jennings every once in a while. Nothing that lasts more than a week or two. Something to do with his sister and the car crash; girls think he has too much baggage . . . that he's a proper nutter because of it. They're not at the age where a lanky stoner is considered a great catch. In another five years, though, when they're pining for surfer chic . . . I ditch his advice, need it like I need a hole in the head.

Snogging is snogging, I don't confuse it with anything else. Kel is still mad at me, each of us taking pains to avoid mentioning the Brit-word in case something blows up again, but I know things are forgotten when she comes back from the toilet with a bag of those baby jelly beans that cost about five pounds a pack. Standing above me, and placing them in my hands wordlessly. She lets the beans and the kiss on my cheek that follows do the talking. Payback for taking her shit on the tube, I guess, and also in part for the strawberry milkshake I'd produced earlier without any prompting, because I knew it was her favourite. We kiss, and hold hands, and giggle, and kiss again.

Much later, close to one a.m., once we're back within Surrey's safe

71

borders, and Kel's mum has been informed, and Kel's dad is driving past the station, I spot something standing at the taxi rank.

There's two of them, a man and a boy, the shorty slightly behind the man, both in shadow, and both in trackies I'm now noticing. They're the last in the taxi queue, a line of around twenty people, and are laughing about some bollocks. The kid is cracking up so the older one must be a hoot. He's holding a rolled up Britney poster, identical to the two I picked up outside Wembley after the show; supersized so that the tits are bigger than the average human head – one for me and Jason. The older man is in and out of shadow, but the build, the laugh, the Nike airs with the exaggerated red soles like Coco the clown, are all photo-fit material; match my disgraced ex-Harrier trainer 100%. Someone call *Crimewatch*.

26

Pearson is a volleyball-playing shit-for-brains lump who thinks he's popular just for punching a stupid ball around an indoor court like a faggot. Sure, the volleyball squad are the glamour elite of the school, twelve guys and girls riding the crest of a wave, the closest thing we have to jocks, but even this status doesn't protect him from ridicule.

He doesn't realise that everyone laughs at him behind his back. Thinks of him as an oaf, which, at this place, is saying something. The other members of the squad are protective of him and all, on the court they're like brothers, but away from the sports hall they're not as defensive as they should be. Must be something in his manner: loud, overbearing, know-it-all smartarse. Has a habit of hogging the ball and busting a few solo moves on the court, whether it benefits the game or not. Coming out with all kinds of shit just to get some attention. Dumping the flid kids' clothes in the shower whilst they're in PE, bullying the pikeys in the changing rooms, challenging them to prove that their underwear wasn't 2p from Oxfam. General stupidness we should all have grown out of at twelve.

The team seem to agree. Me and Jase would have got a cleaning from them otherwise.

Moon used to realise this, I think, but seems to have forgotten now that her eyes have gone heart-shaped. Now they walk around the corridors hand in hand, barely out of each other's sight.

Normally I have respect for the jocks. Fellow sportsmen, and all that. It should be a mutual thing. We all give each other a heads-up around school, some more enthusiastic and exuberant than others. Since I do most of my training out of school, do all of my competitions out of school, steer clear from competing in lacklustre class athletics, I keep it low-key. I'm not a show-off like some of these volleyball and footie idiots. But nothing will make me like this guy. Rich boy trying to be like one of us? Fuck off! What's the appeal of that? Putting my feelings for Moon aside, he just ain't right for her.

'They're sweet together,' Kel said once, when we saw them feeding each other chips in the canteen. Thought it was all right now that we were a couple ourselves, thought she could relax her neuroses a little, but she saw my look, realised I wasn't laughing.

'If you want us to stay together, you're going to have to stop saying things like that,' I go, voice so low it's virtually in the gutter; where tone ends and a snake-like hiss begins. 'Don't keep talking about them. Don't even mention them. Doesn't do anyone any good.'

It came out tougher than I meant it to. I was going for jokey, but something in Kel's observation set something off. Made me panic that she was possibly right. Panicked me more when I thought about how everyone else at school might be thinking the same thing; that Moon was better off with a proper boyfriend, and without me.

Glance over in Moon's direction whilst Kel goes to the loo for a discreet cry, waving over Lizzie Jennings on the way. They've finished the chips and she's now biting into his Snickers. They take alternate mouthfuls. She takes it slow, conscious of crumbs falling on her shirt. He grabs the fucker like the greedy pig he is. It's all about ownership with that piece of shit. Then they share the same can of drink. I can almost feel Pearson's gob on my lips. Can't stop watching. Feel sick. Her face is so different. Furrows smoothed, mouth looser, eyes wide, none of her usual defensive squinting. Touches her hair every other minute but all the time certain of herself. None of it's a ruse. She's never looked so settled . . . or sated.

27

Jason has no time for Casey. Calls him various vegetable names, depending on which aisle he's stacking.

'He's a turnip, man,' he goes, on more than one occasion, when I find myself justifying exactly why I'm with him. 'He's a fucking kiddie fiddler. I've got no time for him, however great you say he is.'

I get twitchy at the mention of kiddie-fiddler and Casey in the same sentence. I wish I hadn't been looking out the car window, seeing things I shouldn't have.

Jase believes everything he reads in the papers. Swears by *The Sun*, like it's the Torah or something.

It doesn't escape my notice that the fiddled kid is the same age as his sister would be now. It touches a nerve; his sole defence for starting a little backyard blaze last summer that ended up in Casey's house being burnt to the ground.

I'm not supposed to know, but I do. He told some slag the night he did it, as a way to get into her pants. She told Chinese Peter's sister, who told me. I'd been running as usual, so wasn't around. And I wonder why people don't invite me to anything. But I wish I'd got evidence of it. Something like an MPEG would've been awesome. Like capturing *history in the making*. Totally wild.

It's one of those secrets that Jase keeps from me, the way I keep stuff from him; like when I had to start giving Mum tuff love when she started overdoing the pity party a couple of years after Dad left, and got really close to embarrassing herself. (Jews, delayed reaction.) You gotta do what you gotta do.

We all have our secrets.

28

Kel makes me walk on air and I start forgetting the real things. It's gone eleven at night when I realise that Mum hasn't washed my kit. Or any other clothes at all. I'm half asleep when I work this out; one of those late-night flashes that hits you before nodding off, gets you out of bed and staggering about the utility room with your eyes shut.

Mum is watching TV and says she won't help.

'I'm moving on,' she goes. 'I can't be your maid for ever. You're going to have to learn to take care of your own laundry.'

There's an empty bottle of wine on the coffee table, one of the pocket ones, so I ain't too worried. I'm not casting aspersions, I'm just saying.

'Watch what you're doing with the washing liquid. Don't overfill the machine like last time. If you make a mess, clean it up.'

'Okey-dokey, lemon-cokey.'

When she's in this mood, it's pointless trying to argue.

The reason for the wine bottle and the mood is this:

Mum has decided it's been long enough since Dad. We've been here before, eight months after he ran to Germany with the optician slut, when she said quite resolutely it was time to move forward, but she hadn't reckoned on the fear taking her over. Ever since Dad left it's only ever been the two of us.

This time there seems to be more weight behind it. Far from

coming out of the blue, it's been on her mind for a while; something to do with one of the younger doctors at the health centre fancying her. He wasn't her type, but did something to remind her that she could still cast a spell if she put her mind to it.

She doesn't tell me this obviously, our open relationship only works one way, but I overhear her on the phone to Jason's mum one night. Billie was distraught because she'd spent all afternoon chucking her guts up and needed to talk to someone about it. Listening to one-sided phone calls is amazing. If you can concentrate hard enough, you can pick up just about everything. It's something Moon taught me. She's an expert at it.

Dad's also been threatening to come by for a visit, which may also explain Mum's spring cleaning of self. Bored of life in the Black Forest or wherever the fuck he lives in Germany. Wants to come and bond with his firstborn. A solo trip; new wife staying at home with the kids. Twins, aged five. Killer time manager, my father.

This will be purely a father/son thing, the first time for about three years. He doesn't want to make a big fuss, and he's right not to. For once in his life, he'd judged the mood correctly. I've got no intention of seeing him.

Mum gets herself in on a speed-dating evening in town with another district nurse, one of the showy younger ones who's always down the pub, and persuades Billie to go with them. It's being held at Po Na Na, the smartest bar we have, and also the slimiest. Mum dresses up to the nines, long black dress, feathery shawl, heels. Hair piled up so high that you know she ain't messing. Face made-up by her mate at the House of Fraser counter two hours earlier. I'm left to fend for myself for the evening. Kel comes round and I get lucky. So does Mum by the look of her. Her face is flushed. She tries to tell me off about not clearing up the snacks after Kel's left, but can't help grinning; keeps putting her hand over her mouth to giggle whenever I ask her how the night went. She got numbers, two of them, but won't tell me any more than that.

29

I hate this trend for skirting around issues. I don't see the point. Mum's prone to procrastinate. She knows which tube of toothpaste she wants, but picking the lottery numbers can take most of the afternoon. I'm the other way, happy to charge into anything. Something I picked up from Dad. He's the master at it. He upped and left the country the moment he'd poked the homewrecker optician and got serious. It's the reason I hate him, but if it were anyone else I'd admire his style. I suppose it's like this with any parent. Feelings change from one day to the next.

Coming straight to the point, cutting the bullshit, is one of the few similarities between us. Correction, a similarity I *remember* being between us. I haven't seen him for so long I don't know what he's like any more.

So at next training, I'm ready to grill Casey about what he was doing at Britney with that random kid. It said on the news last year that the subject of Casey's investigation was eleven or twelve, but this kid looked way younger. Either he is a half-pint, or he's really eleven and I'm growing up too quickly for my own good.

It had been on my mind all night. I thought about txting him when I got in but knew it would spook him to know he'd been spotted. Had this feeling it would make him clam up. Dad's approach was far better. Direct questioning never fails. Even if he's lying to me, I'll be able to see it in his eyes.

I get to the park at half-five and warm up, flex. Get through all the preliminary business so that I'll be ready for him. Six passes and no sign of Casey. Six-fifteen, nothing. Six-thirty, footsteps, but only the park-keeper checking to see that I'm not making mischief (he was the one who caught me breaking out of Harriers last summer). Because it's early and I never need it, I've left my phone charging in my room, the battery having been worked to its last nerve.

Casey plans each session in advance so I pretty much know what I have to do. I set myself exercises based on whatever he's been threatening the day before. Today it's starting block technique into the first fifty metres, and I get on with it in the hope that he'll turn up sometime soon.

'Stop slacking, V-pen. Don't think you can put in only fifty per cent just because I'm not here to check up on you, Mr V-pen.'

He's caught me making a balls-up in the starting block. Dammit. I look at my watch, six fifty-five.

'What's with the time-keeping, fruitcake? Thought this was meant to be a full-time gig.'

'Enough of the cheek, young Turk. Get back on those blocks and let me see what you think's the correct starting position. Then we'll compare notes.'

When he's in this mood there's no messing with him. He throws down his trackie jacket, red and white, and we get down to business. I suppose that's why I hired him the first place, because I wanted some seriousness. All this other foolishness is an added extra.

I only get the chance to quiz him once training's over. We're walking up the path towards the car park. Park-keeper hasn't cleaned up the dog shit from yesterday so every step smells foul. He's in an awful good mood about something, telling me some story about a notorious Surrey ref who's as blind as a bat and giving examples of his various fuck-ups. We're both holding our noses and laughing, and he pats me on the shoulder as we walk. Only once, only lightly, but a pat nonetheless. If I wasn't so secure I'd be screaming for Childline about now.

'You never did tell me why you were late,' I go, as he's getting into his car, glad for some distance. 'If I was fifty-five minutes late for training, like you were, you'd bust my fucking balls.'

'I hear that, V-pen, sir, and I sincerely apologise. I'll fix my alarm clock and promise it won't happen again.'

'This training thing works both ways, Casey. Neither of us can afford to be late.'

He laughs at that.

'Shouldn't I be the one telling you that?'

'Not really, since I'm the talent and you're the help.'

Spoken like my father's son. He's a bastard about status, something to do with him being a Tamil and never having had any to begin with.

'Being disrepectful, V-pen, will only get you into trouble with your maker. Did your mother tell you never to mock your elders?'

'She's too busy tending to the sick. So where were you? Late night, was it?'

'Not at all. I went to my meeting and was in bed at eleven. I've been an early bird all week. Not that it's any of your business. Sir.'

A salute and a sneer.

Casey is member of the Christian Fellowship via Catholicism. Didn't think the nuns at St Mary's clapped enough. There's a church near the Common that takes him. You can find him there speaking in tongues most weekends.

'Must have been some meeting. You've got bags under your eyes, Casey. You should take a leaf out of my book. Went to see Britney the other night, got in at one, and still made it here for six. Fresh as a daisy.'

His eyes widen a millimetre of a millimetre, but that's just enough for me.

'Britney Spears, eh? And how was that?'

'An education, Casey. You should have been there. I saw all sorts.'

30

Me and Moon don't have Saturday jobs. 'We're professional spend-whores,' she goes, each time we flash our plastic at the cashpoint or checkout. Practising for the day when we turn eighteen and become eligible for major credit problems.

Mum doesn't want anything to get in the way of my training, and thinks Saturdays should be my day off. Makes sure Dad sends me all the money I need. Moon, like her sister, is a lazy princess who's born to shop and very little else. It's inevitable that we would bump into each other between the mall and the high street eventually.

This is our moment, in the queue at Starbucks. Only the two of us. Jase is at Tesco, Kelly with the traders on the market, and Pearson caddying golf clubs up on the Downs. There are no back-ups or pretending to have prior appointments. We're thrust together, end of.

'I didn't plan it. It just happened with Pearson,' is the first thing that comes out of her mouth, literally the moment we spot each other, and neither of us have our lattes yet. We've both paid our money and are standing at the counter like idiots, thinking of something to say. These Starbucks people are getting slower. If I actually knew them I'd swear that it was deliberate. (But they're foreign, so it's not.)

She looks fantastic. Jeans that cling to her arse, pink ugg boots, cropped red hoodie, gold hoops bigger than Kelly's. Really working a look. I miss hanging out with a fashion plate. A girl like that always makes her boy look equally great by association, a notion that's never been completely lost on me.

The only warmth coming from my body is from the latte I'm now holding. Realise that the pair of us are holding mugs to drink in, out of habit, rather than take-out cups. We find a table, and get it over with. It's the only sensible thing to do.

'I hear your eyes met in a crowded chemistry lab. Were there fire-works?'

'He came to apologise, actually. He's really sorry about all that business . . .'

'Ah, yes. He's so sorry about hanging out with the Paki bashers that he still hasn't apologised personally to the Paki in question.'

Two Pakis in one sentence makes her flinch. Me too, if I'm honest. I'm not part of the radical reclamation camp. I know it's good enough for the niggas, but . . .

'He really wants to make it up with you and Jason. Really, he feels dreadful about it.'

'Did you just say dreadful? What is he doing to you? You've never said dreadful in your life.'

'Piss off.'

'What, family pearls under that hoodie of yours?'

'You should give him a chance, VP, he's really not as bad as you think.'

'Once a tosser, always a tosser. You've been together for what, a month? And not a peep from your noble boy. Just lots of diving into corridors whenever he sees us.'

'Like I said, he does feel bad . . . but he's kinda pissed at you too. After I told him about you snooping.'

Moon found me flicking through her phone on the bus after the Challenge outing to Godalming. I was properly caught out. Didn't think quickly enough. I should've said I was looking for Jase's new mobile number, that I'd programmed the digits the wrong way round. But everything's easier with hindsight. She went fucking ballistic, really fucking bunny boiler, because one thing Moon hates is anyone going through her stuff, even me. Been stung too often by her crazy parents being secretively investigative in the name of welfare. I only have myself to blame. This is the first time we've spoken since.

'How else was I supposed to find out? I knew something was up. You'd been acting funny all day,' I go. 'You were hardly going to tell me otherwise.'

I may be thinking other things, but as far as she's concerned, I'm admitting nothing.

'I was working up to telling you VP, OK? It's just been a difficult situation . . . I was probably going to do it that afternoon, if you hadn't spoiled it.'

'Snogging a boring bastard who's tried to kick your mates to shit. Twice. Can see how that could prove difficult.'

I don't mention my theory about her being in love with him, in case she tells me it's true. Prefer to think I'm being stupid, making up shit to make myself feel worse.

She can't shut up.

81

'I like how I look when I'm with him. I look like I matter. I'm no longer this girl who sits up in her room and obsesses too much. I stop thinking about running the world and how I'm going to be in twenty years' time. I hang off his shoulder like some trophy, and I see myself as I am right now, and I like it. I like how I can live in the moment.'

'We live in the moment, don't we? You and me?'

'Not in the same way. We make out we're spontaneous, but we're just projecting what we want to be. With Daniel, I just live it. There is no projecting.'

'Fucking load of bo-lax, you're on about. You talk shite sometimes.'

A member of staff comes over and asks us to keep our voices down. A couple of the parents on the sofas aren't taking too kindly to our language. They have the timid eyes and weak pallor of secondary school teachers or social workers, but none that we know. Their rugrats are all under three, dribbling gob everywhere, and practically bald. The Starbucks skivvy is Polish or something, so she has to repeat herself about five times before we understand what she's saying. We nod all apologetically when we finally get it, and then, when she's out of sight, back to her milk frother, we give the offending parents the fuck-you finger and an evil eye. Your filthy rugrats look a greater threat than us – hygienically speaking. Like, where's the fire?

Now we're laughing, the pair of us, like it's old times. But it only lasts a minute. Short and deliciously sweet, like the Frappuccinos they make here (the best!). There's still a connection between us.

'How's life with her?' she asks, ruining it. 'I hear the pair of you are like love's young dream.'

Patronising, even if she is three months older. She leans forward, elbow on table, left hand cradling chin, looking like she's interested, even though her tone has become as cold as ice again. Makes Kelly sound like scum. If I come any closer she'll whip her hand out and give me a slap. It's her classic defensive position; I've seen her in action, know all the moves, even the hidden ones. I'd hug her in a second if she let me.

'It's kushty,' I tell her, even though it doesn't always feel that way. 'Kel's safe. We went to see Britney a few days ago.'

'So I hear. I'm sure you looked like a real couple.'

Moon's been hearing a lot of things. This isn't getting us anywhere. Sarcasm can only outdo sarcasm for so long. We used to compete in our rooms, cussing cast-offs that could last hours if our minds were up to it; but today neither of us has top trump. Brains lazy from too much lovin'. Emotional holes filled, momentarily content. We leave the lattes and piss off.

31

Mum goes on a proper date, the first follow-through from the speed-dating evening. His name is Mike and he's a solicitor-barrister-type person. Has his own business in Esher and a staff of ten. I'm more interested in seeing a picture, and clocking how old he is, but have to make do with the information Mum gives me. She's being very limited on this front. There's no time after work to see her mate at the beauty counter so she does everything herself, and makes a pretty good job of it. She's lost a load since joining WeightWatchers and doesn't look bad at all. This was after the summer when she saw our snaps from Portugal and had a fit over the size of her thighs. She's wearing trousers this time, black and flarey, with one of those floaty tops that all the makeover women wear on TV, very bright pink, so Mike will have to wear his sunglasses.

I put a note in her make-up bag just in case there's any first-night wobbles. It says 'Don't Worry. You Look Fantastic! XXX'

She meets him at the new Italian that's opened opposite the library, and leaves just before seven-thirty, giving me an evening of fun. Kel is having tea round her nan's so no action there. Have to make do with Jason's company. Preferable to Kel, what with the mood she's in (I had to let her in on the Starbucks business).

I let Jase smoke a large one out of the back window, whilst I burn the new 50 track from one of those illegal sites, and try and get trapped on a porn cycle. Unfortunately Mum's been fiddling more than she should have done and has activated all the AOL child-locks. This is what happens when your parents start to get too computer literate. Means the only Vs we are getting to see on the computer screen tonight are violins or violas.

Dad calls around ten. See it's him because we have caller ID. Can't face exchanges with him and Moon in the same day. It's too much to ask. Get Jase to answer, shouting down the phone like a madman, saying that the house is on fire. He's stoned, and throws himself into it. Lives the part. Bellows like smoke's choking his every last breath.

We put the phone on speaker. Can hear Dad's panic until he realises it's a wind-up. 'Hello? Is everything all right? Hello? Veerapen, why are you shouting like that? Let me speak to your mum right away.' He only hangs up when he hears the laughing.

We're on the floor, cackling like idiots. Wetting ourselves. Clinging to the walls because our sides are splitting. Lasts a good fifteen minutes. He doesn't call back.

32

Moon can never be subtle about anything. You only get this with spend-whores. Anyone else would have more decency. She has a stayover when her parents go to Tallin for the weekend. They won flights at the Citizen's Advice Xmas Raffle and had been wetting their pants over it for weeks. Mum, who was also there, had been feeling lucky and spent an extra ten pounds on raffle tickets, so was pissed at the outcome, their single ticket coming through, and muttered about it for days.

'Sympathy vote for the Lib Dems, that's all it is. They can't win anything else, that's why they let them win the bloody raffle!'

She still managed to keep it all smiles when she was outside our four walls, their eyes meeting when taking out the wheelie bins, or bumping trolleys at the Tesco car park.

For the sleepover Gwyn invites the gay-boy Goths who adore her, and the sappy Christian mate Ohmygod. Moon includes the top tier of the library posse, these two dozy science swots who think everything she says is completely radical. One of them, Captain Vegetable, has a lazy eye and used to wear an eyepatch. These are the kind of people she used to hang round with before I rescued her. Jase and Pearson complete the set, the pair of them acting as totty for her guests as well as Gwyn's.

The invite doesn't extend to myself, my place being taken by Captain Vegetable and his team of soggy legumes. Botched corrective eye surgery over me. Makes me feel so special. I've had lunch with Moon almost every day this week and she has never mentioned anything about a stayover. Meathead's on a weeklong lunch detention, which is why this is possible. Whenever he's present, I'm lower down the evolutionary scale than even Captain sodding Vegetable.

It's Gwyn who gives the game away when she sees me at the shops after school.

Her: Coming over later?

Me: Uh? (blank potato face like I'm having a spastic attack)

The stayover means nothing, even though Mum's on a late shift, giving me all the time in the world to get up to tricks. I book a couple of movies on Sky Plus and make myself my own comfort zone: duvet on the sofa, Diet Coke, trashy food I'd be arrested for eating if Casey caught me. It's fine. It's real. I'm in my universe and they're in theirs. Same zoo, different cages.

But I can't fool anyone, least of all myself.

First, the TV thing doesn't work. I have one eye on Will Smith, the other on the curtains, and what's going on beyond my windows. *I Robot* is a bucky duck compared to the happenings across the street. I'm too wound up to even touch the nachos. Watching robots go mad isn't the best suggestion for someone who's almost strangling themselves with their self-control. All it makes you do is want to follow suit, start your own revolution.

Next, I get a call from Jase, asking me which races Kelly Holmes won the medals for.

'Why you wanna know that?'

'It's a quiz question. Triv Pursuit. And if anyone knows the answer to that it'll be you, right?'

There's laughing in the background, female, and Pearson shouting his mouth off about something or other. The music is Chili Peppers.

'Where are you playing Triv Pursuit, Jase?'

'You know.'

I give him the answer, one right, one wrong.

I Robot is dead after that.

The best spot is upstairs. I stand at Mum's window and do my watching. Thinking how MI5 need people like me. A Paki who likes nothing better than snooping around. I'd be killer at it.

They are sitting on the living room floor drinking white wine and playing their dumbass Triv Pursuit. Wait 'til I tell the boys down the sports block that Pearson was sipping vino and doing board games! What a pussy joker! No wine for the Jones girls, of course. The bottle being passed round is a concession to the weaker will of their guests. No judgement! They stick to Diet Coke and keep their opinions to themselves.

Moon and Pearson are in the centre of the room by the fireplace. Where else would they sit? They're a couple! Practising their prom pose (and would be in with a chance if Moon wasn't so unpopular, ha!). They are glued together and don't move. When it isn't their turn on Triv, they lightly snog. Gwyn waits on their guests hand and foot, occasionally helped by Jase. Aside from the wine – only one glass each – there's Fanta and nachos and spiral crisps and absolutely NO SMOKING. Everyone seems to find Pearson incredibly funny. The cunt seems to have a goofy answer for everything. After some question that one of the gay-boy Goths asked, his answer took about five minutes. How does he know enough words to last five minutes? He can barely say the days of the week let alone anything else. Everyone's laughing at whatever the retard is saying, including my so-called stoner mate. It's excruciating.

Watching a room of people laughing whilst you are standing alone feels as if you are being stabbed repeatedly. It's fun.

I wonder about the sleeping arrangements; where Moon and Pearson will sleep. Thinking about it takes up half my night, and now, the jumbo bag of nachos. Turns out everyone crashes on the living room floor. Sofas moved back. No excuses for creeping away.

I make a couple of crank calls to kill the boredom and the hurt. Two calls to a reflexology woman's house down the street (she's always leafleting her details); one call to Pizza Express. On each occasion I scream down the phone like I'm being murdered. I stuff a sock down my throat so that no one can guess it's me. In one of the three calls I also cry. I've done it a few times. People seem to find it very realistic.

I know this makes me a weirdo, but you have to do the things that make you feel better. Ease the pressure in your head.

I save the best for Moon's place. The silent caller act. The lights are off at my house, car out the drive. Can't pin anything on me. The beauty of *1471.

Darth Vader breath.

I give up after the sixth ring. Gwyn keeps picking up.

The next morning me and Moon take the bus into Kingston to buy Jase a birthday present. I call for her at eleven-thirty and the house has already emptied, all evidence cleared away. I tell her about a boring night watching daft movies, and ask about hers. She says she had a quiet night in.

33

Jase makes no attempt to hide where he's been when I ask him about Moon's sleepover.

'They didn't want you there, mate. End of. Knew that it would kick-off with Pearson otherwise. You can't act all surprised about it.'

'But we're supposed to be friends, Moon and me. Us. How come you can be there and I can't? You've had fights with him too.'

'I don't hold grudges, VP. I think that's the difference.'

Again, this can be attributed to the Jew gene and the Tamil gene, both parents being natural born grudge-holders.

'Anything to report, from this A-list-only, cream-of-the-crop party?'

'Not in the way you're thinking. It wasn't X-rated,' he goes, in his fake LA accent, which is so dumb it sounds like he's from Bristol or something.

'Look, it was a laugh. Simple as. Turned up, had a few drinks, watched a video, played games, acted stupid . . .'

'Yeah. "End of." I get it.'

'I was out of my box by about nine o'clock anyway. Didn't pay much attention to anyone after that. You know what these things are like. I'm only good to have around when they want me to get things going. After that, it's "See ya." Look at what goes on at all those park parties I get asked to. I ain't stupid. Watch how Gwyn's friends will blank me at school next week. And Pearson. He'll act like he never met me.'

'Unless we're together, of course, then he'll act all matey just to wind me up.'

'Just ignore it. Stop getting yourself wound up. Concentrate on what you *do* want, and then one day you'll have forgotten why you got so angry in the first place.'

'You think?'

He pats me on the shoulder, and looks me in the eye. Sort of thing my dad would do.

'You can't bottle all your anger all the time. It isn't healthy. You have to open the lid from time to time, and let all the unnecessary anger just dissolve. Trust me. I know.'

34

I'm having lattes with Gwyn. Same Starbucks, same red hoodie. Says she wears it 'cos it makes her feel closer to Moon. Gywn's a bigger girl, so she really has to squeeze herself into it, but I get her point. If I could fit into any of her clothes right now I'd be doing the same.

Only see her back at the counter when I arrive and my heart stops beating. I don't register that the hair is longer, the waist thicker. And then she turns round, and the reality is half horror half let-down, like in that mad seventies film where you're faced with that midget hag that wants to kill you. This was a pretty similar set-up.

The txt had come out of the blue, several days after the ghost passed me in the Mall. Starbucks midday — time we talked. Over that night I gave myself a hundred and twenty-four reasons why I shouldn't be sitting across a table from Gywn, why I should be wringing her neck for making sure that I was the one landed in it, but somehow I found myself leaving the house, getting on the bus, walking through town, turning up.

Sitting on the same table that me and Moon used to hang out on is too much of a head-fuck, so we're on the sofa. Not sure how to take Gwyn today. Her face is red, skin around the eyes inflamed from more crying probably, but she doesn't look mad at me. Buys the lattes for a start, and biscotti. You don't do that unless you really want to give your enemy a false sense of security. I should have my guard up but find myself melting into her. Maybe because of how cuddly she looks in the hoodie, securely round, the weeniest touch of belly poking through the bottom, or possibly because of those tender just-dried eyes. Or maybe, and this is the reason closest to the truth, just because we both need people to be nice to us. There's been more than enough hate.

She's holding my hand and talking about how nice the funeral was, and how she wished I stayed for the whole of the service. I couldn't bear it as the vicar did his final wrapping up, so I bolted. Went AWOL for about two hours. Even now I have no idea where I went, only that I managed to get myself to their house for the wake. Really, that day was one long AWOL with brief reality breaks for the church and the wake. No wonder everyone is treating me strangely.

When I got to Moon's house, looking like it had always done, just with five hundred cars parked outside, I wasn't sure of the reception I'd get, if they were going to punch me or feed me sandwiches. Relations at the church were civil enough, but that was church. Hardly the best place for a dust-up. But at that point, walking up to the door and ignoring the bell, banging the knocker very hard, twice, I was fearless again. I'd lost everything, a door slammed in my face is a pinprick in comparison.

'Why the about turn?' I ask. 'Thought I was public enemy number one at the Jones household.'

The funeral changed their mind it seems. Seeing me in that state struck a nerve. Also, the parents are Christians, the kind who have the fish bumper sticker on each of their vehicles. Fish-wavers aren't fighters, they're forgivers.

She's telling me that her parents want to see me for dinner. That they're ready to talk, if I am. That's the point of her meeting up today. That Moon would have wanted us to get along in some way, no matter what happens.

Now it's my turn to have tears in my eyes. Everything she says is unexpected. We're now turned inwards towards each other as we speak. Eyes are on me the whole time, not like her sister. She's still holding my hand in both of hers. We talk into each other's ears so none of the mothers can hear the sound of our hearts being bled dry. If she comes any closer I'm going to have to kiss her. If I close my eyes, it would be like . . .

Only Pearson's mother comes in and drops her shopping when she sees us. An albino giantess, almost the same height as Jase. Pearson is a shorty, five-nine, and dark like his father. That was always comedy seeing the two of them together, mother and son, like something from Monsters Inc. Her eyes pop out as if someone's strangling her. The billion nerve endings under her skin unite and put together a show of fury. Pure. There's no other word to describe it. Face blood red and getting darker by the second. She always thought Moon and her precious boy belonged together. Hates the fact that I may have had something to do with ruining it. Scares me shitless. So scared I stop thinking about kissing my dead girlfriend's sister.

'*My son's not a liar!*'

She screams it so loud the whole of Starbucks drops a load.

She steps forward, oblivious of the looks around us, but I'm already up on my feet. I'm not staying to hear any more. I drop Gwyn's hand, and the biscotti, say that I'm sorry for the five hundredth time, and leg it.

35

Winning my last races meant something. Kept me on the road to receiving a tin cup at the end of the season, as well as rubbing Brendan's nose in the shit. This next race doesn't have the same kudos. You don't even get a certificate. But if it gives me another chance to piss all over Harriers, I'm there.

I've still trained like a mother, friendly trial or not. Stopped daydreaming and started knuckling down. Putting in mornings and afternoons. Clearing my mind of the bullshit happening at school or anywhere else. Who cares who Moon's going out with? Doesn't matter that the trials have nothing to do with the national championships. Once I'm on the track, there's no such thing as being friendly.

Mum should be coming to wave a flag and cough up the traditional post-win KFC, but is having another date with whatsisname, the man I haven't met yet. He's taking her to some stupid event at

Silverstone. Mum has absolutely no interest in cars, but is acting like she's the one who's driving or something.

'I'm going the see some of the best racers in the world,' she goes. 'Mike's really gone to a lot of trouble to get these tickets.'

They're also non-refundable, and whatsisname sounds too dopey to have ever heard of eBay. *Loser!*

'Go. Have fun,' I tell her, seeing how she's bought a new leather jacket and got the hair straighteners out again. 'Just make sure he treats you like a queen.'

She laughs like she knows something I don't.

'My hopes aren't as lofty as yours, kiddo. As long as he treats me better than your lovely father, then that's good enough for me.'

The bonus result of not having Mum around for the race means that I can get touchy-feely with Kelly, all in the name of celebration, on the way home. But Kel blows me out as she has to work the stall at the weekend. It has to be something major for her parents to give her a day off – none of them think that this is it.

Location-wise, the trial is a Guildford special. Thirty minutes on a train each way. Moon and Jason come for company. Mum gives me the money for all three tickets and says 'that's that'. Looks happy at the prospect of a teen-free day, of having her eardrums blown-out all in the name of romance; but guiltily so, because she can't be happy unless there's some kind of baggage attached. If I ever bother-ed to ask her why that was, she'd say 'It's because I'm a mother.' At least, that's what I'd imagine she'd say.

She coughs up another twenty quid.

Need to spend the next couple of days settling my head for the run. Physically everything's great, but something about the way Pearson looked at me the other day in the school caff has ruined all my mind-work over the last couple of weeks. I go to sleep thinking of that face, it's that bad. Puts me nearly back at square one.

I try and make arrangements for Casey to come down to Guildford and watch from the sidelines. It's a big-enough track, so he could quite possibly slip into the upper stands without attracting any attention, but like Mum, and Kel, he seems to have other plans. He has no obligation to me, other than training me for races that he never gets to see. It's the kind of half-arsed job I want to have when I grow up.

He calls up as I'm packing up my kit ready to go, saying he has flu in the clearest, most non-congested voice I've ever heard. Doesn't even sound remotely sorry. Says there'll be another time. Like in another twelve months! It makes me feel all reactionary. Start wondering if he's taking that kid out instead. That he's lucked out. Bonding over Britney, stars in everyone's eyes. Bet the kid will go anywhere with him after that. It's obvious.

On the train it's like everything's the same as normal, except we're all wearing each other's clothes, or something. Moon and Jason act like they're the best friends in the world, which isn't helping any. Yacking way too much. Every approaching promise of a silent vacuum extinguished; filled, filled, filled. And they're not even saying anything interesting, it's all nonsense.

'Can both of you keep your traps shut for just a minute?' I go. 'I'm meant to be visualising.'

'OK,' they say, and carry on talking.

This puts me in a really bad mood. They don't even think to ask about Kelly. By the time we get to Guildford, I'm ready to explode.

It's an indoor track, which I hate, big time. Running outdoors feels more real somehow, less poncey. I like things to be natural, to feel the sun on my face. I like it that you can see the sky. Enclosed tracks give me claustrophobia. I become a caged rat, anxious and scratchy, something that works wonders for my running. I get revved up good and proper. If anything, I run faster in these places. This isn't reverse psychology, no matter how many times Casey tells me it is. It's just fucked-up.

Brendan meets us in the foyer. He's the closet thing we have to a guardian this afternoon. We're stuck with him for the duration, being his sole charges, since none of his precious Harriers even qualified for this thing, they're so crap.

'Welcome to Guildford,' he goes, big smile and flaky arms wide open, like he's the Ambassador for Guildford or something. Dry-skinned freak.

We all nod. No one makes any attempt to shake his hand.

'How are we all feeling? Has everyone eaten?'

'We're feeling *great!*' says Moon brightly.

'Yup. *Really* excited for V's chances,' goes Jase.

Brendan has no children of his own, and it shows. He's nodding his head like he's taking them seriously.

'That's excellent. Verrapen, you have some really supportive friends here.'

'It's Veerapen,' I go, for the five thousandth time.

'Well, look, *Veerapen*, why don't I take your friends up to the seating area, whilst you get changed and get yourself ready? It's an hour until you'll be called, so if you're going to eat anything, make sure it's something very light, like a piece of fruit. Though it may be better if you don't eat anything at all.'

I touch his arm. It's safe, he's wearing his trackie top, so there's no danger of any skin flaking off on me.

'It's alright, Brendan, I've done a few of these before. I'll steer clear of the steak and kidney pies.'

Moon gets a call on her cell and starts looking all shifty. Jason too, as their mutual friend checks in. But Brendan's whisked them away before I can think any more about it.

I hit the showers as soon as everyone's out of my face. Can't be going on the track smelling like a used Astra. The changing rooms are posh, 'cos we're in Guildford. My shower cubicle has it's own private changing area and door. It's like being in the Ritz, but without having to be old or wear a shirt and tie to get in. Proper posh.

I'm steaming in the shower for a good twenty minutes. Let all the irritation and niggles escape from my pores.

When I make my entrance into the main changing room proper, hair slicked back, towel wrapped low around my hip bone, a thin line of pube just about visible above the yellow terry cloth, the room is empty, aside from a couple of fatties (they'd call themselves muscular distance runners 'cos they've done weights, but they're fatties to anyone else). Peter Platinum, Under 17s champ, also passes through, or should that be prances through. Runs like a woman on and off the track. All the real dudes are on trackside starting their warm-up. Major disappointment. I look fit when I'm wet. The two fatties aren't interested. They take one look and go to the showers, where they're probably going to bum each other furiously.

Brendan's back by the time I'm dressed. Chucks me a bottle of water, and makes himself at home.

'Everything all right?'

'Yeah, fine. Look, Brendan, I know you're responsible for me for the day, but you don't have to keep checking up. I'm a big boy, I know how these things work.'

'I never said you didn't. Just thought you'd like some encouragement before you start warming up.'

Better the motivational lecture here than on the track when I'm getting myself in the zone. Don't want people to mistake him for anyone important.

'Why are you here, anyway?'

'Because I'm responsible for all amateur athletics in North East Surrey, and . . .'

I give him the W. *Whatever.*

'Come to claim all the credit. I don't even run for your scabby Harriers any more.'

I shouldn't be getting riled up like this, but I do. All Casey's techniques on taking your mind down to semi-meditative state before warm-up, of eschewing drama for focus, are gone, thanks to this dry-skinned donut.

He gives this broad smile as I'm saying all this, raises his eyes like he's humouring me, and then, when I'm done, his face tightens, eyes darken. All the tension showing in his brows and neck.

He gets up and shuts the door, but doesn't move an inch more than that, standing dead straight, hands crossed behind his back like a police sergeant on a fun run. The authority figure.

'You might be on the margins, young man, but you're still a part of my remit whether you know it or not.'

'Like fuck I am! You've had nothing to do with me since I was booted out! You're only sniffing round now 'cos everyone else at the center runs like a spastic.'

'How do you explain Casey?'

'Dunno what you're talking about.'

'Did you really think that I wouldn't know you two were working together? That all your progress this year was down to you training solo? I'm not stupid.'

'I haven't seen Casey since . . .'

'Yesterday. You haven't seen Casey since yesterday. You can stop pretending otherwise.'

'You can't be bothered with me, Brendan, so it's none of your business who I train with.'

'I knew he'd been training you since that friendly in November. It was all in the technique. You were so bold all of a sudden. So assured. Pure Casey.'

'He's the best, that's why. Not like these amateurs you have running about the place.'

'Casey's no hero. He's a nothing. He's lost everything. Self-esteem. Passion. Bravery. When a man like that caves in, and lets the fear take over him, it's open season, lad. I could impose my will any way I like. Break him, just for fun. Wreck your chances. There's nothing you could do about it.'

'Bullying belongs at school, mate. Not here. What gives you the right to deny Casey a second chance?'

'But I have given him a second chance! I've kept my mouth shut. He wouldn't still be training you otherwise.'

'Feels like Casey ain't the one people should be watching. What are you getting out of this, aside from making his life a misery?'

'I'm not immune to wanting some praise every once in a while. Anyone who isn't honest with themselves about that is a liar. We all want to be a Johnny Big Potatoes. That's one of the reasons why I do this job. So combine the notion of rescuing Casey with getting my hands on his young protégé . . . the young dark-skinned protégé that everyone's talking about. A potential Asian hero. Do you see where I'm coming from? It doesn't get any better than that! He could develop you into something this country could be proud of, and if I got some of the credit for that . . .'

I go and lock myself in the bathroom for the next few minutes. Turn on the shower and all the taps so that I don't have to hear any more of his talking. Knock my head hard against the mirror a couple of times until I get scared at the idea of cutting myself and stop. I can't deal with the stress. All this chatting to people I shouldn't.

Brendan's fifteen minutes of local fame will have to wait. I run my race and come second. It's good, but not good enough.

36

Post-cinema, all the girls want to do is stuff their faces at the Golden Arches, but make out that they're only here for our benefit. They shout their order for milkshakes as they run upstairs to the ladies to apply yet more MAC, all of us knowing that there'll be trouble if said shakes, strawberry for one and chocolate for the other, aren't delivered on a tray complete with jumbo fries and two dozen nuggets. Pearson already has the Moon fear written all over his face and gets the order down pat.

Friday night. Double date. Moon's and Kelly's idea. Something they cooked up in art class whilst Ms Jackson locked herself in the cupboard and had a nervous breakdown. An hour of chaos apparently, a display of pure lawlessness, started by three of the hard kids from the Rose estate. An environment where the hardest of enemies can melt into something resembling friendship, laughing in unison over the fighting pikeys. (Year Head was virtually ready to call the police. It was only the three-thirty bell that stopped things.) Me and

97

Pearson didn't have any say in the matter. We just had to turn up.

Outside the Odeon the girls hug each other. Kel hugs Pearson, I hug Moon (strangely exhilarating doing this in front of that shit-for-brains lump — even if the actual touch feels like we're strangers). And then the girls wait for the boys to do their thing. Passing the love is the fakest thing in the world, and the two of us are the worst at it. We're nowhere near achieving the levels of fakeness that everyone else seems to display so well and with so much flair. He's hating this as much as I am. His smile is out, full blast, but the eyes harden when he realises that he's going to have to press the flesh. It's only because he's so besotted with Moon that he even contemplates coming into contact with brown skin. That much is very obvious. We do the black handshake, give a wassup, and the girls relax. I don't.

New slasher flick, everybody's doing it, so screen is packed. We are glued to each other. Me and Pearson are separated by the girls for safety. No escape. Mine and Kel's snogging has to compete with theirs. Not as much tongue on their side, I notice. His ineffective-ness makes me feel like a right Don Juan. With people on all four sides there's no chance for anything else. Shame. The only *Bo' Selecta!* nudie antics are all in my head.

I have been lying my pants off. Things on the love front are muddy, not rosy. It's Moon that I want. Whenever I kiss Kelly, it's Moony Suzuki that I'm thinking of. There's no competition. But I don't confuse snog-ging with anything else. A warm tongue, an open mouth and all that . . . I act my socks off. Oscar material. The other three are none the wiser.

Down at the Golden Arches, Pearson starts acting like a motherfucker the moment the girls are out of sight. He doesn't quite pin me down, but makes pretty damn sure my face comes close to the counter top. My lips kiss the charity box by the till. Penance for molesting Moon in my head whilst I was physically molesting Kelly. Know there's no point in struggling when he's got my neck down like this, not just yet. I need to see his body, and I can't from this angle. Need to plan my moves.

'Don't listen to every word my girlfriend tells you,' he goes. 'I ain't apologising for nothing.'

It's about nine o'clock and the place ain't busy. There are some younger kids on the front tables who are hanging in two groups of about eight – Year 10 grungers, seen 'em about the place – chatting and not eating anything. A couple of mental home nutters, and an old guy about thirty with bad skin and no date complete the scene. The High Street is like tumbleweed for anyone respectable after dark. If you have any sense you avoid it like the plague.

'What? Got all chicken to do the manly thing, now that it's time?' I go, knowing that this isn't the time to be all cocky, but not being able to help it. 'Should've guessed you wouldn't have the bottle.'

'I'll show you bottle, scum,' he goes, all tough guy, ready to drop a fast one.

This is when I find his body. Push my leg backwards and out so that it goes straight for his gut. It's easy 'cos the hurdles make me flex-ible. He doesn't quite fly across the room the way I expected, but stag-gers back a few paces nonetheless. I peel my face from the charity box.

'Show me bottle then, scum. Show me. I'm ready for it.'

This is when the staff decide to get visible. We've been at the counter all this time and no one has come to take our order. Too busy shoving down Big Macs out back. The manager is some kid two years above us at school who was mad into Buffy like some freak. He gatecrashed Lizzie Jenning's park party last summer, pissed, with a couple of Goths, and tried to get everyone to jump naked into the Hogsmill, spotty little herbert. The other two counter monkeys are Sri Lankan/Tamil-looking, so I have to treat them like bredren. As if. I might show them a smidgin of respect if they didn't have those looks on their faces, like I'm letting them down. I'm all out for the brothers, but I can't be carrying the expectation of a nation on my shoulders. I'm way too young for that kind of pressure, and I resent even the notion of it being offered up, as their eyes hit mine from the deep fat fryer to where I am on the other side of the counter.

A millisecond thing, but I still manage to feel it.

The three of them start shouting the moment Pearson's got my head down. Half-hearted shouts coming at me from behind the fryers, weak and ineffectual. Too busy on their nuggets and apple pies, I guess.

'And stop trying to steal my mate from me!' I go, meaning Jason. Trying to find a shoulder that can lead me to an arm to twist.

'That dopehead? You can have him if you can stop him following me around like some lapdog. He's pathetic.'

Suddenly it becomes about Jase's honour, as much as mine. It's all about upholding stuff in round here. Diss me and I'll smack ya. Diss my mate and you'll get a double kicking. Gets tiring after a while. This would be the perfect moment to stop the physical stuff; get my phone out and show Pearson how pathetic his dad can be, if he really wants to play the game of who can be the more pathetic. But I don't. I'm waiting for the right moment to play that card, and this isn't it.

So I leave the cerebral out of it, and keep things as physical as fuck.

One of the bredren, the youngest one, who looks all right, makes a move to come over as I struggle on the counter, but backs off when he sees I have it locked. They only start going ballistic when a handful of straws and their precious serviettes go flying. Bunch of arseholes. Want me to get all nationhood, but only get annoyed when I make a mess. What kind of nurturing relationship is that?

Girls, like cats, always seem to know when there's been trouble. Their backs are up from the moment they walk down the stairs, fingers out like claws, all kinds of words coming out of their mouths. In this situation, when me and Pearson only have eyes for each other's throats, their gabbling comes down the lugholes like white noise. Can't make head nor tail of it.

They, on the other hand, are working out plenty. Might have something to do with the state of us. Shirt not so pristine, and forehead as tender as fuck; must be a bruise coming. Pearson is still winded from the kick and leaning against one of bins, hand on his belly like the big baby he is. The milkshakes are everywhere. I'd taken a punter's supersize strawberry and lobbed it. Pink processed muck floods the floor and splashes across the front window, A second shake, medium chocolate, collects in pools under the counter. Turns out, I needed something more than the kick to get Pearson's manky hands off me.

He was bang in the shake's trajectory so copped plenty of the strawberry, some on his hair, the bulk on his precious Ralph hoodie. Ha!

But neither of us were going to admit anything. Athlete's pact. What happens in the locker room . . .

'No trouble,' he says.

'No trouble,' I go. 'What gives you that idea?'

Now, the only aggro we can hear is coming from the outraged milkshake-robbed punter but we pretend not to notice.

37

You can afford to do Shabbat dinner if you're in a family where the father stays at home and doesn't run off with his optician. Those families have it locked. When you have a mother who works shifts with very little let-up, Shabbat becomes a less rigid state. We still have our Shabbat dinner but, depending on when Mum gets in, we could be eating at either six or ten. Don't pay as much notice as I should do to Mum's shifts, so getting back from school most Shabbat afternoons are like a lottery. Dunno if I'm going to be playing on the computer or drawing the curtains. Wouldn't be so uncertain if I wasn't such a cretin and actually read the post-its she sticks on the fridge. I'm a loser with no attention to detail. A big one.

It was only after Dad left that Mum showed any interest in Shabbat. He never liked routines. Now he's out of the picture, she seems to depend on hers.

Once we do the business, it becomes a dinner like any other. Food that sticks to the diet sheet and the pair of us talking about our day. She's in an unbelievably good mood since Silverstone. I'm drinking juice from the carton *at the table* and she doesn't even notice. Too busy telling me about giving CPR to the relative of one of her old biddy house calls. This one lived, and she's quite pleased about it. I keep the conversation away from the subject of being the worst runner in the world in case I have some episode and try to cut one of my legs or something. Tell her instead about finally cracking 1000 on my ab crunches. That's not for training, that's just for vanity. Getting a stomach like Beckham.

'How's school?' Mum asks casually, when I run out of things to say. (My fast talking's worse than my fast running.)

'Fine,' I go, almost choking on my Kiev.

'So why did I receive a call at work today from your Year Head?'

Shit. Hiding letters only goes so far. Fucking dried-up bitch Year Head. Hate her. Late thirties and still hasn't got a man. Hasn't got anything better to do than stalk my mother over a stupid fight that we all forgot about weeks ago.

That's the thing with teachers, they never let anything go. It all comes back to haunt you eventually. We finish our dinner with a very long talk. Once Mum is certain I'm not being bullied – and I do consider that tack very briefly, but know it would be more time-consuming than the other option – I'm floored with a tongue-lashing that lasts most of the evening. Even the night birds are making zeds by the time she's finished. My phone and computer are seized. For a week, she says, and then she'll review it. Only, when we're up in my room disconnecting the thing, she comes across the second letter from the Year Head enquiring as to why she hadn't responded to the first. It came last week, when I was busy with Kel and didn't have time to hide it down the ropey. Mum almost believed me when I was spilling about the clerical laziness that goes on in that school. They lose exam papers, class reports, do you think that fat school secretary mails out all the letters she's supposed to? No way! Too busy sitting on her arse reading magazines and confidential files that are none of her business. They lost my SATs last year, so it's a viable story, but I fuck it up with my own sloth. Now she really explodes. Clip round the ear, and another, even harder, which I have to take without snivelling, even though she's a foot shorter than me – because she's my mum – and because she's really mad, she takes a leaf out of Moon's folks' books: grounded for a fortnight.

PART 3

38

Long before her death, there are vanishing acts. When Moon first disappears from my milk-crate during my supposed grounding, I do something similar — leave home and crash at Casey's. I've no idea where she is, only know about her state of mind. That she's really fucking pleased with herself hanging out with a bad boy before her sister. Hate that she's pipped me to the post.

We've always talked about running off; usually when we've not got our way about getting some old knick-knack that means fuck-all out of our parents, or when forced to obey the rules that are waved in your face every once in a while. Yeah, we'll run away, and that will show *them*. Spitting the words like they're the worst scum we've ever dealt with.

And now she's really done it. Being away from home, like she is, away from our street, is the one solution I can think of that will stop me from going mad with worry. Helps me to stay closer to her somehow. Can't explain why.

Mum knows all about Casey at this point, about all the alleged filth, and the untruth behind it. Thank Kelly Button, the girl with a bad case of sour grapes and a big rubbery mouth that can't stay shut. Or should I say, vindictive fingers. Sends Mum a txt, the nearest thing a market girl with too much jewellery can muster up as evidence.

Mum's excited for about a second, this being the first txt she's ever received from someone who isn't family. She shouts, slaps me a little, and then comes down the track and watches him put me through my paces, and something clicks. She doesn't quite welcome him into the family, but she gets it.

It helps that she doesn't particularly like Kelly Button, and didn't want to believe everything she came out with. If she was a patient she'd change her dressing without prejudice, but this . . . She virtually broke into spontaneous applause when we broke up.

'Let's face it . . .' I tell her, '. . . he's been my trainer for almost six months. If he'd have wanted to do something he would have done it by now.'

'I beg your pardon?'

'My blacked-out face would be all over the internet, right?'

Me talking about Casey being a PPP so casually isn't quite what a mother wants to hear from her fifteen-year-old son. Think she'd rather I got Kelly Button pregnant, far simpler to deal with. Casey comes with way too much baggage. None of it savoury.

But Trisha and Oprah advise compromise when dealing with stroppy teenagers so that's what she does, albeit unwillingly. She lets me stay at his, so long as it's only for a weekend (finals are coming up, so we are training morning and evening). She has all his numbers for emergencies, and psyches herself that it's all about reassurance, not drama. She doesn't realise that one night will eventually roll out into a full weekend, Casey neither for that matter.

His place is a tip, just like his car. Messy, dirty, stinky. It's only on the track that he pretends to be a clean freak. This is the first shock. Thought I'd love hanging with a laid-back guy, dropping my shit wherever I like with no one to nag, but it feels odd, not what I'm used to.

My hood is where the show palaces are. Where we show off our stuff. Streets like rows of blank canvases: our place, Jason's, Moon's. Aside from the heavy wooden stuff, nothing is more than five years old. It's the Surrey way. We are all constantly reinventing our homes. Always tip-top and ready to receive visitors, to spotlight the new Morrocan-style tiles in the bathroom, to have dinner in our brand-new conservatories whilst finding a way to casually drop into conversation that we are now on Sky digital. We parade our purchases 365. What would be the point of buying them otherwise?

Trainer's palace, with its eighties furniture, all black wood that looks real cheap, and its beige-gone-yellow walls, is something else.

The only clothes that aren't on the floor are the tracksuits, hanging on a rail in front of the wardrobe. They are ordered in tones, darkest colours to the left, and working along. The kind of thing you might see at P Diddy's house but on a micro scale 'cos Casey's only got ten tracksuits. A pad for the guy who never leaves the locker room, or who never grew out of it.

Can't work out whether or not Casey is pleased to have me. You'd think it would be his wet dream, young boy sleeping over and all. Virtually forcing his way in. But there's none of that. I get there around six, and he's pretty distracted. Points out where I'll be sleeping, mentions there's a bowl of pasta and chicken with my name on it on the kitchen top, and leaves me to do my thing. Something to do with the news being on and not wanting to be away from the set for even a minute. Casey is news obsessed. You don't have a summer like he had and not be, I guess. Trevor McDonald or whoever it is sounds more sinister than usual, as his voice rattles around the flat. Doom-laden. No wonder Casey has this mad look about him if this is how he spends his evenings. Even I can see that it's torture.

The flat has three bedrooms. Thankfully my room and Casey's are about as far apart as they can be. I don't even know why I keep thinking these things and still find myself sleeping over. I'm a joker. A big one. If I wasn't so mature I'd be throwing my head out the window and shouting for help. Except . . . the flat is at the very end of the Rose estate. Almost dropped the phone when he gave me the address. I always knew he had to live somewhere on here – where else would the council put him? – but I hadn't thought he'd be dumped on its outer reaches. I'm Earth. Casey's Pluto. The view from my window is of the closed-down health centre with its open car park where the boy racers will dump and sometimes burn their stolen Unos or 205s. Only the wetlands lie beyond it, no other houses in my eyeline. I suddenly understand how where you live can make you sadder than you already are, especially when you run out of choices.

Half-expecting Mum to be sitting in her car outside, just in case.

It's the kind of thing she does. The Florence Nightingale influence and all that corny stuff. This has been the insurance policy in my head the moment I set foot inside. I crane my head at every angle for the Astra. No sign of her. She must have really believed me when I told her that there was nothing to worry about. But then, she doesn't know how this part of the estate is the boy-racing centre of Surrey.

I'm in the box room. The kid's room. Everything in here, as with the rest of the flat, is curdled yellow and floral. Combined with the dirt, the custard flower prints, big and bold, on the bed and across the curtains make the room seem even more depressing than it would normally be. Have a feeling that maybe all rented accommodation is like this. Dad's emergency flat that he stayed in just after leaving us and before leaving the country gave me the same feeling. Flower-print normality papered over giant worry cracks; nothing fooling no one.

Mum tells me to make sure I unpack all my stuff once I get there, but all that goes out of the other ear once she's out of sight. Bag slung across the room, jumper on bed, coat on floor. Freedom! Can't help, though, coming back into the room five minutes later and hanging the coat up. Hate the idea of Hackett soaking up germs and who knows what else from that skuzzy old carpet.

I sit and scoff the pasta whilst Casey stays glued to the news, the local bulletin now taking over from where Trevor McDonald left off. News is the most boring shit I've ever seen. I try to avoid it. Here, it's local hospital scandal and various stupid triumph-over-adversity stories about plucky pensioners who should be put out of their misery. It's the kind of nonsense that makes you want to move to another country (only they probably have their own equivalent). Casey takes everything in without a word. He only starts to pay me some attention when the bloody programme is over. I'm sent to the fridge to get us some drinks. It's full of beer. No sign of any vegetables. Can feel it's going to be one of those nights so bring back a four-pack.

'Everything good?' I go, meaning, being sued by the greedy parents.

'My people are working on it. Can't say any more for legal reasons,' he goes, flippantly, meaning that it's looking deadly and he's shitting his pants.

Casey has an embarrassing tin-box stereo and about three CDs. He used to be a music man, kinda like myself, only all his stuff — a couple of hundred CDs, he reckons — got lost in the fire. The stereo, a plastic thing that looks as if it came free with a packet of cereal, and the CDs, The Corrs, Coldplay and Fatty Bedingfield, are recent acquisitions.

'You're telling me you've spent six months without music?' I go. 'How did you live?'

'We're not all millionaires like you and your mates,' he laughs. 'Some of us have to work for our stuff.'

He's kinda self-conscious 'cos I'm scanning round the living room as we speak, seeing that, beside the hired eighties furniture, the sofa bollocks etc, and the TV and the stereo, Casey doesn't really have much of anything.

'It's not as bad as it sounds, young Turk,' he goes. 'You get used to it. Fewer possessions focuses the mind. It's an important lesson for a young person to learn.'

'Ha! I'll, uh, take your word for it.'

'You're never without music anyway, if you have the radio, and the internet.'

Ah, yes, the internet . . . but the less said about that the better.

Until this moment I'd never given much thought to what Casey did for money. The council pay him for training me — I'd worked the 'promising young kosher Tamil boy in athletics' angle. Somehow thought that what they were giving him probably covered it. Didn't think that the dodgy stereo and the empty fridge would prove a different point, that he's skint. Sounds like he needs a couple more promising runners to mentor. Maybe I could set him up with . . . no. He's a grown boy who needs to sort his own finances out. Not my problem.

I stick Coldplay on the stereo. They're too grim for my taste, but anything is better than the Irish harpies or Fatty.

He doesn't mention the tense ten minutes when I have an episode and have to lock myself in my room. Out of my depth and too frightened to move.

Ten minutes later, we're all good. I wouldn't have minded chilling in front of *EastEnders*, it's what we all do, but somehow in front of Casey it doesn't feel so manly. He gets the cards out and we play a series of poker hands. I forget about having any objections to group participation; as a houseguest, this kind of mid-evening shit is mandatory. Partly the reason why I've never taken up Dad's invitations for holidays in the Black Forest or wherever the hell he is: because I don't want to miss my favourite shows (they don't let you down the way your parents do), and I hate anything to do with sitting round a metaphorical campfire. Moody teenagers are best left to their own devices. That should be the rule.

But I backtrack, like I always do. I seriously get into the poker and start whopping his ass. Ha! Casey wants to play with 2ps, but I insist on matches. He was going to use the coins from his copper jar, but I still wasn't feeling it. You have to be strict this way with PPPs. If you start gambling with money, however innocent . . . This is far safer . . . says the boy in a flat on the Rose estate, on his own with a PPP. I'm a joker, ask anyone. I'm a headcase.

'My father taught me how to play poker,' says Casey. 'When he left the army he was out of work for about a year, so we'd spend afternoons after school, kind of like you and me tonight, playing poker on the kitchen table. He'd tell me to close my eyes and imagine we were in one of those big casinos in Monaco.'

'And?'

'We became frequent visitors to Monaco. He'd do some voices. Make it believable.'

'He can't have taught you very well, if you've got a fifteen-year-old beating your fruity behind.'

'What have I told you about calling me that?' he says, laughing so I know he's not really annoyed. 'Anyhow, I'm letting you beat me, that's the point.'

'Yeah, yeah, Case. Whatever you say.'

I'm way happier talking about poker than I am hearing about grown-up sob stories. He should have dealt with that stuff ages ago, not left it smouldering to foist upon unsuspecting teenagers at a later date.

'Why did you start running?' I ask him on our fifth hand, when he's as good as his word and thrashes me good and proper.

I forget for a moment that I'm trying to act cool and uninterested.

I'm expecting some poetic sub-Irish nonsense about the non-existent green hills of Wandsworth, of training in grotty back yards and pounding inner-city pavements. A glorious display of pure talent over poverty and all that bollocks. There's none of that. I thought Casey's buzzes might be the same as mine: enjoying the sudden drop you feel in your stomach as you arrive at the racetrack for a meet; breathing in that mixture of petrol, sweat and freshly cut grass at trackside (this being in Surrey means you're never more than fifty yards away from the nearest car park); hearing the slightest of scuffles coming from behind when you first make it into the lead, as botched runners start to feel the power of the lion and strain to catch up; of positioning yourself in the starting blocks and waiting for that moment to descend when you cut out all the shit around you, disengage yourself from the people and the noise, and make yourself believe that you are the only winner on the track. That you're not a loser who won't amount to anything.

All he says is, 'Because I was good at it.'

'That it? Because you were good at it?'

'OK, Mr V-pen. And when I was on a run, and my legs were working, really working, so that I was ahead of everyone else, I felt fucking invincible. There's no feeling that can beat that. Not that I know of, anyway. And believe me, I've been looking.'

'And now?'

'Now nuthin,' he goes, draining the last of the four-pack, the half Carling that I've left on the table for the past few minutes because it tastes like piss, and heading towards the kitchen. 'I don't run no more, so I'm never going to get those feelings back. What I can do, though, is help you sustain them. That's what I'm here for.'

'And is it enough for you? I mean, the Olympics . . .'

'Ah, that was a long time ago. For the moment, this is fine.'

And then, because I've had some beer and am feeling brave, and because alcohol can suddenly make you very clever, 'Why didn't you tell me you were training someone else?'

'What?'

'The kid you've got. The one I saw you at Britney Spears with. You're training him, aren't you? Why didn't you tell me about him?'

'Because you didn't ask.'

'Very clever, fruit loop. But really, why didn't you tell me?'

'Because you didn't ask! And I've told you about the cheek. Once more, and your mum can come and collect you. I mean it.'

The reply comes sharper than before, the tone not what I was imagining. I know it's not 'cos of the fruit thing, no matter what he says. He likes it, really.

'Has Peter Platinum been talking to you?' he asks. 'He told me he'd told a couple of friends, other runners, but I didn't think you'd be one of them. Fucking bigmouth, that kid. You know how little boys like to blab.'

He laughs in a dirty way that I don't like. Ordinarily I would have joined in with him, seen the joke, appreciated his rare display of irony, but alone with him on Pluto, I'm not in the mood.

'Track talk, y'know,' I go, wishing that I actually listened to track talk once in a while.

'Ah, that windbag! Jesus! God forgive my taking your name in vain. Means that everyone knows if that fairy's been talking. Christ!'

Peter Platinum, a kid my age, is the gayest runner you'll ever see. Runs like he's in some fricking stage show. Eyes and teeth. Eyes and teeth. Hands swaying all over the place. Shame he's faster than the wind. On a good day he can beat everyone. Pete hasn't told anyone about the kid, apart from me; no one else knows, but it seems to satisfy Casey. The cupboard doors in the kitchen stop panic slamming.

'Keep it to yourself, lad, same as Peter. This kid's a good runner. I don't want to ruin it for him by having gossip started.'

'I wonder if you're doing the same for me?'

'What? Speak up, young Turk. What have I told you about mumbling?'

I'm thankful for the kettle boiling and leave it. Now is not the time to be asking about my place in the world, where I fit in the scheme of things. I think for a minute.

'What was your dad like?' I call.

'My dad . . .'

'Did you get on with him? I hate mine, that's why I'm asking.'

'Your dad's your dad,' he calls back.

'That's helpful.'

'He's the only dad you've got, so you have to lump it. Make the best of a bad situation.'

'Don't see the point.'

'Well, maybe it's time you should. My dad was the most sociable man you'd ever meet. Loved to talk to people. Big drinker. Never caused trouble or nothing, but he did like to have a drink.'

'Was he what you'd call a good drunk?' I go, thinking that it made me sound clever. I'd heard Mum use it before when she used to talk about one of her old patients.

'Yeah, you could say that,' is the reply that doesn't make me any wiser.

'Sounds like Jason,' I go, trying to stop him from getting serious, but he's not listening to me being a smartarse, he's on a roll.

'Loved my dad. Had some of my best times with my dad. Whether you drank with him or not, he always treated you good. Wasn't the type of greedy bastard to sue a poor man 'til he has nothing. I think about him every day.'

Cuckoo. Best not to ask about the mother. Hear she had a heart attack in her warden-assisted flat in Hackbridge when the Harrier news broke. It was one of Mum's district nurse friends out on one of her rounds who found her. Last summer's business, all twenty days of it, nearly finished the pair of them off.

We bump into each other in the kitchen. He's about to poke his head into the fridge, I'm taking my plate to the sink like a good boy. If I stay at that table one moment longer, he's going to come over and hold my hand or something girly. Too much sincerity brings me out in a rash, but . . . what do I expect? I'm the one who asked him about the emotional stuff. I'm an idiot. A big one.

'It's not too late, you know. There's no shame in having your dad as your best friend. Look how I turned out.'

My head's full of more steam than his poxy kettle. Him telling me off about something is preferable to hearing any more talk about dads. I smash his plate into the sink, reducing his crockery capacity by fifty per cent. The bollocking comes like a summer shower. It drowns out everything else.

39

Summer holidays. Mum working; not a district nurse yet, still at the hospital. Dad has the day off from the office and is babysitting.

I'm eight years old, too old for babysitting, I tell him. I'm the tallest in my class. If you passed me in the street you'd think I was ten.

'Don't listen to him, Jeya,' Mum goes, ratty because she's late and can't find her keys, looking everywhere but in her pocket. 'He can moan all he likes. He's being looked after by his dad today and that's final.'

Yesterday, me and Jason were caught trying to pinch a Twix from the newsagent by the stupid old man that works there, who isn't as slow as he seems. Bloody double mirrors. I don't tell Mum that it was my idea, that I bullied Jason into it, almost having to knee him in the nuts to get over his wobbles, as we asked the old man to hunt in the back for a spare couple of cardboard boxes for our den. And we almost had it too. He popped back out just a microsecond into the crucial moment, when hand stashes gear into pocket. Next time we'll know not to pansy around and be quicker.

Mum has a different version of the story in her head, something related to Jason's dad being investigated by the council for fraudulent accounting. Lumps the criminal minds together. The mammoth tongue-lashing I receive only stops when I agree to spend as little time with him as possible — hence Dad being here.

Dad was looking at us funny last night. He doesn't always seem used to how me and Mum go on at each other, snapping and moaning and nagging. Doesn't realise that we don't mean half of it. Some days it makes him fractious and prone to shout, especially when he comes home tired, but today, because he's had a big fry-up and relaxed, he takes it all in his stride. Like *Kindergarten Cop*, he rolls his sleeves up, no nonsense.

'I'm not babysitting you, my big grown-up Veerapen,' he goes, quite seriously. 'I'm just hanging out. Every dad needs to hang out with their son every once in a while.'

'Uh huh,' I go, dropping the Godzilla and listening to what he's got to say.

He gives me a rundown of what he's got planned, and the food we're going to sneak into the house and eat, and he makes it sound good. Less babysitting, more day camp. It's an excellent plan.

Dad is always working, home really late, so it feels like I never see enough of him. His office at the chambers in town is like his second bedroom. If he's worked late on a file and drunk a bottle or so of wine, he's been known to sleep there. Been stopped drink driving once before, and too tight to take a taxi. If he's not home and the phone rings around ten-thirty, you know where he'll be kipping, in an office the size of the cupboard, on a sofa covered with a blue check blanket, which smells fuzzy, like how your mouth gets when you haven't brushed your teeth for three days. And absence does funny things to my memory. The odd day goes by when I forget him completely.

The day is a scorcher. One of those when I'll be able to take my T-shirt off and still feel like I'm wrapped up like a roti in the oven. I already have my plans, to run wild around the garden like an Indian boy all day long – especially as Mum can't do her hourly sunburn check. Examining my shoulders and back like a mortician, cool palm never leaving my forehead. But Dad's plans come first. We're hanging, those are the rules. Also, I am not allowed to use the garden because Dad laid turf at the weekend. If I'm found running over it between now and next weekend, I'll get a bigger verbal than the one I received for the Twix. And a smacked bottom too, probably. Dad's words, not mine.

Mum has been shouting at him all summer to get the garden fixed. It had been OK last year, but winter had messed things up real good, and nothing had been done since. Mum and Dad have this deal – Mum will cook dinner every night if Dad does a spot of painting every once in a while, and more importantly, tends the garden. And what with Dad's sleepovers, nothing has been done. It had all come to a head last Thursday. It was a beautiful day and Mum exploded, fixed her radar on Dad and let rip. Annoyed that she couldn't sit outside because it looked so fucking ugly (her words, not mine). A couple of plates were smashed, nothing as bad as normal, but enough crashing about to create an atmosphere. I hid at Jason's on the pretext of Playstation. In these situations home becomes how I imagine Mars to be: gassy and unbreathable. And usually I'm right. Two days and two sets of shattered glasses later, Mum gets her result: a stony, weedy plot levelled and transformed into parkland. It's lush. All you can see is green. Thick, flat green that runs for miles – or so it seems.

It feels too hot to be laying turf. It's like saying that the best way to freeze an ice cream is by putting it into an oven. Too scared to tell this to Dad, though. He busts a gut with the clearing, cleaning and laying; huffing and puffing all the more because he isn't sure about what he's doing, and making me go on drink runs every ten minutes. By the time the day is out he's gone through a five-litre water bottle, which takes me a long time to carry back and forth to the fridge because it's so heavy, and ten tall bottles of Stella. That is some thirst.

'I'm a working man, my Veerapen,' he goes. 'I need a drink.'

'But I'm tired.'

He lets me have a sneaky sip of the Stella when Mum gets bored overseeing the makeover, and goes indoors.

Now the garden is fixed, Dad waters his plot religiously morning and evening. On the nights when he doesn't come home, Mum takes over. But none of this can stop the afternoon sun from doing its worst. The scorched patches that soon appear are first shrieked over, and then, when calmer, watered with more attention, and then, when that fails, discreetly ignored. By next weekend we'll have a fully functional lawn all right, only charred to a crisp, with blades sharp enough to cut our legs to shreds.

Once Mum is safely out of the way, Dad drives us to Sainsburys to stock up on junk. For me, that means Pringles, cheese string and all the Milky Bar buttons I can fit into the basket. Dad goes for all the spicy stuff Mum doesn't let him have because it irritates his belly – jalapeno peppers, chorizo and a giant jar of Indian pickle, which he will feast on with one big spoon. The kind of mix that will keep him on the pot for the next three days, but neither of us care. Right now, the afternoon ahead is all about pleasure.

I might be eight and look ten, but I'm not grown-up enough to stop holding Dad's hand as we wander around the aisles, or too old for Funny Feet ice creams, which he tosses onto the conveyer at the last minute. There's something nice and safe about holding Dad's hand and swinging our arms as we walk back to the car; swinging and laughing over the thick girl at the checkout because she gave

Dad change for a twenty instead of a ten. And Dad being Dad, he wasn't going to pull her up about it.

'I thought you're supposed to be a lawyer,' I say, once we've reached the far end of the car park, safely out of sight. 'Honesty is the best policy, and all that?'

'Course it is,' he goes, 'but you saw how stupid that girl was. If they're going to employ a thicko, they can't complain when the till doesn't add up at the end of the day.'

Dad has no time for shop people. It's where him and Mum differ. She can happily talk to the woman behind the till all day, but then Mum's a very chatty woman, when you catch her in the right mood. Dad, on the other hand, can barely hide his contempt and keeps all conversation to a minimum.

'These shopworkers are too pushy these days, with their friendly-friendly "Call me by my first name" nonsense. All this pretending to be friends,' he once complained to Mum after a particularly chatty session at Dickens and Jones when the pair of them went to look for a new hoover, and left an hour later. 'Shop people should employ the same code as servants, as far as I'm concerned. Speak only when they're spoken to.'

'Says the man from Mauritius,' laughs Mum, giving him a hug and ruffling his hair, which he hates. 'Such snobbery! And where did you learn that? On your twenty-acre estate?'

Dad tuts and disappears into his study (the dining room). He hates any reference to his poor childhood. If anyone asks, we're landowners.

I'm still worried about the checkout girl. Think about it for most of the ride home.

'S'pose she gets into trouble?'

'*Suppose* who gets into trouble? Speak properly, Veerapen!'

'I'm *supposing* about the girl at the supermarket. Maybe we should give her the money back.'

He gives this laugh, this loud hiccup thing that I hate. Goes on for ever. Means that I'm being a baby.

'Forget it, my Veerapen! These big supermarkets can afford the odd loss here and there. In fact, they build a loss in. If we didn't take this money, they might not reach their loss target, and then someone would really be out of a job.'

'OK,' I go. Taking his word for it, like I take his word for everything. He's my dad. He's the law.

'But are we going to tell Mum?'

He laughs again, like I'm suffering from insania.

'Absolutely not!'

We take out the ladder and climb onto the garage roof. It's either hang out here or stay indoors, what with the garden, and I like the idea of having lunch on the roof. I bet Jason's never done it. We can eat our naughty food and then lie on the black-gone-grey asphalt, prickly rather than scratchy when you first sit on it, and fry like eggs – Dad's words, not mine. Getting the food up is tricky, as Dad insists on using a tray (Mum's influence), meaning that I spill the drinks as he passes them to me at the top of the ladder and get shouted at. I want to cry, or sulk at least, but that only lasts for a minute. The weather's too good, and it's an afternoon of just me and my dad, and no irritating woman company.

We sit over the door with our food, dangling our feet over the edge. Dicing with death. This must be what it feels like for people who jump out of buildings, except they probably don't have cheese string and Funny Feet. Only tears. They probably aren't wearing Buzz Lightyear flip-flops either. The flips themselves are kinda gay, but the Buzz picture on the soles are boss, that's why I'm wearing them. Jason takes the piss every time he sees me wear them, which is every day, but he's only jealous because I got them first. His feet have been sweating it out in a pair of Reebok all summer. They must stink.

Dad is also sweating like a pig, but that may be because he's eaten most of a microwaved chorizo and a jar of Indian pickle. He joins me on the Funny Feet. Him on his first, me on my second. I follow his moves, biting the big toe in one large chunk, and then nibbling the shorties; Dad making both of us laugh by pretending they're Mum's corny, bunioned feet.

Everything feels the greatest it's ever felt. I'm with my dad up on the roof, tops off and getting tanned, and now each of us on our second Funny Feet. He doesn't disappear off into the house for the rest of the afternoon with the woman who later turns out to be the optician for another hour. Leaving me on the roof, ladder tucked away so I can't get down, until I fall asleep and get sunburnt, and for Mum to find me and go mental. That's all to come later. Up until then, living at tree height, sun shining, eating our favourite food, making fun of the women in our lives, it doesn't get better than this.

40

Me and Jason are being thrown out of the mall for being lairy. This is Surrey, so it's done in a very polite way. There's no one to say you're out of order or anti-social, especially if you've got brown skin or look halfway poor. Those kind of confrontations make everyone uncomfortable. We're booted out for causing a nuisance and upsetting the old people. The security guy who escorts us out is an all right bloke actually, and quite apologetic, like it's going to break our hearts if we can't poke our heads back into Dickins and Jones or Clintons.

'Sorry, lads, but you can't stay in the centre any longer. You've made it impossible, I'm afraid. The police are already on their way.'

'You can't ban me, mate. I work here,' goes Jase, flashing his Tesco pass in the guy's face, back and forth like he's performing a magic memory trick.

'I'm, like, staff, you get me? We're, like, colleagues really.'

The pairs of us giggle like stoners, even though Jason's brought nothing to smoke. Hasn't smoked all week. This cracking up for no reason in front of adults is habit, I guess. Making out to them that we have secrets, it's a stronger impulse than even the weed. We need it.

Casey knows too much about me. Moon knows too little. I have to feel in control of something.

The mall post-lunchtime is like a feel-good convention for the elderly. They are all out and being smug about still being so mobile. You can see it plastered across their faces. They almost need mugging just to bring them down to earth — Jason's words, not mine. Aside from a handful of unemployed scum, there is no one here under the age of sixty. Am not including the young mothers here because they are invisible and don't count. We can see every defect associated with age on display, from rickety old bones clinging onto zimmer frames, to gum disease, to white-stick blindness, to skin cancers. It's enough to make you bring up your salad.

'I'd keep that store ID to yourself if were you,' nods the guy, with a matey-I'm-OK wink. 'If the centre supervisor sees that, he'll be onto your bosses in a flash. You could get into even more trouble.'

Something about us being cheeky to the man at the handcrafted mug stall. Paying our money and then demanding that he inscribe the mugs 'Happy Birthday Cunt' (Jase) and 'World's Biggest Foreskin' (me). The banner said 'Personalise your mug! Any dedication.' We were just holding him to it. There was no mention that the dedication had to be some lame ass bollox.

Obviously I don't have an anorak for my dick, but this guy isn't to know that. I could have asked for 'World's Biggest Kike-Basher' and he still wouldn't have put two and two together. Trus', not having an anorak, it kinda makes you obsessive about having one. It's fucked up.

The mug man, this old guy around thirty-five, with one of those ratty free-for-all beards that's supposed to tell us that's he's so organic or something, had no sense of humour. Put down the pen and refused to inscribe anything. Gave us our money back. That's when we started kicking up a stink, demanding to see the manager.

'This is my stall. I am the manager,' he kept saying, which made us crack up all the more.

We were shouting a little and kept picking up all the mugs and pretending to inspect them. He looked almost scared of us for some reason.

'As consumers, we have rights,' I go, remembering a few of Dad's best lines. The ones he gave whenever he wanted to show how he was better than anyone who worked in a shop; usually as retaliation for being given too much attitude by shop girls who didn't like serving anyone with brown skin. I still get that shit even today.

'I am outraged by your treatment and will be writing a letter of complaint.'

'I'm happy to inscribe anything, lads, so long as it's not offensive. And those words, I'm afraid, are offensive.'

'Which words would they be, mate?'

'I'm not going to be drawn into your childish games by repeating them. You know the words I'm talking about.'

'Fine. Then my letter shall also be copied to the Chamber of Commerce and Trading Standards, *and* the local paper.'

If there was a letter to be sending Moon, I'd send it. Dear Miss Jones, please can you explain why you now prefer the company of psychos over us? I'd update my MySpace profile in a second if there was any guarantee she'd read it. But she's too busy for computers these days. Being drunk on dating makes you forget all the weird online obsessions you relied upon so heavily to pass the time when you were single and lonely.

'Mate, don't be such a wuss. Put the pen in your hand and inscribe cunt on my mug, you cunt,' goes Jase, precisely at the moment the security idiots are doing their rounds – for the sake of the CCTV. They are all questions. If there was a girl with us we'd probably be left alone.

'Why aren't you at school anyway? It's two o'clock.'

'Library studies.'

'Mate, haven't you heard of library studies? What kind of school did you go to?'

'Enough of your lip, cheeky. So why aren't the pair of you at the library?'

'Because they're getting some local history files out of storage. Told us to give them twenty minutes.'

I've used this line before. It's a winner.

We are asked to move on.

Then it's about them not liking how we were spinning the free-standing pine units on display outside Dickins and Jones. We were on one by this point. We just wanted to see how sturdy they were. That's why Jason was sitting on them whilst I was doing the spinning. Formula One speeds.

Jason picks me up when I fall over 'cos I've been laughing so much. Puts his arms tightly round my middle and lifts me from behind. My stomach does cartwheels.

Admittedly, the corner unit shouldn't have been pushed in the direction of the old people but, as we were trying to tell the security after the accident, the casters on the things were fucked. Shoddy workmanship. All we were trying to do was push them back into their original spots. No idea that they would shift in the opposite direction. If Mum took one look at them she'd say they were tat.

The security guy is standing with his feet apart, like he's trying to make out he's had police training. Gives his cheap blazer a brush across the buttons like its fucking Armani and not some synthetic bollox from TK Maxx. Now we're out of the building, he doesn't touch us. S'pose he can't, legally speaking. He does that thing that teachers do when they want you to be reasonable, giving you full eye contact and talking in a conspiratorial way that's supposed to make you think that it's the system that's making things tough, and not them at all.

We nod like we get it but, man, we're past the age to be swallowing fairy stories. Too old for that good-cop routine. We puff our chests up and make out we're scared of nothing. Inwardly, though, cacking it because we're both in uniform like a pair of retards. Standing out like two unkosher beacons.

'Like I give a shizzle. 'Cos when the police get here, we'll be, like, dust.'

Have been listening to too much Wiley lately. On top of Dizzee, I'm sounding as black as you like. When I get all 'You get me?' like this, especially in front of the dry security suits, it makes Jason lose his mind with joy. He always wanted a homie for a mate. Surrey — Hackney. There's no difference.

We can't get our bikes, but still manage to have some fun on the way home; a Sri Lankan muppet who has to run all the way up the Downs Road 'cos we've jumped him and grabbed his shopping. Sounds a good idea in theory, but running up a hill with five litres of water in one hand and about three thousand potatoes in the other ain't as easy as it looks. (Not helping 'cos I'm trying to make it look stylish, being a near-professional and all.)

The bloke's about twenty-five and darker than my arsehole. When we start attacking the meat of Down's Hill, getting under a long, wide canopy of treetops, where much of the sunlight gets eaten up, you can barely see him, only judging his movements from the flouro flashes on his Nike, and his gob from when he shouts at us. Pearly whites as a compass, better than any lighthouse.

'Come back with my shopping, you cheap motherfucking bastards! Get your arses back here!'

He's got an accent, so I ask him to repeat himself. Several times.

What kind of manners has this one got? The ruder he gets, the angrier, as I continue to ask him to repeat what he's just said, running backwards so we're teeth to teeth, the more certain we are that he ain't gonna get his aloo gobi gear back.

'Paneer, mate. Say "Paneer",' goes Jase, as we reach the top of the hill and the start of the Downs. No longer shielded by the tree canopy, we are overwhelmed by light and sky. Three specs, dotted onto the simplest of natural equations: ground and sky. Feels like we're running on top of the world.

'What?' calls the Sri Lankan, still under the canopy, but nearing its end. 'You want some Paneer? I haven't got any Paneer.'

'He's asking you to say cheese, you muppet,' I call down, helping out. 'We just need to take a picture.'

Jase gets what he wants, before we start rolling the guy's gear back at him down the hill. Asylum-seeker skittles. That, together with the pics, cheer us right up later when we're round my kitchen, drinking tea and waiting for X Box to load up.

41

Pearson doesn't even try to hide it. I get to my locker at lunch to find YID LIVES HERE tagged onto it. An address card that wasn't there at 9 a.m. Feel like my insides have been kicked inside out and then some, but get over it in about a minute. The corridor is kinda busy so there's no point in letting people see you fall to pieces. It's the kind of evidence we are all looking out for. Some gigantic public fuck-up that you dine off for weeks.

I know that it's Pearson because it's written with a navy Sharpie, and you would never use that if you were a serious tagger. Only pranksters write abuse with a Sharpie. And by pranksters, I mean boys. Girls have more creative forms of torture. Also because I saw him and a couple of the shadier volleyball boys tagging Year Head's door last year with a scrawl that was too similar to make it a co-incidence – something about her being a lesbian with one of the PE teachers. Gossip that we all knew was pretty much true. Tall, uneven block lettering that looked like the work of someone learning to write the Western alphabet for the first time. The V in LIVES clumsily morphed into an E. Fucking retard. He can't concentrate for a minute.

The thin sharpie ink on the locker is dryer than a nun's cunt, meaning it's been up there from at least morning break. The corridor where my locker is is mainly for my year and out of bounds for the younger kids. The lettering isn't big, but it ain't exactly tiny either. The words running along the bottom of the door like ticker tape, reaching about halfway. Making it clear that a return visit is more or less obvious.

Pretty much everyone I'm remotely bothered about has probably seen this diss between break and lunch, and no one has seen fit to give me a heads-up on it. That's a great feeling to start the afternoon with.

Jason's got the day off so I can't blame him. Moon is walking around like someone has kicked her. Tittle tattle getting on top of her. When she's not hiding under Pearson's protective chimp arm, she's scuttling towards the library and the warm arc of Gwyn and Ohmygod. Wonder if she knows about the tagging. Wonder if she worked out how the gossip started in the first place. Egged him on. Maybe she even suggested it. You have to be extra-perceptive to know that I'm part-Jewish. Most people are too caught up in my Tamilness to notice anything else.

Pearson's diss fires up an unforeseen reaction in me. It makes me laugh. He may have done his homework, but I can only see the funny side. That Yidding me out is going to tip me over the edge or something. Anything but. I ain't dropping from any ledge yet. I like the attention too much. Agree or disagree at your leisure, but I find that anti-Semitism makes a pleasant change from Paki-bashing. I'm a strange boy, I admit it. At times, I'm fucking warped.

PART 4

42

Moon makes me wait forty minutes as she turns foxy into FOXY 'in case the paparazzi turn up', leaving me to make excruciating small talk with the stern mother. Jason got blasted all night and woke up late. Billie's still asleep, so we have five minutes absorbing the dampness around his stoop whilst he gets *his* shit together. I chew my lip inside out in the meantime. Moon takes advantage of the extra minutes to add an extra coat of lipgloss, her fiftieth, judging by the thickness of the final result. We get to Casey's an hour later than we should have. You can tell he's been pacing up and down all this time, wondering what the hell is going on, 'cos he opens the front door as soon as he hears our footsteps. Cap and coat on, keys glued onto a sweaty palm. I shrug when our eyes meet. When Moon is getting dressed and whatever else, there's no point; like, how long is a piece of string?

'You're late?' he goes. 'I didn't even notice. I wasn't expecting you 'til after five.'

I give him the W. *Whatever.*

'Now get out,' I say. 'Give us an hour. Go for a run or something. Mum will be here any minute.'

He eyes up our serious amount of baggage with suspicion. We're loaded with carriers and mysterious unmarked holdalls.

'You're not gonna mess up anything, are you? I don't want any of my stuff touched up or played around with.'

'Casey, you've got nothing *to* mess up, remember?'

'Hey! I might not have much, but I like what I have. Just respect my things, that's all I ask.'

'Case, this isn't a makeover,' I say. 'We're just doing a little summat summat. Chill, guy.'

'Go on,' goes Moon, giving him a little push the way I would never dare. 'Give us time to make everything nice.'

Jase won't stop staring at Casey, but we all pretend not to notice.

Kicking someone out of their flat before their surprise party isn't ideal, but we didn't have anywhere else we could do it. In real estate terms, there was a scarcity of premium locations.

Mum was keen on helping, part of her new phase in 'Understanding the Child', but refused outright to have the party at our house.

'There's no way we could have that kind of event here, Veerapen. Casey's or any other party. I mean, come on! I'm busy enough as it is.'

'You wouldn't have to do anything. I'd take care of all of it.'

'That's what I'm afraid of.'

'This is pathetic. Being in this house is like living in a dodgy African state. I can do whatever I want, so long as it's your way.'

'My way or the highway, son. Your choice. I've told you I'll help, but we're not going to do any entertaining here.'

'Is that what you told Dad? My way or the highway?'

'What?'

'Do you want me to go to Germany? Is that it?'

I didn't get a slap, but she did try to shake me. Small woman five-foot-five trying to shake the brains out of a six-foot lug. I would have laughed if she hadn't thrown herself into acting so crazy.

We didn't speak for two days, which isn't that much different to how our relationship can be from time to time, when she's got stuff on her mind and gets drawn back into the arms of the pity party. She couldn't work out whether she should continue to 'Understand the Child', or if she should throw the book out the window. If anything, episodes like this, with the full-on silent treatment, leaving me to get my own dinner, give unexpected freedoms. Gets her off my back.

The compromise was that we'd hold the party at Casey's, so long as he was up for it, but I hadn't hedged any bets on Mum or anything.

During our two-day skirting around Coventry, I pursued up every other opportunity. Jase said over his dead body, even though Billie would appreciate the company; Moon loved the idea but knew she wouldn't get it past The Rottweiler™, who was only liberal when she wanted to be. I even thought of swallowing some pride and chatting to Brendan about using the Harrier Centre, but stopped myself when I realised that even if he did agree, there was no guarantee that Casey would set foot there. And then there was the Christian Fellowship . . . but there was no way I was asking about that. If Mum can't get me into a synagogue, there's no way in hell I'm going to be organising raves at some backstreet chapel where they're too forgiving for their own good.

It was this or nothing.

Jase has been saying the same thing for the past ten minutes.

'He lives on the Rose estate? The council put him on the Rose estate? Man! How fucked up are they?'

Casey's house, the one that was burnt down, wasn't council, but was only about five streets from here. Seems worlds away from what he had before. That's the power of arson, I guess. Your last bastion of security stripped in the time it takes for your house to be levelled to the ground.

Me and Casey never talk about how warped the relocation decision was; 'new home, new start,' is the most I can get out of him, but Jase is right, as always. It *was* twisted.

'He's innocent, Jason. He can live where he pleases,' said Moon. 'And also, you guys, he keeps it low-key round here. Kids too busy racing cars to notice him.'

Jase doesn't let it go, like he should.

'But the Rose estate? Man, someone in the council's got a sick sense of humour to be sending him here. It's like being thrown to the piranhas.'

'This part of the Rose estate ain't bad. They've put him in with the Poles and the Afghans, and whoever else has rolled over here to milk our welfare system, so aside from the odd wife-beating incident, and the cars, it's one of the areas where everyone keeps themselves to themselves.'

If you talk for long enough, and clearly enough, with no distraction, and pure conviction, you can stop any amount of needless digging. Even if it makes you look like a first class W to the A.N.K.E.R. It's something I learned when Mum and Dad were at their bloodiest. Anything to stop the elephant from being in the room.

I give Jason the bag with the balloons. Me and Moon get busy with the banners and arranging the furniture.

'This is the last time, by the way,' goes Moon, as we lug the sofa more centre-stage. 'From tomorrow, I'm officially the girlfriend. I'm strictly by appointment.'

She's wearing his yellow plastic cancer bracelet on her left wrist. It legalises everything.

I go through the top kitchen cupboards for glasses just so I wouldn't have to listen to any more. Mum had said she'd get a pack of plastic party cups, but it's better to be prepared. Even with a list she's liable to flap and forget things.

Moon had pushed the low coffee table into a corner and sprung out the camp chairs we'd brought over. Jase was fiddling about with the stereo.

'This tuner is bo-lax. All I can get are the talking stations.'

'Oh! No music?' goes Moon, disappointed, like it's her party or something.

'Nada. Left my iPod at home. Anyone bring theirs?'

Chorus of No's all round.

'It's because we're on the outer reaches of the Rose,' I go, explaining the tuning, 'it's like being at the end of the world when everyone thought it was flat. It's like being in Portugal or New Zealand, depending on which century you choose.'

'We can't have a party without music, boys. A party without music isn't a party.'

'I think he's got a Bedingfield CD somewhere.'

'Fuck that shit, I'd rather have the talking station.'

'Jason! Can you try and start the afternoon without being so sour?'

'The guy might know something about running, but that doesn't stop him from being a giant sleazebag.'

'Hype, Jason. Spin.'

'Spin, my arse. Tell that to V. He had him running about in the rain last week 'til he was soaked through. What was it you were wearing, again?'

'Vest and shorts.'

'You see, vest and shorts! So you ran in vest and shorts until everything was see-through. Does that sound normal to you?'

'It wasn't like that. We were running out of time, and we had a lot of exercises to cover.'

'Stop stirring, Jason. I think Casey's all right. He helped me out the other night when he didn't have to.'

'Your mini-meltdown at midnight. When you needed a lift home from the station. I heard.'

'I'll pretend I didn't hear the sarcasm in your voice, Jason, only your deep concern. So let's just give him a chance, eh?'

Moon was throwing a couple of those big paper serviettes over the coffee table as she played peacemaker, placing the glasses and plates on top.

'It's all about dressing the table. The Rottweiler™ taught me when she hosted a couple of parties for the Lib Dem candidate, Peter whateverhisnamewas. "A tablecloth will transform a table," she'd say, "or at least a couple of napkins, if you're pressed for time and don't have the desired facilities."'

'So your mum's become a one-woman finishing school?' I go. 'What happened to Oxford?'

'Of course I'm going to Oxford, that's a given. But she wants me to be a lady too.'

Me and Jase giggle like idiots.

Bedingfield is found and chucked on. We put the garage track on loop, 'cos that's the only one we can stand. We perch across the stools and sip the last of Moon's Tango from the rinsed-but-not-dried glasses. No one is keen to sit on the sofa.

'Remind me why we're doing this again?' goes Jase.

'Because it's Casey's birthday and he deserves to have some kind of party. If it was left to him, he wouldn't tell a soul, and it'd go unmarked.'

'Imagine how you'd feel if no one knew about your birthday. Wouldn't it make you feel lonely? Gwyn went round one year saying that birthdays were just a Western extravagance, and that, as she was no longer a child, she didn't want to celebrate it. But on the day, she was still gagging for her cards and presents and a piece of cake.'

'Sounds fucking brilliant. No obligations, or having to fix your face when presented with cheap useless shit you never even asked for.'

My phone goes.

'I'm coming up the stairs,' says Mum, 'so get the door open. I don't want to have to set down all these bags just to ring the bell, and then have to pick them up again.'

I want to tell her that she could use her nose or her forehead the way paraplegics do, but know when to keep it zipped.

Mum's brought most of Tesco with her.

'It's too much,' I say, 'you've spent fortunes.'

'Don't make a song and dance. Most of it's on offer.'

Once unpacked, the table groans under the weight of crisps, nachos, chocolate cornflake treats, cupcakes, cold sausage rolls, hot turkey twizzlers, cheese and tom sandwiches, egg sandwiches, baby Yorkshires, crudités, dips, hummus, salad, mini muffins, mini quiches, apples and satsumas. It was the kind of display you want to show any passing alien: this is the food of our people, come taste.

With the balloons up in each corner of the room and flanking the banner (fixed, refixed, and fixed again) across the doorframe, Bedingfield turned up to seven, everything feels right. Party in waiting.

Mum and Moon took the stools, leaving me and Jase to stand around the place, unsure whether to lean against the wall or kneel at their feet like lapdogs. We held our glasses clumsily. There was much watch-fiddling on Mum's part, followed by tutting, followed by discreet snacking.

'He's cutting it a bit fine, isn't he? You know I'm not staying long, as I'm meant to be going out with Mike.'

'That's a shame, Vivienne. You could have brought him to the party.'

Mum laughed as if the likelihood of that suggestion would kill her.

Her eyes had been taking in every inch of the place since her arrival. Her training as a district nurse taught her not to turn her nose up, as on a day-to-day her workplace varied from Edwardian mansions on the Downs to caravans on the industrial estate. Her job was to dispense care to whomever required it and not necessarily to pass judgement on how they lived, except in cases where it had an impact on health. I knew that Mum prided herself on her ability to take her kit bag and go anywhere and make herself welcome. Still, she couldn't escape the pull of her two strongest genes: Jew and Bexhill. She could hide it from Moon and Jase, who were unschooled, but not from me. The tiniest pinch across the bridge of her nose, a tick repeated every few minutes as she came across something else she found distasteful: an absence of skirting boards, the dull sheen on the carpet, the lack of furniture, the thick balsa doors that looked faintly institutional, the smell, one that was unapologetically male, which permeated every room, a window-sill free of any birthday cards other than the ones that we've brought. Far from being angry, as I should have been, I knew I'd only giggle if our eyes crossed to share her secret assessment: what a loser, what a dump.

It was the first enjoyable thing that we'd shared for several days — a little piece of nastiness at Casey's expense.

We got the bell because I still had his keys. Whilst Mum went to answer the door, I left them on the corner of the table, between the French Fancies and the Turkey Twizzlers. The music was loud-ish, but we could still hear their voices as they spoke in the corridor. Mum had her work voice on, which meant, as friendly as she was being, he was one step removed from her. No matter what part Casey played in my life, he'd always be an acquaintance, a contact, nothing more. He could help me win the Olympics and she'd still shake his hand like a stranger.

Moon and Jase moaned the moment she left the room.

'She didn't bring any wine! What's going with that?'

'I only said I'd come if you got a couple of bottles in!'

'As if that was ever going to happen,' I go. 'This is the real world, guys, not some fantasy free-for-all. She isn't going to leave us with a load of alcopops to get pissed whilst we're in suspicious company.'

'So even *you* are calling him suspicious now,' said Moon, suddenly suspicious herself. ''Cos if that's the case, I don't know what we're doing here.'

'I mean, suspicious 'cos that's what Mum thinks, in spite of all the good intentions. Casey ain't guilty of nothing. I'd trust him with my life, you guys.'

'That's going a bit far, isn't it?' goes Jase, the most nervous I'd seen him looking in a long time.

'Not really,' I said, ''cos it's true. Just spend an hour or so with him, alcohol or not. You'll see.'

We're all on our feet and gravitate towards each other, until we're standing in a line facing the door to greet the reception party; like a trio of waiting diplomats from Planet I'LL KICK UR ASS.

43

When Mum and Casey re-enter the room, she already has her coat on. Guest arrived, time to piss off. She pushes him towards us like we're playing Tag Team.

I've been waiting so long my mouth shoots off ahead of itself.

'Casey! Happy Birthday! I know technically it isn't your birthday, because the actual day is on Tuesday, but Happy Birthday! D'you like it? Do you? Really, we should have had one of those Happy Birthday songs to play on your entrance, like maybe that Stevie Wonder one, 'cos it's classic and not too cheesy, though it would have most likely been the Fiddy Cent one, where it just goes on about it being your birthday and everything, but we didn't get it together in time.'

Everyone looked at me as if I were a mad person, not getting that this is how me and Casey talk – all the time.

Casey took in the table, the balloons, the banners, Bedingfield on loop, and his house-guests, and his eyes were moist.

'It looks like you've done a pretty cracking job to me, young Turk. It's a blessing, truly it is.'

Over his shoulder I could see the younger guests rolling their eyes and making faces.

He shakes everyone's hand, including mine, distantly and self-consciously. Even before he's got through the procession, all 'Nice to see you again, Miss Moon Jones' and 'Ah, yes! Jason, SIR, the rock n roll rebel!', Mum's vanished; partly to do with the countdown to Mike, and partly to do with a major decrease in patience. On her days off I think she takes exception to wheeling the patience out when she really doesn't have to.

Casey's been to the gym or somewhere whilst we've been balloon-blowing and party-planning. Scrubbed up a treat. Hair still damp, and curly and tight, still too short for a full comb, but forced into something resembling a side parting, a definite shift to the left in any case, clean-shaved, skin rosy and scrubbed. Out of the tracksuit and into *cargo pants* and a white polo shirt. I'd never seen him look smarter.

First impressions: if you saw Casey looking like that in the street, you'd think manager, David Lloyd Centre, or maybe Head Lifeguard if he was ten years younger. But I'm not malicious in my appraisal, the way Moon and Jase are. I'm just absorbing their judgements so that Casey doesn't have to. I'm a big brown sponge who mops up the bad energy so that you can only see the good. If I were a wire, I'd be Earth. Ask anyone.

He pulls a bag from one of the lower, more voluminous of the cargo-pant pockets.

'I stopped at HMV on the way up. Thought you'd want something a little more feel-good than my usual selection.'

He handed the bag to a dumbstruck Jason.

'Pop-Dance Hits? You think we like Pop-Dance Hits?'

'Also, don't get too excited. I've got you some beers. Just some light beers, 'cos I don't want to get into any strife with your folks. Just, seeing how you've gone to so much trouble for me, the least I can do is give you a little something in return.'

The scorn plastered across Jase's face immediately vanished on mention of the B-word.

'Mate, why didn't you say so sooner? Go get them from wherever they're hiding. A couple of those, and I'll be happy with your Pop-Dance anything.'

By the time CD 1 has finished and CD 2 begins to creak into motion, all party activity is at its peak. Moon hasn't been eating, so the 0.25% of alcohol in her system is determining her every action; still straight-edge, but no longer horizontal, a degree or two above terra firma. Turfing Casey from his favoured spot, she's dancing on the sofa to an audience of three. It's some cheesy mix of 'Crazy In Love', which she's claimed to have always hated, in spite of the tribute to Beyonce that now twists and shakes before us. Jase, after looking delighted, then uncomfortable, then bored, disappears to the loo for a smoke. Casey looks bemused, with thoughts like 'Do people really dance like that?' crossing and criss-crossing his face as he struggles to follow the variety of moves.

Which leaves a two-horse race. In normal circumstances, i.e. if we were in my bedroom or hers, I'd be up there joining her, bus'ing my head up, throwing my set around like Jay Z. I'm not as keen to do that in front of Casey. Also, I haven't had my 0.25% of alcohol to sozzle my inhibitions.

'It's a party, guys. Come on! Get up here!'

We stay grounded and wait for the show to end, which is about ten minutes later when Moon throws up due to motion sickness (the spins were crazy, bra), or the cupcakes, or the 0.25, or maybe just a combo.

I'm not smug. I just know that all straight-edgers shouldn't get so carefree with their drink. It only leads to trouble.

Casey takes it all in his stride, making her a slice of toast and giving her weak, sweet tea, but Pop-Dance Party does lose its earlier euphoria and becomes more subdued after that. We sit in our circle like a bunch of old women and pass the sausage rolls.

'Did you not have any mates you wanted to ask down?' goes Moon, when she gets her voice back. 'A crowd is always good for a party.'

'A couple of my muckers from the church I go to said they'd try to make it, but y'know, sudden commitments and all that. I'm quite happy with the crowd I got here, to be honest. I think we're happening enough without the addition of more cautious influences to cramp our style.'

'If you say so,' goes Jase.

The buzz from the door forces everyone to check themselves; that maybe Casey had invited friends who'd be mad and funny and show us that he wasn't all loner and grudge.

It was a pizza boy. Brendan had sent his apologies with a twenty-inch American Hot with extra mushrooms.

'I didn't even know we'd invited Brendan,' said Casey, dumfounded. 'Where did that come from?'

'I just thought you might appreciate it, now the dust has settled. Should have known he couldn't be bothered to make the effort.'

'Let's not discount the pizza, though,' said Jase, grabbing the box and inhaling the contents like some deranged knicker sniffer, 'seeing that it's here, and hot and everything.'

'I would never have thought to appease a no-show by sending a pizza,' said Moon, thinking aloud, eyes lighting up with possibilities, 'but the more I think about it, the more I like. Pizza is good.'

'Let's open presents. Presents is better,' I go, hating the idea of being palmed off by that dry-skinned snake, and them falling for it. I clap my hands to break the mesmeric hold of melted cheese, jalapeno and ground beef.

Casey tries to hide his pleasure, but is useless at it, a thick smile spreading like an oil slick across his cheeks and raising all the muscles across his face. For a moment he looks almost normal.

'You can't have got me presents after everything else you've done. It's too much.'

'Shut up and take it like a man, C. It's your birthday, innit. Expect presents. It's the law.'

I'd asked all guests to come up with a present to the value of five pounds. I would have said a tenner, but you only do gifts for a tenner for someone you really like.

'It's manners,' I'd explained to the disbelieving. 'You can't go to someone's party and not bring them a present. It's really rude.'

One of the disbelieving asked whether a punch in the mouth could be considered a gift, or maybe pissing on the TV.

'You needn't be so generous,' I said. 'Something that comes from a shop will do fine.'

We got our shit together and assembled. I was first and last in line, so to speak, presenting Casey with Mum's gift, which she had neglected to put forward in her rush to leave: a white orchid in a square cut-glass vase from Tesco. She'd wanted to go for geraniums, which is what she gives to any old dear on her rounds that she gets friendly with. Bribes them with flowers so that they produce their stool samples without any fuss. The conservatory was full of geraniums for shitty occasions. This wasn't right for Casey. I pushed her for a slightly pricier option.

'I know he looks like a sad figure, but he's a man about town. A player on the scene. You wouldn't give a Premiership footballer a fussy old trail of greenery.'

'I'll decide what I think is an appropriate gift, thank you very much. I'm not going to break my habit of giving plants just because you think he'd rather have a bottle of overpriced aftershave. I always give plants, Veerapen. It's what I'm known for.'

'She says it's for colour. Said it'll brighten up any room, or something. Just be sparing with the water. They hate it, apparently.'

Casey handled the plant uncomfortably, struggling to take off the yellow ribbon that had been affixed with some kind of gum glue around the top of the vase. He got halfway, before feeling the weight of collective eyes on him, and gave up, placing it on the table amongst the food, the bow at the front falling low like some slapper who's showing you what's under her skirt.

The orchid looked funny sitting there. Aside from bacteria, his flat looked like a stranger to botanicals.

'That's very generous of your mother, on top of everything else. Very posh. I don't know what to say.'

'Save it for later, mate. You can write her a note or something. Here's mine. Happy returns and that.'

Jase had bought an Odour Eaters three-pack. One size fits all.

'And mine.'

Moon produced an olive oil and balsamic vinegar set, looking rather similar to the gift boxes The Rottweiler™ kept in the dining room cupboard for emergencies. Just saying. His grip of this was clumsier than with the orchid. He looked suspiciously at the bottle of balsamic like he didn't know what the hell to do with it. If anything, he was happiest with the Odour Eaters.

Then I got out my present, which made Casey's eyes fill with tears, and made the disbelievers think that I'd gone too far.

44

'Friends are friends, right? They tell each other everything?'

'Course, son. Unless you're a mass murderer, in which case I'd rather you keep it to yourself.'

'But you should be able to share everything with them, right? Even things they don't want to hear?'

'Even things they don't want to hear.'

This is the kind of phone call that Jase likes to make at one a.m.: mashed up, just back from hanging with one of the older college dudes from Produce, and wanting to right wrongs. These were the kind of calls I was used to, where he'd show his regret for giving beatings to whichever muppet had crossed his path that day, or be wondering why no girl at school was ever interested in him. My job wasn't to say anything, it was just a case of being there, listening. If Mum hadn't been out on an emergency visit, another old girl who needed an urgent check-in at the nearest NHS hotel, she would have wrung my neck to be up so late, as well as Jase's.

Also, what's spoken down the phone stays down the phone. There is never any mention of this stuff at school the next day. It's like we were both imagining it.

'I've done something I shouldn't.'

'We've all done something we shouldn't have, Jase.'

'Are you just going to repeat everything I say? I'm phoning you for a reason.'

'All I'm saying is that we're meant to get off the programme once in a while. Don't give yourself such a hard time over it. If everyone just does what's expected of them, things are bound to get boring. Tonight, your stray dog is Stella, three cans, possibly four.'

It's not that I don't have the patience to be a good mate, just that Casey's party has given me the warmest feeling that I want to carry into sleep. I don't get this often enough, the comfort zone, so want to hold onto it for as long as possible. My own stray dog, I guess, #645.

'I thought I was being really clever. I was acting so smug this afternoon, didn't you notice?'

'I just put that down to your natural exuberance, bra.'

'And I just feel dumb about it now, 'cos I know I've done a really nasty thing.'

He says Casey's name, and it's like stray dog #645 has been killed instantly in a hit and run. The warmth, everything I'd been holding onto since I got home, evaporates.

142

'I was going to his house, V. You were taking me to his freakin' house. The temptation was too great.'

'What the fuck have you done?'

'I left pictures, V.'

'What d'you mean, you left some pictures?'

'If you don't stop repeating me like some fucking parrot, I'm going to hang up, I swear.'

'OK. OK. Just tell me what you did.'

'Like I said, I was in his house. The temptation to leave a souvenir was far too great to pass up. It's not like I was gonna get another invite, was it?'

'I still don't understand. What pictures?'

'I guessed Casey might be feeling a little lonely in his new place. Without the old comforts of home, if you see what I mean. I just thought I'd leave him a few things. So he could take a stroll down memory lane whenever he liked.'

'You can't be serious.'

'I left five. All about twelve years old, eleven. All starkers. No sex poses or anything. Just nekkid. Thought that'd do the trick.'

'What were you trying to prove? Can't you see that there's nothing wrong with him? That all that shit was made up?'

'Well, yeah. *Now* I can. I mean, there's no way you'll ever really know, but he does seem all right once you've spent a few hours with him.'

'That's what I've been telling you all this time!'

It's a minute or two before one of us speaks, both of us lying there listening to the other's breathing. If this were any other time, I'd be thinking something else about Jase and his breathing, not the anger that is wringing my guts inside out. I clamp my jaw so tight my teeth feel like they're about to shatter. I feel wired and gritty, like those people on the ECT tables, when they're being tortured for wanting to hold everything in.

'Why would you want to hurt someone good? What possible satisfaction can you get from it?'

'We bus' people up all the time, V. I never hear you say anything then.'

'But not people that mean something to us! There's got to be a line. Otherwise . . .'

'Otherwise?'

'Otherwise . . . we're animals. We're council-house-and-violent. We're nothing.'

'We're not nothing. We're not *worth* nothing.'

'Where the hell do you get pictures of naked twelve-year-olds? It's not like you've joined one of those Camera Clubs.'

'The guy in the photo department. He has to hand over any dodgy pictures he develops to the police. Always manages to make a few copies first, though.'

'What a sick fucker. And you think Casey's weirder than that?'

'He said I could do what I wanted with them, so long as I didn't post them on the web.'

There's another pause for more breathing space. Jase's pulse is fast and shallow, either because of the panic or because he's looking for a way out. I keep my breathing even and deep, breathing techniques designed to help through anything. Lion power. Have to focus on summat, else I go round Jase's and bash his head in with a lead stick.

'I didn't leave them in his face, so there's a chance he might not have even seen them yet.'

'Don't give me hope like that, 'cos if it isn't true I'm liable to start throwing things.'

'Put it this way, I didn't put them some place he'd find straight away.'

'This isn't the time to be talking in riddles, Jase. If he ain't seen them, I want to get them out of there.'

'He can't have seen them. He could have called you, wouldn't he? He would have said *something*.'

'S'true. He's never one for holding anything back when it's on his mind.'

'His bedroom.'

'What?'

'I left them under the mattress.'

'Jesus, Jase. You're all for originality.'

'I thought it was a good place. Funny. He'll see them when he changes the sheets.'

'He never changes the sheets. I mean, didn't you see the state of the place? He's a pig.'

'But he's your pig.'

'Yeah. I guess he is.'

You can only make statements like this at one a.m. when the person on the other end is mashed and unlikely to remember your blatant sentimentality.

45

It's hard to make a loaded call sound casual when it's been playing on your mind for most of the night.

'What are you talking about? It's Sunday morning. Haven't we seen enough of each other so far this weekend?'

Even though it was early, I'd made it down to the kitchen and had the TV on, trying to keep everything sounding up and laid-back. If he even sniffed the mechanics behind every *hey*, *yay* and *yeah*, I'd be done for.

'It's out of the question, young Turk. I have church, and then I'm giving a talk to the youth group.'

'Your church has a youth group? How many kids are in it that aren't disabled?'

'If you got your head out your arse every once in a while, Jesus pardon my language, you'd see that the church is an active and vibrant place to be a teenager.'

'That still doesn't tell me how many kids you've actually got there.'

'We've got enough.'

'More than ten? Less than ten?'

'I haven't got time to have this conversation, young sir. I've got to get ready.'

Casey's tone wasn't so much busy as exasperated. Most mornings you couldn't get anything out of him until I'd run at least 800m. Why should Sunday be any different?

There needed to be a window, day, evening, anything. The subsidence of the rot I was feeling in my guts hinged on me getting in there and performing my magic spook trick: thirty-second wonder. Blink and you'd never know I was there, in your room and hunting under your bed.

Casey hemmed and hawed for infinity. Off the track, where indecision rules, he could be a champ at it; greater than anything he ever achieved on the field. He was sensitive about being spied upon, but that couldn't be helped. He could be in the most secure and non-judgmental environment ever and still feel the paralysis of paranoia. We could discuss the pitfalls of the Surveillance Nation we have become until we were both blue in the face, and he still wouldn't accept my argument, that the cameras actually give you more freedom rather than repress you. He wouldn't have any of it. He's the kind of guy who's going to spend his old age living off tins in a nuclear bunker somewhere.

My voice crackled with an enthusiasm I wasn't feeling, cranked up to warp speed like some kids' TV presenter who's spent half the night hopped on coke but still manages to turn it on once he sees the red light. Anything for Casey to think that I was in need of his mentoring presence. Hell, I was even prepared to sell Mum down the river if I thought that would do the trick.

I didn't have to. He gave in once I started going on about how I thought that whilst church was probably a good thing, what was really important was the church that people carried within them in their everyday lives. He laughed for a full five minutes over that one.

'You're full of shit, young sir. You know that, right?'

'You're not the first person to have come to that conclusion.'

He said he could spare me some time late afternoon, a period of around an hour or so, before heading over to his evening session, Café Worship.

'What the hell's Café Worship? Do they make a devilishly good cappuccino?'

'It's the informal setting for our evening services, boy. And let me tell you, the coffee's pretty good. You're welcome to tag along to that too, if you like.'

I assured Casey that I'd spoken all the church I was liable to for one day, if not for ever.

I felt so relieved I could have smoked a fag. I rang Jase's mobile about five hundred times before he rose from his Produce-influenced coma. There was no point calling the house phone, neither he nor Billie would answer it. He isn't good on details generally, so that time on a Sunday morning, with weed buds performing all manner of power-tool excavations in his head, his directions were woolly and to be taken with an unhealthy pinch of salt.

Much of what we argue about, then and later, will stem from Jase's inability to distinguish between top, middle and bottom.

'It's under the mattress, man. Who gives a shit about the exact location?'

'I'll be bothered when I'm having to dive into Casey's room under the pretext of going to the bog.'

'It's a small bed, cousin. It'll take you less than twenty seconds to find them.'

'I might not have twenty seconds, dumbass. It's a secret mission. Every second can be crucial.'

Jase offers to come with me to provide diversion services, but I knock it on the head. Casey'll take one look at his face and clock that something's up.

I shouldn't get complacent, but I do. After the calls have been wrapped up, I get my feet on the sofa and keep the blueberries on tap. MTV Base on blast, with some X Box to vary the mood. I sleep a little. I could keep my mind clear until I got to Casey's at four. He was out all day, so there was next to no chance of him finding something he shouldn't have. Where's the fire? It comes at just after one when Casey phones to blow me out.

'You won't believe it, kiddo, but my church buddies hadn't forgotten my birthday after all. They're throwing me a party!'

'You're getting two parties, at your age? How spoilt are you?'

'So we're going to have to take a rain-check on our coffee later, unless you'd like to come to the church hall, and meet my friends.'

'I've already told you, I'm not setting foot anywhere near that place.'

'Suit yourself, young sir, but I know everyone would love to meet you.'

What I experience is the battle of extremes, a very real panic over the prospect of not getting into that flat, versus a flush of pride that he wants the church goons to meet me. You wouldn't make an offer like that unless you really meant it.

I sweat out a third anxiety: the possibility that I have a more permanent place in Casey's family-free family.

'There's got to be some time when we can hook up later, kick back. I could come round after your café thingy, if you like. Watch *Match of the Day*.'

'The only time I've got is at this party, Mr Prendrapen. What a whirlwind social life! Check me out!'

'But I . . .'

'What's the big deal with you wanting to come by my place, kiddo? Anyone would think you were desperate to get into that dump.'

It wasn't the muted laughter in the background that told me he was making a big show for his church goons, more to do with him calling me kiddo all the time, like he was some big carefree guy who never worried about anything.

I'm at a loss. I have no idea what to do, short of coming clean and dropping Jason in it.

'A church rave sounds great. I'll see you there.'

46

Casey lives in a big fat circle. He starts and ends with the crucifix. Everything else is gaseous, insubstantial. Inside the circle he's as safe as anything, paranoia banished and fears displaced. He becomes the person he always wanted to be, if you push aside the tracks and the medals: impenetrable, *an example*, so long as he stays in the circle.

His sense of humour is reborn. It's like I'm witnessing the fucking resurrection, God pardon my language and blatant blaspheming.

The church hall rave sounded like it was going to be stuffed with a busload of spastics, but they turn out to be a really racy lot. Women outnumber men by 3:1. Single women outnumber men by 2:1. No one dresses like Lil' Kim or anything, but there are calves on display, and cleavage, drop earrings and plenty of big hair. I ask Casey if they are like this because of the party, but he tells me that they look like this pretty much all the time.

The men give me discreet cups of punch and tell me to keep it under my hat. About five of them do it, so I'm near pissed within an hour. The women take me outside whenever it gets too stuffy and slip me contraband cigarettes. Everyone asks me whether I have a girlfriend.

Inside the circle, Casey is the bloody funniest person to have ever walked the streets of North East Surrey. The way the men and women laugh at him, you'd think he was channelling one of the old boys like Tommy Cooper or Eric Morecambe. Put the exact same act in a different kind of church and it would have been like a one-man séance.

I call the numbers for the raffle. I dance with the married ladies to S Club. I am the perfect guest of the guest of honour.

I am seduced by the wisdom of the circle. I share their

joy-without-agenda, putting aside the J-word, and the crosses that decorate every available wall space. I forget I am here with an agenda of my own. I forget the anxiety that filled me as I ran to the hall. Too many hugs from smiling Christian strangers. I see the fellowship. Makes me wonder what the hell I was worrying about.

It's a different story when the punch runs out. My buzz, alcoholic and spiritual, evaporates, and I remember the reason why I'm here: to create my own lull, a Jew–Tamil special, my own homegrown illusion of security. It's a case of flattering my bollocks off – the women, some of the men, Casey. Anyone within my line of vision gets it. If you were looking in, you'd think I was the most polite and charming young man in the world. That the future would be safe if all the young people were as centred and loving as me. They wouldn't believe that I could be the King of the Switcheroo, leaving the party early and breaking into Casey's flat and pulling the pictures from the bed.

The only person in that room who'd believe it would be Casey, and he was all for acting upon his beliefs. He catches me as I'm trashing the place in a bid to make it look authentic. He only looks at the first picture in my hand. He doesn't wait to hear about the rest.

PART 5

47

Three things.

He thinks of manners before himself. Casey pops a note through the door, getting his arse out of bed extra early, as I find it on the mat before I leave the house for training. I wasn't expecting him to be there, but I was getting ready anyway. I can't stop training just because I think he's gonna be a no-show. Who knows what's gonna happen to me? I may have to go through twenty more trainers before I reach Olympic level. The note tells me to go back to Harriers. The C scrawled at the bottom is so wispy and random, it's like the note isn't really signed at all, the C itself looking like a scribble someone does to check whether there's any ink left in the Biro. Left-handed, careless business. Block lettering, brown envelope. It could have been a Paki Go Home note if I hadn't read it properly, or if we were in the 1980s.

In the fold of the letter is the 9-carat St Christopher I'd spent most of my cash on. I wasn't trying to be sentimental when I gave him that gift, more that it was the most appropriate thing I could think of. If it forced him to think about me each time he wore it, that would be his lookout, not mine.

Now it sits in my hand uselessly. I'm not feeling anything. Just static. There's no point in going to the flat and pleading for anything, as I know what I'll find there: a clothes rail cleared of tracksuits, Bedingfield CD packed up and away. He didn't say much when he found me, but what he had said sounded final. The look on his face only seemed to back that up. Softness over anger, but still incredibly resolute. I knew when I left the flat that there was no reverse decision. When it comes to disqualification, all decisions are final. I've been trying to run all my life, but I'm never going to run the way Casey does. I'm not scared enough.

It takes Jason a couple of days to say it, but he manages it eventually. No longer feeling so fucking clever. That only three of the five pictures I gave him were the ones he originally left under the bed. Either a magic trick or something we don't want to voice an explanation for. When Casey started shouting, I thought it was because he was shocked at the pictures, I didn't think about *which* pictures.

I move on because I have to. Driving yourself mad because you're missing your mentor is only going to fuck with your head. Trus' me, I've been there.

48

I'm a bright boy. Pearson's bullshit keeps me off the streets a little. Yid graffiti follows me about the school. Hey, replaced with Shalom. Simple things.

Simple doesn't bother me. Simple is the easiest thing to handle, but I keep myself to myself only 'cos I don't want to waste my energy, or pull a muscle. I train with Brendan. I go to school. I come home. Strict routine. Mum twigs after about three days. She isn't stupid.

'Are you on drugs? Is that the problem?'

Then again.

Mum wants to know everything all of a sudden. Doesn't like that I'm always in heavy fight mode on X Box or scrubbing myself in the shower. Outside of training and school, I haven't left the house for nearly a week. Won't even go with her to Tesco.

'Are you being bullied?'

'No!'

'Then what's the matter? I don't understand. You shouldn't be indoors all the time like this.'

'Teenage stuff,' I say. 'Growing pains. Nothing I want to discuss with my mother.'

49

Jase on *his* mother – this came last Christmas when he stayed over one night. A stayover sandwiched between my first two times with Moon, so I was feeling manly and all-knowing. We'd played on X Box until we were virtually blind, but still unable to sleep. It was one of those three a.m. conversations that adults are so fond of having.

'Her sticking her fingers down her throat is the only happiness she gets. It sounds fucked up, but that's how it is.'

'I get it. It's like her high, right?'

'You should see the look on her face before she locks herself in the bathroom. And then the look she has when she comes back downstairs. It's the closest thing I've seen to contentment. Since Sophie, anyway . . . Why would I want to take that away from her?'

'Don't say any more,' I go, but not for the reasons he was thinking. More to do with me looking at him in his boxers on my floor and thinking things I shouldn't.

Everyone pretends they don't have a gay phase, but they're all liars. This was mine.

50

The nights when we meet are when she practises sex with me. All socialising has gone out the window. I'm banned, thanks to the volley-ball idiot and his Surrey fatwah.

She'll turn up at eleven when Mum is doing a night shift and Pearson is safely tucked up in bed, saying things like, 'I need to try it out with you laying on your back tonight,' or 'Let's see if I can get you off in five minutes without taking my clothes off, and by neither using my hands or mouth.'

She says these things before she's said hello.

Having Moon this way, in secret, is better than not having her at all, even though I know that the next time I see her, outside her house, or in the school corridor, she'll be looking at me like I'm some deranged dependent muppet who can't let go.

If I wasn't so angry, I'd find the urgency in her voice, the hot hot heat of her breath, fucking sexy.

'This is sick,' I tell her, usually when she's on top of me. 'You're just trying this stuff out like it's a recipe you're perfecting for a dinner party.'

'That's exactly what it is.'

'Why don't you just do this with Pearson in the first place? Forget the dry run. It's not about making mistakes, sex. It's about the moment, the connection, or something.'

'Like you're the big expert all of a sudden. I suppose we have Kelly Button to thank for that. I'm not interested in the unknown, Veerapen. I'd rather get the new stuff or the tricky stuff out the way with you, so that when I'm with him I'm in control.'

'That doesn't sound too healthy.'

'Well, it's either this arrangement or exercise control over food. Which would you prefer?'

Moon had a problem with food for a couple of years when she was about eleven. It's kind of common round here. Everyone looking for perfection and not finding it, having to keep it all in their head and out of their bellies. Her parents had to get outside help to sort it. It's why they always go crazy at the first sign of trouble because they never know if she'll cave in and pull the inner trigger. Wheel out the crutch when things aren't going her way. It's also why they don't like having the computer on in their house, after she tried to make her own pro-ana webpage, sending a hyperlink to her dad instead of saving it.

It's like living with a suicide bomber who'll never take his coat off.

I hate her. Right now, I hate her, but there's no way I want her going back to how things were before she got help; a skinny unsatisfied undernourished hell.

'No, it's fine,' I say. 'Keep fucking me 'til you think you've got it right.'

We carry on, silently, like Scientologists.

51

Stoicism is bollocks. I'm no good at letting go. Ask anyone. When Dad left, I'd creep downstairs after Mum had gone to bed, and sleep in the garage, pulling down his old sleeping bag that he'd used about three times on a fishing trip and then forgot about, and the cardboard boxes from the Christmas stuff that no one had got around to chucking away. (Mum was never very good at getting rid of clutter, maybe that's why he went.)

I slept in the garage every night for two weeks, thinking that he was going to find me, or that I'd wake and find his car towering over me and realise that it was all a bad dream. Kids are so stupid. No wonder people lose patience with them. First sign of trouble, and they start doing rubbish like that. Like that's going to solve anything, retreating back into your shell, regressing to toddlerhood.

Looking back now, I get it. It wasn't so much that I wanted it to be a dream, I just wanted to be near him. The garage was *his* place, it had his stamp all over it. He wasn't a practical person, the only things he knew about were books, food and screwing opticians, but he liked gear. He liked having the kind of stuff all dads have, even if he wasn't ready to use it: tools, nails, tins of paint, ladders of varying sizes, lampshades, varnish, off-cuts from the old carpet, stacks of old magazines. Wonder why Mum never noticed.

She didn't notice a lot of things. Too fucked up at the time to notice that her kid had stopped speaking. She was taking a few pills to get her through the day, pills that made her rabbit on. She talked to me, to herself. All the time, yak yak, trembling tone, everything's rosy, what are we having for dinner, yak yak. Never a comment to register that no sounds were coming from my mouth, that I'd become Dad's unwilling counterpart, the silent ghost. It took the same amount of time, a fortnight, before I started talking again, when I realised that Mum needed more help than I did.

Not sleeping in the garage, making myself not do it, was the biggest hurdle. I tried tying myself to the bed, but it didn't work. I had to rely on willpower. It was like I was being operated on without any anaesthetic. Doctors ripping my guts out and me feeling every second of it. Knowing that I could stop feeling so empty in a minute, if only I'd get my ass downstairs and meld my body into the concrete floor, the site of multiple botched DIY attempts and car repairs. A place where it was just the two of us. But I didn't. I gritted my teeth until I felt my incisors sinking into my gums, and I stayed in bed. You can't always be a baby. You have to grow up eventually.

52

Mum's moved the computer from the bottom of her wardrobe, where it's been confiscated, to the dining room, and creates her own tech area. Whilst I'm at school, she clears out some of the crap and pushes the desk right into the far corner, next to the piano that nobody uses. It's all for Mike, of course. She and him get online and swap instant messages on the nights when they're not on dates.

I've got so much going on right now, I've forgotten about being a cyber-geek. It's the real world I want, not the one that comes in a flat screen, but Mum's taken the baton and is pegging it for all she's worth. She's hooked. You know it's getting serious when you start eating in front of the thing. Mum says she's got a strong mind, that it's hard to pull the wool over her eyes. She isn't. She's putty. Three days in and all her snacking time is at the keyboard instead of during *EastEnders*.

'What's a grown man doing cruising the internet all night? Doesn't this strike you as odd?'

'He's not *surfing* anything. I thought you were supposed to be one who knows everything about the internet.'

'That's how I know about the cruising.'

'Veerapen, he's chatting to me, nothing else. There's nothing very strange about that.'

'Why doesn't he just pick up the phone like normal people?'

'Online is better. Cheaper, for one thing, and he likes to mix it up a little.'

'"He likes to mix it up a little"? Mum, that's what young people say.'

'Oh, yes, I forgot. Your generation invented everything, including, it seems, the English language.'

Mum's a proper joker when she wants to be. It still doesn't make me trust whatsisname. I don't know anything about him. He could be the world's biggest internet pervert, for all we know. These legal people are very good at hiding their sick sides. Best alibi in the world.

53

Like all couples, they have their places: Yates' Wine Lodge if one of his older mates is riding with them, or up the Bowl if he isn't.

Bowling's different. It isn't about the booze, it's open to anyone. You can just bump into people by chance. There can't be any talk of following or creeping about when you're down the Bowl. You have as much right to be there as anyone.

Jase's idea, the bowling.

'Nothing else to do round here, unless we want to watch some shitey film, so we may as well show our faces.'

Also, the place stays open until one.

Double also, the new guy behind the bar used to do security at Tesco. Means we get our beer poured discreetly into Pirate Jack kiddie cups without having to drop our voices to baritone or flash the fake ID, which looks ropier and more bogus by the day.

'Yeah, Keith's a good bloke. He'll get us loaded, and if we're lucky we won't even have to pay for it.'

What could be better?

The Bowl kids itself that it provides entertainment for all, but in reality past nine o'clock the only people you find here are the fifteen-year-olds. Every so often you come across a group of twenty-some-thing couples, the men usually being lardy meatheads with Alpha-male competitive streaks, their girlfriends with fat asses in their ponchos and bootcut jeans, who spend more time deciding on which size ball to use than actually throwing the thing.

You see, this lot still have these phases where they kid themselves that they're young, and that's when they start hanging out at our places and getting under our feet. Mate, you're over the age of twenty, forget it! Unless you can buy us a proper drink, or find us someone who sells decent weed, you're redundant. Stay out of our faces and we'll stay out of yours, yeah?

Just sending out the signals does the trick. Crossed arms, the kind of stares they shy away from returning. They stay mostly on the outer lanes where they're out of harm's way and near-invisible.

The staff are acting like we're a pair of dorks without dates, but we're not actually here to play bowling. That'd be ridiculous. We're just here to hang out and take the piss out of everyone else. If we bump into certain people, we bump into certain people. No need to make a whole song and dance about it.

Jase doesn't tell me that the guy behind the bar is a Sri Lankan. Birthname Roospen, stage-name Keith.

Short. Moustache. Thick black hair that's both wiry and wavy, cut into the style of a university lecturer circa 1975. Pudgy. A face that looks like it enjoys a great quantity of food. He has round and heavy cheeks that were born to be smothered in curry sauce or mayonnaise. He looks like a guy who couldn't stop traffic, let alone stop thieving down Tesco.

'What's all this Keith business?' I go. 'Couldn't you have given me some prior knowledge or something?'

'Leave him alone. Keith's all right.'

Don't start loading me up with Munchausen's By Proxy or whatever it's called, I don't have Sri Lanka-phobia or anything. I just have a problem with anyone whose eyes start gleaming whenever they bump into a guy who's painted the same shade of brown. Don't get me wrong, I'm nowhere near as dark as Birthname-Roospen-Stagename-Keith, but I doubt that's going to stop him. In the ethnic desert that is North East Surrey, I appear as a mirage, an oasis. The temptation will prove too much.

'All right, lads,' he goes, friendly enough, but still proving me right. Looking me up and down in a couple of seconds like he's getting a biometric print, going at it until he's satisfied he's identified my full genetic history and is able to tell me the exact vendor from which my great-aunt gets her milking goats. Is it any wonder that I do my best to avoid eye contact? I just want my beer, not a layman's account of my family tree.

'How's things going at home? Your mum looked much better when I saw her outside the pharmacy last week.'

'That's great that you think so. She has been a lot better the last couple of weeks. Having my auntie down has helped. You met her, didn't you? That time they came down to Tesco.'

'Ah, yes. Maureen. Tall lady.'

'That's the one. She got Mum to break some of those routines she'd gone back into. You know, staying in bed all day, keeping the curtains drawn, that kind of thing.'

'Your auntie sounds like a good person.'

'She's amazing. She, like, saved my life. And Mum's.'

'I'm pleased to hear it. Is your mother ready to be receiving visitors? This place has a shift system too, can you believe it? And I'm on earlies next week, so I could come by after work one afternoon, if that would work.'

'That would definitely work! She'd love that. So would Auntie Maureen. Any excuse to get the china out.'

Jason's voice had changed completely. He lost the drawl and got a grip on his consonants, kept the vowels tight and clipped. His hair wasn't parted to the side with a cowlick like some under-the-thumb church boy, but it may as well have been. The grown-up conversation with an adult without an ounce of cockney, it wasn't how I was used to seeing him. I stood there, my mouth open like a fish, looking a dork.

Second time tonight, the dork-isms. I was keeping count.

I don't know what I was more surprised about, that I didn't know he was so friendly with the darkie, or that I was completely oblivious to how bad his mum had gotten again. I was too busy checking the darkie out to wonder why Jason had stopped confiding in me.

The thing with Sri Lankans is that they have this kind of dark skin, kinda like old sodden wood left to rot in a derelict house, which makes it impossible to tell his age. You can call me racist if you like, but it's my own parents' fault for not making a proactive effort with me to mix with other darkie children when I was growing up. There were a couple of brothers I vaguely remember when I started infants, father from Madagascar, mother from Uganda, and there was this Brazilian kid Gabriel who came round to tea a few times and who Mum used to think was so polite and charming, though that didn't stop him nicking five pounds from my birthday money jar. But they were only moments, brief friendships that never came to anything. Once we moved to Surrey it was game-over at the Commonwealth Institute. Not that my parents did anything underhand, they were busy working. We were the only spot of beige in an area that was blindingly white. They just didn't think. And then Dad ran off, and I was the only brown spot left. It's the kind of upbringing that's meant to turn you into a radical black panther, or, in my case, an enlightened Jew-Tamil Tiger. But I'm dead inside, man, blunted by TV, and girls, and the promise of what I can do when I slip on my running shoes, and the sniff of freshly burning weed at five paces. I got no energy left to be all radical, no time left for brotherhood – maybe for a kid who's grown up the way I did, but not for some be-pleasing-you-sir who's just stepped off the boat. They mean nothing to me. It might sound rough, but that's just how it is.

We did get what we came for, however, two kiddie sippy cups filled to the brim and covered with a lid to avoid any awkward questions.

'Christ! What's his game?'

'Leave him alone, I said. He's all right.'

'Your mate "Keith" has given us shandy, like we're kids or something. Go on, taste it!'

'What's the problem? You never drink more than half a bottle anyway.'

'I thought we were getting real beer, not this watered-down muck.'

'You're very picky all of a sudden, V. We haven't been entirely swindled, there's still beer in there.'

'Whopee-do!'

'And if you start drinking up, we can go back and get a top-up.'

'I think I'll just chuck mine in this plant pot and dream of the real thing.'

'Suit yourself. Give it here then and I'll drink it. Stupid to waste it, now it's in our hands and everything.'

'If you're going back for more, Jase, you're on your own. I'm not going to forsake the sanctity of my family history for another teensy cup of warm shandy.'

'What are you going on about?'

'Long story. Listen, how come he knows so much about your mum, and I don't? What's that about?'

"Cos you don't ask, V. You don't ask.'

If there wasn't anyone around, and I was a more comfortable kinda fella, I'd put my arm round his shoulder, and tell him that I'm always around to talk about his mum, that I'm not as selfish as I appear to be. It's what I really want to do, slip my left arm over his left shoulder, turn my body into his, feel a little closeness, try to make real some of the stuff that sits in my head. But I'm way too scared to do anything. You don't get this shit going down round here. Jase is looking out onto the lanes and shifts a little, feels my breath on his cheek and moves back, seeming to read my mind, the way I'm unable to read his.

There's a few kids in our year who are making the most of the lanes, but no one worth talking too. Satellite mates, you know the kind. Fine for five minutes but not the kind of folk you'd miss if they were killed in a road traffic accident or anything. Jesus, what is with my mind tonight? We get chips, soggy with vinegar and criminally anaemic from the microwave, and sit on the banquette that overlooks the centre lanes. It's only place worth sitting. If you sat in the diner section, the way lot of the kids do, you don't get to see anything: who comes, who goes, the aggro over scores, the fights. It really is the best spot.

An extra order of chips later and there's still no one about of any note. Jase txts a couple of troublemakers to see where they're at, both of them bouncing back notifications of Park and Odeon. Even with a shandy inside me (I changed my mind), the night feels like a washout.

And then they're here. They're here. I'm not saying that I've gone all soppy and hear some kind of special music every time I see her these days, but I'm not exactly lying either. There is something special that happens when she enters a place. She's still not the most popular girl (quite the opposite – none of the high school bitches can work out what she's doing with Pearson), but somehow she manages to alter the vibe of a room, the chemistry as soon as she appears . . . or as soon as I see her anyway. We were sitting on a banquette covered in crumbs, watching a load of kids make a cack-fisted attempt to bowl, with some lame watered-down R&B coming from the speakers above our heads. Wacko on a big scale, a painful excuse for a night out. But then Moon's in the room, and everything starts to fizz. The music gets slightly better, the shandy seems to have a stronger kick, the kids bowling start picking up a rhythm, with that hefty and satisfying clack of bowl meeting skittle becoming faster, harder, more frequent.

Pass the cheese, please, but it's true, man. Moon's the reason for everything.

She's the only girl in Pearson's group. It's him and a couple of the volleyball idiots. We give a couple of whassups. Pearson nods his head up and down at me so quick it's like he's got palsy. He's not even looking at me when he does it, just the side of his head does a quick move in my direction. That's not respect, it's some bogus bollocks just to make him look friendly in front of his crowd. Jason, Jesus, Jason gets a fucking hug! It's enough to make me want to kick things off, but I know what the deal is with Pearson. It's a given. I can't go crying every time he tries to shut me down like that. Which is why, still seated, unlike Jason who's up on his feet, I'm Pearson's mirror, less palsy-like but still the same up-down; whassup, mate, good to see ya. This muppet is looking at the king of shut-downs. I ain't going anywhere.

'Hey,' goes Moon to the pair of us, but no hug, what with her being a taken lady and all. This week, hugs are no longer appropriate. She seems to have forgotten about how she last visited me a week ago . . . when we did more than just hug.

'We're just going to start our game. We'll catch up with you guys later.'

Is that all I get? I ain't greedy, but is that all I get? I haven't seen Moon for two days, haven't spoken to her for three. She talks at us like we're people who took a science class together, like, four years ago or something. Married lady stuff – this week at least. A fake brightness in the voice, and facially, shutters down. Her way of avoiding an argument; a maturity that's hard to swallow.

I look at their feet and see they've already got the stupid shoes on, ready to take to the floor.

'Hey, Pearson,' I go, 'aren't you gonna change into your bowling shoes before you get going?'

He's so thick it takes him a few seconds to get the diss. Not the others, including Jase, they're already cracking up. I've kept it upbeat, so it sounds friendly and not like I'm dissing the arse of the cunt.

'Yeah, funny,' he goes, but he doesn't rise to it. Been there too many times before, we're both tired of it. And he's got the girl on his arm, that's the clincher. I can try and make him look like a muppet all I like, it ain't gonna make any difference.

And then, when I think he's swallowed it like a lemon, he calls back.

'Yo, Jase, we got a spare place on the team, if you wanna play. Go get some shoes, if you're up for it.'

They're already on their way to the far end of the lanes, playing by the twenty-something couples because they're oh-so mature. They don't wait to see the look on Jason's face, they don't have to. They know he'll come. So do I. And I get it, I do. Jase is loyal, but he's lonely. For him, bonding with someone at a mate's sleepover means friends for life. I'm pissed, but can't be really pissed if he wants to go play. It's Jase, innit.

Moon is the one who looks back, sees Jase as his ears break into a should-I-shouldn't-I dance. Flapping like Dumbo. She watches as I take his shandy and push him in the direction of the fit black girl with the good honey weave in the centre booth where they swap the shoes.

'Go on, mate. I'm cool watching here with my watery shandy.'

You gotta do it, haven't you? Getting into a denial twist with your closest friends is only gonna get your head messed up otherwise.

I'm like some old hippy, really. Everyone should be free to do what they wanna do, or something.

Moon is wearing the top I bought her, the H&M number I picked up when she had me over a barrel over some evidence. A baby-blue sweatshirt with some OK-looking graffiti on it, old-fashioned New York subway stuff that makes you look like a rapper from 1982. It took me ages to find that jumper. Had to go to three different branches to find it. So she's got no right to stand there and give it the silent lip in support of Pearson whilst she's wearing the top I bought her. Does she even remember where it came from? When she takes it off, she can give all the wordless judgement she likes. Until then, she needs to shut it. I'm not afraid of going over and taking it off, if I have to. I'm not.

Jesus. This was only s'posed to be a random night out, no aggro. I've only said about five words and I'm a fucking mess.

The shandy in my hands is now tepid and gag-inducing, but I force the last of it down. Martyrdom is what I do best, ha ha. I go to Keith for a top-up. All things considered, he's probably my best friend in this place right now.

There's a grubby little Goth kid working the bar too, but I wait for Keith to clear his side of the queue before I place my kiddie sippy cup back on the counter.

'You're back for more? Boy, you can put it away, Veerapen!'

'Yeah, I'm a regular big drinker. I'm like the guys back home,' I go, 'where they sit under their coconut trees drinking rum.'

I've got no idea what Sri Lanka is like, but presume they have coconut trees like they have in Mauritius. Same colour skin, same lifestyle I reckon. This is closest I've got to breaking my self-induced racial autism. Normally I can't even look these people in the face.

'You want something stronger than shandy?'

He's laughing now, at my brazen Tamil-ness. Also, the Goth kid has disappeared somewhere now that the queue has been dealt with, leaving us to talk freely.

'Whatever you can give me, my man. Load me up.'

'That kind of night? It looks like you're having fun over there, now your friends have turned up.'

'Don't believe everything you see, Keith. I'm hating every minute.'

He smiles the way people do when they think that they know everything: teachers, mothers, disgraced trainers with persecution complexes.

'What I like to do, when I'm having trouble with a girl, is to rise above it. I'm not saying that I do rise above it, just that I want it to look that way. I act like I don't give a damn. Make out I'm busy, really busy, that I've got all kinds of things on my mind that have nothing to do with her.'

'Who says I'm having trouble with a girl? I've just come for a drink.'

'Man, grant me some intelligence. I got eyes.'

'I'm only here for the drink.'

'I've been looking at your face, and how it changed the minute that girl came in. You were all teeth smiling, and then your brow knotted. Still smiling, but brow knotted. Classic sign of holding something in. It's gotta be about the girl, right? I can't see anyone else in that group making you feel that way.'

'Yeah. Course it's a girl. I'm not stressing out over a goat, am I?'

Heart sat firmly in my throat, hoping that if he's this good, he won't strip back the layers and find what I was thinking about Jason minutes before that. How much more can a thick old illegal Sri Lankan be capable of picking up?

'What d'you think I should do?'

I have to ask. There's no one else here, and I need something. If this was Casey I was talking to, I'd make him take me down to his church, see if the Fellowship brothers have the answer; but even though I've only known Keith for about five seconds, I know that I can talk to him about girls the way I never can with Casey. He's too busy watching his back to think that I might need to talk about *les bitches* and the messed-up stuff that comes with them. I'm not latching onto anyone. Keith is here, and just looks like he wants to help.

He has customers, three kids the year below me who want Supersizes and keep changing their mind between Coke and Tango, and then diet over full-fat. Two girls and a guy, meaning that they're all giggles and no focus. Getting a drink, changing your shoes, going for a slash, everything's a fucking holiday for these retards. I have to butt in and tell them to speed it up before I start hitting them. They shut the fuck up after that.

Between the kids, and then the beer tap, presumably for yours truly, Keith is kept busy whilst he thinks over his answer. The beer tap is one of those slow runners, it's not like the taps you get on sinks. Obviously I don't spend my time hanging out in pubs, so I've never seen how beer taps actually give. If you're desperate for a kiddie cup, you need to place your order an hour beforehand. It's millilitre by millilitre, something like the way his thoughts are beginning to ferment and distil: drip drop, drip drop. It's only when the cup is filled that I get anything out of him.

'Take a leaf out of the Jamaicans' book, man. Relax. Take it easy.'

'I ain't no Yardie. I don't smoke weed, and I don't drink rum.'

'I'm not talking about that, man. Just a little island mentality. Stop and breathe a moment. Don't get all hot-headed around the girl and start acting like a fool.'

'Why not, Keith? It sounds like the best idea to me.'

'Because that's what she wants!'

And it was like someone had switched the light on all of a sudden. Moon, out of the shadows and illuminated, like under proper harsh fluorescent strip lighting, not the rosy-tinted bollocks I'd been using all this time in my head. Sri Lankans speaking sense, revealing the mysteries of the world like a bunch of fucking yogis. If I wasn't so sober, I wouldn't have believed it . . . or been dazzled by the way the new light was shinning on Moon and her not-so-flawless face.

'It's what she wants, man. You're making trouble for yourself. And it just does the opposite of your true intentions, all the shouting, the pushing, rabble-rousing, makes her think that she's right. Not you. Her.'

'Are you a misogynist or something? Like, do you actually like women? 'Cos the way you're talking sounds you're the one with the chip on your shoulder, not me.'

'I've been married to my wife for seven years, and I'm very happy, thank you. This isn't about hating women. It's about understanding their tricks.'

'So you think that I'm right, then? Not her? How do you come to that conclusion? You don't even know me.'

A sip of strong beer plus wound up tension equals dark-skinned contempt. I can't help it.

Keith is too busy wringing out his beer towels to notice. He looks up and gets the stumpy brown thumbs out. Gives me the Fonz.

'Because we're brothers, man. That's how I know. Brothers of the Indian Ocean, innit? Us guys are always in the right, no matter what other people think.'

'What makes you so sure of the Indian Ocean connection? I could be from anywhere.'

'Not with those genes, man. You can travel halfway round the world. You could be in some Penthouse in New York in ten years' time, but you can't escape your genes.'

This is less to do with smart talk, his intuition, I think, and more down to Jason and his slack gob. Become a friend to Jason and he'll tell you anything.

I go for a piss and take my sorry ass, now slightly calmed by the voice of my people, and my new Supersized sippy cup back to the banquette, moving closer to the end lanes so I get a taste of the action. If I'm going to act aloof and unaffected, I may as well do it from a position where I can hear exactly what's going on.

Moon isn't playing. She stands around the score-zone acting cheerleader.

'SEVEN YEAH ! . . . THREE YEAH . . . STRIKE YEAH!'

She could be reading a magazine, the amount of interest she's showing.

That's why they needed Jason. Pearson wasn't joking about needing to make up numbers. The four of them are clustered around the foot of their lane, virtually breathing down the neck of whoever's up. Anyone who manages to ignore that and bowl in a straight line is a bloody miracle-worker.

This is why Pearson will never become a sportsman of any note, not because he's fucking useless, but because he has no respect for the rules of play. There are times when it's more important than ability. It's why I have to swallow my temper down if I don't win a race the way I should've, 'cos one day, when I'll really need it, some doddery old track official will remember my humility and vote in favour of the Tamil Jew. When it's down to a photo finish, this shit counts. It's something Pearson will never learn, because in his head he has all the arrogance in the world to carry him through.

They're not being quiet about it either, all taking the piss and calling whoever's holding the ball a blind spastic cunt. The prohibition beer goes some way to explaining their enthusiasm. Jase, getting busy whilst

I was in the bog; as far as he's concerned, kiddie cups are for sharing. He's the one who's the most excited, shouting the loudest, cussing the hardest. He's happy to be included, wants to show that he's nailed it, this being-part-of-the-gang business. He can take it or leave it, but tonight he's happy to take it, yes-sir-thank-you-very-much. I have to concentrate on staring at Moon, 'cos if I look too long at Jase and see how's letting himself be so happy with these idiots it'll break my heart.

No one wants their mates to be hurt in any way, but people gotta learn lessons.

Pearson throws a look in her direction at every other cheer.

'This one's for you, babe,' he goes, before each one of his rounds, like he's John Travolta in *Grease*, and we're the fucking muppets with nothing better to do than egg him on. He's giving so much cheese you can smell it from here. There may be a kiss in it for her if he gets a strike, or if he can be bothered to move his ass the several steps it takes to reach her, what with heckling the other guys proving to be more important.

I stand as close as I need to be heard, no closer.

'Why would a person want to come up the Bowl if all they're going to do is change their shoes and then stand around the sidelines?'

She gives a hollow laugh that sticks in her throat, the kind she uses when she's about to put the boot in. Also, walking me in the direction of the arcade games where we won't be overheard.

'Yeah, you really are wasting your time, aren't you? Standing around . . . on the sidelines.'

'I'm not talking about me! I'm talking about you.'

'So stop trying to be so clever if you don't want to be wound up! What business is it of yours where I go? If I wanna change into bowling shoes, I'll change into bowling shoes, who gives a shit?'

'Isn't it an expensive way to watch a stupid game of bowling?'

She looks at me as if I'm stupid.

'I don't pay, twat-head. He does.'

'He knows how to treat a girl. I bought you that top, and he takes you bowling.'

'Why do you always have to make this a competition? Jesus. He's my boyfriend. You were never my boyfriend. End of discussion.'

'Don't get het-up. I was just making an observation.'

'Keep your observations to yourself. No one's interested.'

Jase hasn't looked at me once since I've come over here, talking of observation.

'Moon, I . . .'

'Veerapen, look. We've had the conversation, more than once. Let's not have it again. Just sip on your illegally obtained beer like a good little boy, and go and growl somewhere else.'

She's hard. He's made her so hard. In the old days, she'd have given me a funny face or something to show that she wasn't being malicious. Any chats we'd have about my welfare or hers was because we cared. This is anything but. Her face frozen in its finality, copied from dozens of shabby daytime soap operas, she turns back to the scoreboard like I'm no longer worth bothering with.

I go back to the toilet where I punch the cubicle door a few times. It makes me feel better. The knuckles on my left hand are bashed to fuck, but it's fine. It's my feet I need to look after, not my hands.

When I get back, Jase is thrashing everyone with a fifty-point lead, and Pearson compensates by bitching about Keith, who won't serve him with any more beer.

'I'm going to get that Abdul kicked out. One bad word from me and he'll lose his job.'

'Fuck off, Pearson, who are you kidding? You don't have that kind of power,' I go. 'This isn't some country club that your parents are members of. This is a cruddy bowling alley. They couldn't give these jobs away.'

''Kinell, Dan,' goes Jase. 'Keith's all right, man. Leave him alone. We wouldn't have got that round of beers in the first place if it wasn't for Keith.'

'Keith, Abdul, whatever his name is. He can't just decide to stop serving us when he feels like it. If he felt so strongly about us getting pissed, he shouldn't have given you anything in the first place.'

'Jase has only got one round in. You can't be pissed on one round of beers, surely?'

The knuckles might be fucked, but there's still a way to put the boot in, if you know what to do.

He talks some stupidness about having a few before coming out, which everyone knows is wack, even the thicko in-breds he came out with suss that. His parents won't let him take a shit in that house without knowing about it, now he reckons he kicks back in his room with a bottle of JD?

We're all laughing at his foolishness, even Moon, who looks at him like he's an idiot. One more move in that state and she'd be well over him. If only . . .

'I'm gonna give him a kicking when he gets out of here. I hope he's a fast runner.'

'Who are you talking about?' goes Moon, though we all know what he's saying.

'That fucking monkey at the bar. He can't be embarrassing me in public like that. I ain't having it. Who the fuck is he to decide who can drink and who can't?'

Jase is pulling at his shoulder, 'C'mon, man, leave it. No biggie, eh?'

'Dan, stop making an issue out of it. You're acting like a prat.'

Moon's voice, suddenly acquiring the authoritative tone of her mother, cuts through the bullshit; the pitch, like diamond cutting glass.

Taking a third toilet break (it's the sippy cups, they kill any semblence of tight bladder action), the others are back on their game, and he's still talking about it. If the guy at the bar had been some cockney wideboy from a longboat on the river, you know he wouldn't have said anything.

Jokers, man, these guys I hang round with.

Now he's talking about cleverness, instead. Of brain over fist, which gets my ears up, 'cos I thought I was the only person who worked in that department.

'If I tell my dad how shocked I was to see a Sri Lankan gentleman serving beer to clearly under-age Indian customers, and how I was worried that it was going unnoticed, he'd send a letter up to that place like a shot.'

I feel this thing rising in my chest that I haven't felt for a long time swamping my upper cavity, powering the acceleration of my heart, filling my brain. Working my legs as I move away from the still-arguing/still-pacifying group, heading over to one of the free shelves where the extra balls are kept. Looking for one just light enough, but weighty enough, to deliver a blow . . . if it was thrown at someone you had an issue with.

It's a beauty. Blue, puke-making blue, like the top that Moon is wearing, and small-sized, like the dinky pumpkins you get in those growing competitions. This isn't a kiddie bowl, it's heavy, and solid, like it was designed for midget men with strong throwing power. I have height on my side, and can't get my fingers in the hole, but it's the kind of prize that fits tight in the ball of my hand and I lean down and cup it. I think about the shot-throwers at school, their form as they run, body turn and throw, all this still powered by the continuing swelling in my chest, like a wave still a mile from breaking. Beautiful, euphoric, deadly.

Moon's hand covers mine.

'Don't.'

'What are you talking about? I was just looking for the bowl so I could join the game.'

'That's not what it looks like.'

'I don't care what it looks like. You don't even know what I'm going to do. What are you so worried about? Me and the trouble I might get into, or just concerned about the damage I'm going to inflict on laughing boy's perfect face?'

'I care about the one that's going to make me most happy this minute. I'm bored of thinking about the long run.'

The building wave that's in my head is more important than pleasing Moon.

'You think an answer like that is good enough for me?'

'Yes, I do. And don't, Veerapen. Just don't.'

Bowl taken from my hand. Wave crashed. Idiots carrying on as normal. Miserable night.

54

If you're going to cry your eyes out, you may as well do it to country. Whoever worked that one out is a genius. Blubbing to Missy E doesn't make you feel so shit, in fact, she hinders things by trying to get funny all the time. Believe me, I've tried. This is why you need the serious stuff when you're seriously down. This is what those songs are for. Mum's off with her fella, and tonight feels like the time, finally, the real time, to let things out. I'm not talking about a trickle here, the little waterworks I've been giving previously, under the impression that this was grieving. I'm talking delayed reaction here, the full-on real deal.

It's been brewing all day, chest feeling choked, neck, throat. Barely able to get a word out to Mum in case I started. Alone in the house now, I'm safe.

I play the Cash tunes Moon used to loop on her iPod during her night visits. I loved those songs almost as much as I looked forward to seeing and touching her. She was only the body on those visits, Cash was the soul. I went out and bought the same CD after the funeral.

Cash's voice feels heavier than my heart. He sings like gravel on a dirt track, a phrasing that tries to prise open my insides line by line. By track three the floodgates open. I take off my shades and cry non-stop until nine o'clock. Mum's due home at nine-fifteen. Crying for Moon as much as I'm crying for myself.

There's a time when you need to put your faith into music. At the point when you run out of friends and your family stop understanding you. Music can be the only window you have. As Cash continues to

175

bellow his fury, I kick the door in. The spare-room door. Smash the glass pane. Something to do with Moon, I suppose, and me feeling as angry as fuck all of a sudden. And it is sudden. If I'd heard Timberlake's 'Rock Your Body', a Moon Jones favourite, me having a turn would be far more understandable. But this? Old man Cash? I don't explain it, I just do it. Realise that it's a replacement for crying. And I kick just as hard as I've been crying only a few minutes ago. What a joker. I can't even be a good cry baby in the privacy of my own home. I have to have a hissy fit and start breaking things. I'm a loser. A big one.

My foot is cut up real good, lower leg too. Like how the blood soaks through the part of my white sock that hasn't been slashed. Like it's in a rush to play catch-up. Don't leave me out, you fuckers! Let me bleed too, yada yada. It's a Cartoon Network newbie someone has yet to think of. The self-harmers and other tales of bloodwork. You could see how it could run and run. Those crazy red blood cells, always getting into trouble and spilling all over the place, hahaha. I think of these stupid things sometimes, ask anyone.

It's like watching Moon's blood all over again, except her cut was much bigger and there was more of it. Way more.

It's only when the music stops I hear myself. Realise that my breathing is becoming shallower. I'm hurting, not just my foot, but all over. I wait for the whole sock to emerge as a thick red, as evenly as possible, from the cut-up toes to the top of my ankle, before I shout for Mum.

55

Gwyn calls me the next morning. Saw me crying at the window to Johnny Cash. Says that it broke her heart. She doesn't mention that I was wearing shades indoors nor about the Surrey ambulance that screeched its arrival outside my house about five minutes after Mum found me. Mum had it sorted, but wanted professional help just to be sure all the glass had been removed. Some of those tiny shards can be buggers.

You would have had to be dead not to have heard the panic wagon as it rolled down our road. Ambulances are never discreet. The bleeding had stopped by the time they arrived. Most of the street popped their heads out as I was being carted off, the full siren encouraging everyone to get their wheelie bins out, but interestingly that didn't include any occupants from the Jones household. I couldn't make out much, being strapped to that stretcher, but that much I did see.

So Gwyn is round and has persuaded Mum that I am fine to be left with her if she wants to pop down to Tesco. She doesn't ask me how I am, and I don't ask her how she's doing either. We've done all this on the phone. There's no point. And she is too polite to mention my bandaged leg, from foot to knee, which makes me look like one of those old people who burn themselves in the bath. The only benefit of the bandage is that I have to stay in shorts for the next few days. Make sure I'm wearing my new adidas, yellow ones. Know that I look as sexy as fuck. Wounded soldier and all that. Girls love a wounded puppy.

'Have you heard from the police again?' she goes.

'Have you?'

'Yes, but in your case I would have thought . . .'

'It's going to be a while yet. My mum says these things take ages. I might not even get a call until next month.'

'Our letter came the other day. Morning after the funeral.'

'Do these people have any tact? Jesus!'

Gwyn makes a grim face.

'Not really. Just doing their jobs, I suppose.'

'No need to make a big deal about it. You've got a letter, I've got a letter, Jason's got a letter. They're interviewing everybody. Year Head. Even people like Lizzie Jennings, I heard.'

'It's worse than that. They're talking to everyone at school. Using the staff room to interview the kids.'

'Yeah? So why are you singling me out then? If they're interviewing everybody . . .'

'You know why, Veerapen.'

'Do I?'

'You were there.'

'So was Pearson.'

'He can't speak. He hasn't come out of his shock. Can you not bring up that bastard's name?'

'I'm sorry. You've just rattled me. I'd rather not think about the police. It makes everything feel so . . .'

'Final? That's because it is. Once they've done what they need to do, everything will be over.'

I'm too dead inside to be angry, the cut bled the last bit of emotion from me, but her words still manage to sting. Why has she got to go on about things drawing to a conclusion? Moon's death, the mourning, everything being over? Trying to get on with our lives? Like I need to be reminded of any of that? I can't do it. I want to keep on feeling this way for ever. I don't want to feel like a normal person ever again. It hurts too much.

She makes some tea and we sit together on the couch and drink slowly, both staring out at the garden, like it's the first suburban seventy-footer back yard we've ever seen; acting like a pair of Eastern Europeans just off the boat. And when we finish the tea, both of us acknowledging that we only have a short amount of time before Mum comes back, it's all on. We don't talk, just kiss.

56

'Are you going to tell me what's going on?'

'Nothing to tell. Nothing's going on.'

'Veerapen, you are standing in a pool of blood, with glass all over the floor, and you tell me that nothing's going on?'

'That's right.'

'Have you just kicked the glass out of the door? Why did you do that?'

'I don't know.'

'Tell me how you're feeling? Are you angry?'

'Duh!'

'Cut the crap, right, OK? Just stop it, Veerapen. Because I've had about as much as I can take of this. And I've done as much pussyfooting around as I'm prepared to. So if you want me to fix up your leg, you better start telling me what's going on, and quick, because if I'm right, you've only got a couple of minutes before your foot *really* starts to hurt.'

'Mum, it's really hurting now.'

'Good. So get talking.'

57

I open my eyes when Gwyn starts slapping me. Turns out she didn't want me to kiss her at all. I got excited, misread the signals and dived in. She only wanted to tell me about the police letter, pulls it out of her bag and starts waving it about angrily, just in case I didn't believe her.

Also, wanted to check that I was OK, but now wishes that she hadn't bothered. Looks really pissed about the whole thing. Says that she knew it was a bad idea to come here. All this mixing in these circumstances is never going to work out. She's on her feet now, and keeps pulling her skirt down as low as it will go, making it look like I was molesting her. Honey, if you wanna know about being molested, this most definitely wasn't it.

I thought it was a tender moment, nothing to do with wandering hands, all about our eyes connecting, and our lips. Some kind of acknowledgement towards Moon, but she doesn't see it that way, only wants to see the dirt. What is it with people wanting to see the bad in everything? That was a beautiful moment we had, and now she wants to soil it because of her guilt.

I try to have a look at her letter, change the subject, but she snatches it away as soon as I come anywhere near. Says that she wouldn't be surprised if it *was* me that Moon had been talking about, the guy who kept pressuring her into sex. She had presumed it was Pearson, following that afternoon when she'd discovered them on the sofa, but now she wasn't so sure. Something about the way my hand was aggressively cupping her tits. OK, I touched her tits, I admit it, but just the one, and I didn't go any lower than that. It was all about our lips at that point. Really.

When girls are like this, there is no point in arguing. The sisters seem very alike all of a sudden. The way Gwyn's eyebrows join together as she calls me a slimy piece of shit, it's like looking into a Moon mirror. Couldn't see it when she was around, but now . . . I tell Gywn to take her poxy letter and to get the hell out, the way they do on most of those TV shows when they're feeling mad and completely misunderstood. First time I've done it, not counting whenever I row with Mum. It's surprisingly effective. Better than Eva Mendes, she takes her coat and her mysterious letter, warns me that I'm in big trouble, and is gone in less than sixty seconds.

58

People, especially old people over the age of thirty-five, are creatures of habit. They're like little hamsters running in cages, from wheel to wheel to wheel. Unless they go for spontaneity and do something drastic like buy a Ferrari, or run off to Germany with an optician, they seem to be happy sticking to the same old routine, day in, day out. Up at seven, shit at seven-fifteen, out the house by eight, lunch

180

at one, dinner at six, fuck at ten forty-five, bed at eleven. No more so than this part of the world, where it's routine central. If I ever get that boring, I want someone to come along and kill me. I don't ever want to become another hamster.

I knew where he'd be even before I set out. The train pulls into the station at 6.58. He'd be at the bottom of the hill on Auriol Park Road at ten-past. He'd still have the same coat on. Same shoes. He'd still have the same briefcase, but he'd hold onto it tighter; he'd be warier. That's the difference.

Solo mission, no Jason. Not interested in taking photos either. If I get a couple, that'd be a bonus, but the point of the job isn't about collecting evidence. It's strictly snatch and run. Beat and run. Pearson needs to feel some of the hurt by association. This seems to be the only way.

His dad's still walking the way he used to: slow slow quick-quick slow, this lumbering rhythm that always seems to be playing catch-up with itself. If running does anything for you, it gives you an ear, makes you listen to the rhythm of steps. Even before you see someone coming, you can listen out for the steps, and get a measure of what kind of person they are; skinny or obese, good-tempered or twisted. Runner's second sight, innit, the listening. When I'm retired I can go on stage with it, my second sight, turn it into a big travelling show. Make a fortune.

The walk is a tired walk. Nervous, but tired. He hasn't gone back to his old comfortable self, the quick-quick steps speak volumes about that. He still feels the fear of what we did to him, and that's good, because he needs to.

If you're worried about being out after dark, you really shouldn't wander the streets where the lighting is useless; where the only sounds you hear are your feet as they go pad pad pad, the thickness of your breath and the thump of your heart as it breaks out into a drum & bass solo. It's all your own fault really, if something should happen to you there, on the dark and empty streets, so neat and clean, that you shouldn't have been on in the first place.

But once I get there, it becomes less to do with the briefcase and more to do with getting some colour back into his cheeks.

'What's the matter, you've gone pale,' I say. 'It's not right that you don't have rosy cheeks. Not healthy. We better do something about that.'

'What's this about? Didn't you get what you wanted last time?'

'I forgot something.'

'Don't think I'm not going to fight back this time.'

'Show me what you can do, grandad.'

'You stupid shit. You have no idea what you're doing, do you?'

Pearson's dad spits the word out at me like I'm the filthiest street scum alive. He's standing up straight, back arched like a cat preparing for danger.

Taking the initiative, he pushes me, but that doesn't work because I'm standing tall with my feet wide apart. Toes pointed. Keeps me welded to the ground, like a pylon. Unshakeable.

Next minute, he's faffing about trying to get something out of his briefcase, but I've prised it out of his hand and flung the thing over the fence into Auriol Park before he manages to flip the second catch. Combination locks are the bomb for people like me. Secure as you like, but no good in an emergency.

Probably lucky he didn't get his hand inside and make contact with the pepper spray or whatever it was he was after. He's so angry he would have been lethal with it. Eyes bulging like a maniac. Hands stiff and outstretched like the Auriol Frankenstein, ready to grab my throat. I've got all the respect in the world for technique, those self-defence masters that are all about showing you *the right thing to do*, that *preparation is the best defence*, which is why I haven't taken any of his abuse seriously. Why I don't feel the threat. No amount of self-defence seminars are gonna prepare you for my level of preparation. It's why I've floored him even before he's finished speaking and drawn breath.

But then he's running after me, so I may have been projecting when I said that he was lumbering. He's on his feet quicker than a person his age should be. Sprints after me as I head into the park. Probably not a bad thing. Gives the old boy the chance to have a bit of a run round. Tire him out a bit. I'll get him on the floor again, easy.

My heart probably shouldn't be pumping the way it is; like one of those cheesy Vegas showgirls giving a succession of rapid-fire high-kicks. Thump thump thump thump thump. No let-up. I'm not scared exactly, but I'm feeling the pressure. Most of the time you punk someone, they stay on the ground inert, like a broken doll. I'd long stopped holding out for that extra variable, where they'd get up and start getting all vigilante on my arse.

This is what fucks my head up. I start thinking too much about the piousness of the Surrey viligante who wants to keep the streets clean. Who probably wants to keep the streets white. I start seeing red . . .

I probably go a bit too far when his mouth becomes filled with blood, but that's always been my problem: obsessive attention to detail. It's cool that he has my scarf as his own little souvenir of Punking #2, as I have another one exactly the same at home. It's soaked with his own blood anyway. I only would have slung it. Who's gonna think that a kid will have the brains to buy two of the same scarf six months earlier, just in case? Will he be able to identify the silver Mongoose I rode off on? No problem if he can, as I lifted it earlier from outside the video shop. I ride a mountain bike, and it's stayed in the garage all night, wheels bone dry, not an ounce of dirt on it. Walk my shoes in the mud round my way so they can't place me round Auriol's green spots. Down to the details, every last one.

This isn't the work of a criminal mastermind. I just gave it a little thought before I came out. Grown-ups are always asking kids to think before they act. They shouldn't ask such things of us if they're not going to like what they get.

59

I know even before she's said a word that she's had a drink. I get this feeling when I put my key in the door of what kind of afternoon I'll be having. When Dad left, there was a couple of years when I'd get that feeling every day. We lived this real-life Groundhog Day for longer than we should've. The reason I spent so much time at the Harrier Centre when I should have been up in my room reading about dinosaurs or battering my Playstation. I had to go somewhere.

Since secondary, the feeling's evaporated, and I forget about the sharp intake of breath pulling from deep in my chest as I shut the gate and walked to my front door. It's nearly banished to memory, bar the odd day when someone's made some thoughtless remark that she takes to heart and then mulls over, like whoever it was had pinpointed her exact place in life, leaving it down to me to get some food and coffee down her and re-set her axis.

Now I'm a grown-up boy, I'm an expert at it. But I won't lie, there are days when I'm on some fucking high cloud, like you've had a good race, or an afternoon where you've clicked with a girl, and you get home, and turn the key in your lock and sense immediately that she will be on the sofa with a wine glass, and all your good spirit disappears, popping loud and clear and irretrievable like a needle stuck into a balloon. All the private things that made you feel happy earlier no longer exist. All you can do is assess the state of the drunk woman and try for the thousandth time to sort her life out. (And start mentally planning on when you are going to get the hell out.)

Also, the hall light is on. We only have that light on downstairs when someone is getting ready to leave the house. You put the key in the lock, and clock the hall light on through the glass panels in the door, lights on in the middle of the day, and you know that she must be distracted and feeling careless about wasting electricity, and if she's feeling that way about electricity . . .

If I'm too happy or wrapped up in myself to listen to my sixth sense, the clue is in the light. Always in the light.

'I've done a terrible thing,' she says, not waiting for me to sit down. When she talks in that deep tone, hoarse, using the back of her throat, like she's channelling a dead spirit or something, you know it's going to be something heavy, not some stupidness about one of the old coots on her rounds calling her a stinking Jewess or anything.

'Please don't tell me you've hit someone in your car,' because that had happened before. A cyclist whose wheel she clipped and then pegged it before he could get her details. On her way to do a fill-in shift and well over the limit. If she had to care for people under the age of seventy-five, someone would have sniffed out the problem a long time ago. Maybe that's why she's still there. So the only person who has to deal with it is me.

'Nothing like that,' she goes, but she's still using the voice. She's also still not looking at me.

We both talk to the TV in these situations. It's much easier than staring anyone in the face.

'I've made a fool of myself.'

'How? At work?'

'No. Last night. At Billie's.'

'At Billie's? Look, can you just turn *Countdown* off for a moment? I can't hear you over that racket.'

'There's no need to shout at me like that in my house, Veerapen. I'm not a child.'

'I'm not shouting at you. I just want you to turn the sound down on the TV so that I can hear you better. That's it . . . So, at Billie's?'

'I looked like such an idiot.'

'No disrespect to Billie, but she's not got anything to brag about. She's a mess.'

'Don't start mouthing off, Veerapen. Those are our friends. That family has been good to us.'

'I know.'

'And it wasn't anything to do with Billie, or even at her house.'

'You just said you made a fool of yourself at Billie's.'

'It was on the way home.'

'I don't understand. What's that got to do with Billie?'

'Don't be so impatient and I'll tell you. She was in one of those moods where you could see she'd been anxious and upset all day, so as soon as we arrived, she was trying to get us all drunk. Make the house merry, she kept saying. I was driving and wasn't in the mood to get smashed, but you know how it is when she gets an idea in her head and wants pleasing.'

'Please don't tell me the pair of you were getting trashed all evening like a couple of teenagers.'

It's far easier to talk about getting trashed with Mum if we include Billie. Makes it all sound far more casual and accidental. We've done this before. It's another conversation that I'm an expert at.

'She was trying so hard to be the life and soul. It was pathetic. The woman is seriously depressed, she needs professional help.'

'Yeah, we know all that. What does that have to do with you, and what's going on here now?'

'It wasn't just me and Billie there. She'd invited someone else.'

'Keith?'

'How would you know that?'

'What other bloke's going to spend any time round that house?'

'You're getting very rude about people as you get older.'

'Lucky guess. I met him with Jason down the Bowl and he couldn't stop asking about her. So this is about Keith?'

'He walked me home because, in trying to be a good sport for Billie and act the perfect house-guest, I'd managed to get myself over the limit. I could have got home easily enough, it's only a few roads, but Keith wouldn't have it. I was clicking the locks on my key, and he kept pulling the keys out of hand and clicking the locks back. It was so funny.'

'Sounds hysterical.'

'Will you stop taking that tone with me? I'll ground you other-wise.'

'OK, I'm sorry. So what happened? He walked you home, right?'

'I let him keep the keys and he drove me home before walking to the bypass to catch a bus. His car's in the garage or something.'

'That all sounds fine. So what's making you so upset?'

'I'm getting to it.'

'Have you eaten today? Can I get you something to eat? I could make a sandwich, or put that soup in the microwave.'

'Don't change the subject, Verapen. You're just like your dad, always wanting to talk around the subject, never tackle it head-on. I'm trying to tell you something here.'

'I'm not talking around anything. I'm listening.'

'No, you're not, you're just making noise with your mouth. Yak yak yak, that's all it is.'

'I'm listening, Mum. You either want to tell me or you don't.'

Mum turns off the TV and switches on the light so that we're no longer in darkness. She hasn't combed her hair since she got up, but she doesn't look ill, tiredness overtaking the drunk state; if you were peering through the window, you'd see a lazybones with a bad case of bed head, nothing more. Once we get the lights on, her moving off the sofa to do it, me taking her cue and putting the kettle on, I know we're getting somewhere, movement being the enemy of all wallowing. Get a drunk to start acting useful and you divert all kinds of catastrophe, so long as it's restricted to light-switching and TV control, rather than boiling pasta or giving you a lift to the shops.

The first thing I do is pour the rest of the wine down the sink. It's not even the decent stuff, just a nasty bottle of no-brand Chardonnay bought at the Co-op down the road. It was Mum who taught me about wine, that's how come I can be such a snob about it, and why I get so hurt when, not for the first time, it sinks in how quickly she must have bought that bottle. Probably picked it up without even looking at it. (Which explained a previous time a couple of years back when I got home to find her mopping up the remains of a bottle of non-alcoholic that she'd thrown against the wall on realising that she was living the haste/speed conundrum.)

So I get busy with the teabags and listen as Mum tells me how she made a pass at Keith in her car outside our house at ten thirty-five p.m. How he reciprocated and came indoors. How it was over by eleven. How they never even made it up to the bedroom.

Because I have some kinda respect, I'm silent, but I'm heaving so hard my guts have spilled from my throat and loop round my neck like those big thick hippy rope necklaces the girls are wearing these days. I'd look almost fashion forward, until you realised that I've just scopped my insides out on hearing my Mum talking about shagging on the sofa I've just sat on.

'Why are you telling me this? D'you want me to become more fucked up than I am already?'

'I thought we had a close enough relationship for me to be able to tell you these sorts of things. You're not a kid any more.'

'But I'm still *your* kid! It's not the sort of stuff I want to be talking about. Haven't you got a girlfriend you can spill your guts to?'

'Yeah, Billie.'

'Yeah, OK. I get the picture.'

'Also, in a *gloriously* sick twist, your father called just after eleven. God, he's got a sixth sense that man. Keith had just that second left and he was on the phone.'

'What's he doing calling after eleven?'

'Trying to get hold of you. You don't return his calls, do you, Mister I-don't-have-a-father? You're always out. He thought he'd get you at that time of night.'

'Great. Now he's calling all-hours. Thanks for the message.'

'You don't get it, do you? As soon as I heard his voice, I crumbled, told him what had just happened. That's why we're having this conversation now, so that you hear it from my mouth, not his. So you don't get a distorted, agenda-filled account of what happened.'

'I'd rather you both kept it to yourself, to be honest. I'm sure I don't need to hear this.'

'D'you think I want to be telling you these things? Private things? But I've been going crazy turning it over in my head all day. Had to call in sick because I couldn't face having to pretend everything was OK, and then half the day's gone, and you're home, and you talk about wanting to help, so . . .'

'I get it. Calm down.'

'I am calm, Veerapen. Stop talking *at* me with that tone. I might be feeling vulnerable, but I don't need to be patronised, thank you very much.'

'Sorry. Does this mean that you're going to stop seeing Mike and start seeing Keith? I thought you said Mike was all right.'

'Don't you listen to anything? The reason that I'm in this state is because I know I've made a mistake. Mike's a great man, a really kind man. I never had any intention of hurting him. But everything with him has been moving so quickly, the Keith thing caught me on the hop.'

'What kind of explanation is that?'

'I was . . .'

'It's fine.'

'I was . . .'

'Really, you don't have to go any further.'

'Horny.'

'Fuck! Mum! Just don't say any more. Just stop speaking! Don't say another word. Jesus!'

Tea does fuck-all when you're wasted the way she is. I should have just cleared up the mess, packed her off to bed and gone for a run. Spared myself this cringe-fest. My shoulders are drawn high around my neck in defence. I feel like someone's force-feeding me corrugated cardboard, I'm cringing so much. Jesus, fuck! What other child has to put up with this? Give me their address and I'll go and give them a ten-gun salute. Fuck!

'I'm feeling jittery about where it's going with Mike. The

189

seriousness of it all scares me. Makes me happy, but frightens me to death. Nothing's going to happen with Keith. I was just curious.'

'How, curious?'

'Don't ask, if you don't want to hear the answer.'

'It can't get any worse. Hang on a sec.'

First I go to the upstairs toilet, where I really do heave. My guts are back inside my body and perform an all-out routine. I'd just had a banana and a Ribena on the way home, so it wasn't pretty. Then, when I've cleaned myself up, and stuck my head out the window for some deep breathing, the moment Casey's exercises were made for, I show my face in the kitchen and let her tell me how she just wanted to make sure that Mike was the right guy, because once they became official she wouldn't be able to wonder.

'I'm sorry about saying the F-word,' I go.

'I think we've gone past that, don't you? Though if you think this is a red light for you to start swearing freely round the house, you've got another thing coming.'

'So we do have some boundaries, then?'

'Of course we have boundaries! You're doing it again! Changing the subject. Will you just stop, please? Let me finish what I want to say and then you can talk all you like.'

'I've heard so much my head is spinning. I don't think I can hear any more. What else can you tell me? That you needed to shag some random guy because you were getting cold feet? That you wouldn't ever want to hurt Billie, but it just happened? That you don't how you'll be able to look her in the face? That you were just practising with Keith to get things right with Mike?'

This is when she put the mug down and stopped talking to the wall. Turned to face me. Amazed.

'How the hell would you know a thing like that?'

'Because I'm the Son of God, Mum. Didn't you ever realise? I know everything.'

60

'Did you do it?' goes Moon, first thing Monday break.

Punking #2 was another Friday night special. She's had a whole weekend to think about how she's gonna approach me, and this is the best she can do.

'Do what?'

'You know what. Daniel's dad.'

'What about Daniel's dad, is he sick? Is that why he's not in school today?'

She's just come in from outdoors and is still wearing her scarf, the scarlet and cream woolly monster that's pencil thin and about five hundred metres long. She's fastened it together with the brooch I bought her, an amber tiger studded with fake stones that I picked up when we went to Camden Market with Gwyn.

'What gives you the right to do things like that to people?'

'Isn't that a question you should be asking Daniel?'

We're at my locker, the site of countless mock snog-fests, when we used to pretend to wind people up over our 'are they, aren't they' relationship. But it was all bogus. Like one of those sham marriages that Dad's relatives used to do to stay in the country. The only people we were winding up were ourselves. The rest of it, what people thought of us, was just window dressing. The same people are still walking past us as did three months ago. We were fooling ourselves to think that they were agog with our antics, open-mouthed at our outrageousness. They couldn't give a shit. It's the only thing that hadn't changed. Thing is, who came to that conclusion first, her or me?

'Where were you on Friday night?'

'It was Shabbat, Moon. I was at home having dinner with Mum, like a good little boy.'

'And you stayed in all night?'

'Ask Mum, if you don't believe me.'

'They've been trying to persuade him to go to the police, but he's refusing. Doesn't want to be made a fool of. Says he feels stupid enough as it is.'

'He should go to the police if there's a crime involved. We can't let Surrey become a neighbourhood of silent victims.'

'You'll regret saying that if he changes his mind.'

'How will I? I don't even know what you're talking about.'

'He'd be able to identify you, you know.'

'I very much doubt it. I hear these attackers are very well covered up these days.'

'If they didn't get you on his word, there's always Jason's.'

My stomach goes. It's the kick in the gut I was expecting.

'I wasn't with Jason on Friday night. I was at home with Mum, like I told you. And just in case you want to check, Jase's on a new phone. You won't get the evidence you're looking for.'

'He'll still have his old phone somewhere. All we have to do is switch SIM cards and see what's still on there.'

'True. Except he'll do his best to hide it.'

'You're making it very hard for us to stay friends.'

'I thought we were past that. I thought we hated each other. You've gotta learn to move on, Moon. No one can respect a person who doesn't learn to do that.'

'And you call mugging Daniel's dad moving on? Very mature!'

'Moon, I'm a runner. Putting one foot in front of another is what I do best. I'm always moving on.'

'If I told Dan that I thought it was you, he'd bash your head to a pulp. He'd kill you.'

'If you do that, you can also tell him to bring it on. I'm ready.'

Part 6

61

I tell Jase that Pearson raped Moon and made her take the morning-after pill. She mentioned the pressure he'd put her under once or twice, so this was sort of close to the truth.

There's been no comeback since Dad Punk #2, so this is me just speeding things up. Training with Brendan and his team and having to be so gracious about it, waiting for the moment when Mum would introduce me to Mike. My nerves are shredded.

Also, the very discreet and painstaking trail of Yid graffiti has extended and seems to have pre-empted my moves around school. So beautiful in parts, like a series of ornate classical marks, when you spot them replicated tenfold across your library shelf, on your random textbook, on the underside of the handle of your bag after gym. Replace the Yids with hearts and it could have been love notes he was sending me. It was possibly the closest thing to it since Moon stopped with her visits. I mean, you've gotta be really bothered about a guy to be doing stuff like that. It's a big project.

The proliferation of symbols are scattered like petals, but read like darts. This is the real world, not some jumbo fantasy I'm having in my head. I need to negate all the additional variables that are pushing me off course. What is it they keep saying at school? That fifty per cent of your final GCSE marks are based on problem solving, the other fifty on effort and imagination? This is my big push at problem solving.

Jase is nonplussed at the news, like this is hardly the most surprising out-of-character thing that he's ever heard about that wanker.

'I'm starting to take a real exception to that cunt. This news is only adding to it.'

Something to do with being dropped once Pearson had made his point down the Bowl. He kept saying he wasn't bothered, but I wasn't stupid. He was starting to spend more time with me down the track than he had done for ages.

'Let me speak to a few people.'

That night, after Jase has spoken to a few people, a petal reaches home. Local paper, back sports page, bottom right, under the athletics report. Upside down, but undeniable.

Liberties, man.

62

'Would it make you feel any better if I said that I was into you?'

'Not really,' goes Gwyn. 'I wouldn't believe a word of it anyway. You'll say anything to get me off your back.'

'But I am. I'm really into you, I think.'

'No, you're not.'

'Then why are you holding my hand?'

'Because my's sister's dead and our heads are all over the place. We learned all about it in Psychology. It's called transference.'

'Fuck transference.'

'You're just looking for someone who understands. Someone who's going to make you feel better . . .'

'And it's you.'

'. . . and I'm not it.'

'I can't help how I'm feeling.'

'That's the grief. It's got nothing to do with me. Do you have any idea how stupid we look together? I'm almost eighteen. You're fifteen. It's ridiculous.'

'Not if it's right.'

'Your idea of eligibility and mine are two different things. I'm looking for someone with A levels, not ASBOs.'

'You won't find anyone like that in this part of Surrey. Gwyn, I feel something for you. It's nothing to do with dead sisters, transference, or not being carted off in police cars. It's real.'

63

School is all whispers. From the moment I'm in the corridor, I get it. Everyone in class has a mouthpiece on one of two things: Vera posing for pictures for the local pervert, Pearson being some giant rape machine. You know how Chinese whispers are. Give it an hour and they take on a life of their own.

It's dirt too good to stay in one room, or one floor even. It spreads across our year and the upper years by morning. The beauty of overnight MSN or a bulletin on MySpace. I've seen it happen enough times.

That night it's no sleep and all niggles. Neither Moon or Jase call. No one wants to speak to me on MSN. I ask Mum if I can stay off school.

'Is this anything to do with Casey being off the scene?' she goes, because she's not stupid.

('What you have to understand is that he's crushed. He looked up to Casey like another dad. Had done for months. He hasn't had anyone in his life like that since Jeya left us.'

I overhear Mum and Mike discussing me on the phone, like I'm another one of Mum's cases, but I can't walk in and tell them that Casey isn't like a father figure at all. More like the other way around. It can't be my fault if I have a dad I never see, and a mum who takes her sweet time in finding a replacement. Why don't they just blame my weaknesses for everything?)

'No. I'm just tired. I need a day off to rest.'

I've just left my dinner untouched, which makes it a yes. Mum says I've been training too hard lately, that I need to ease up.

I'm still worrying, not about tomorrow now, but about the day after. Convincing myself of its distance away, I manage to get some sleep. But then, Jason turns up at eight a.m. like he always does, and suddenly Mum doesn't look so sympathetic. I chuck on my uniform and go in. Fuck it.

I'm visualising all the way in. Hawk not dove. Hawk not dove. Now's the time to be moving away from the lion.

'Anything to report?' I ask him.

'Nothing for you to worry about,' he goes. 'Just get on with your day and ignore these idiots.'

Just as I thought, my front crumbles from the moment I walk past the shops with Jase. Rape-machine is yesterday's news. Pearson must have been working overtime on MSN last night. There's too much talk about pretty boys going on in the corridors. Registration feels like something out of the Hutton Inquiry. Way too hostile. Way too much comedy smirking. Everyone throws these looks like I'm the freakboy who's about to run off with a man who's not his dad. It's not enough that they think that I'm gay. They think I'm gay on a BIG scale.

Before lunch I have History, Science, Maths. Laughs, laughs, laughs. No one manages to get any work done for all the gossip and sniggering. It was just a regular training programme, I tell them. Learning the kind of techniques that'll make me a champion. Trying to tough it out and embellish makes it worse. Makes me out to be an on-going faggot with a boyfriend and all that nonsense. I've nothing against faggots, I just don't want to be labelled one. It would have been better if I had been assaulted or something: less sniggering and more sympathy.

There's no sign of Pearson, but then there doesn't have to be. His work is done. Lizzie Jennings, the walking chatroom, takes the baton for the second time in her soft overweight life and runs with it. She has the choice of deciding which should become the lead story. At this point in time, she's probably the most powerful person in the school. Can make or break either of us. And one who decides to right the humiliation heaped upon her best friend Kelly Button by some chancer who dated her on the rebound. For a ginger fatty, she doesn't forget much, and that morning works as hard on her choice as I do on the track. Makes sure there's enough noise about a boy who fancies old men to drown out any mumblings about some rapist and his abortion-magnet girlfriend. I don't even know if Moon has twigged yet.

Everyone at school knows about my bizzle by lunchtime. E.V.E.R.Y.O.N.E.com. The only person it doesn't seem to bother is Jason, possibly because he knows he can fight his way out of anything. We stand in the lunch queue like the bogstandard flashing beacons we are. One hardnut, the other pink and unkosher. But no one dares to shout anything, not with Jase there.

'You're the talk of the school,' goes Moon, who crashes the queue and looks flustered. Still not making me sure whether it's my gossip that's reddening her cheeks, or hers.

'You should be worried too, shouldn't you? With all those stories?' goes Jase.

'Everyone knows the stories about me are bullshit. Even the girls who hate me know that.'

'What makes you think so?' I go.

'Because no girl, however twisted or messed up, really believes that a woman needs to be punished by gossip just for having consensual sex. I'm pissed that my business is public business, but not over anything else.'

What clears things up is the way she's speaking, all matter-of-fact, like some newsreader who keeps harping on with the bad stuff when you don't want to hear about bombs any more, or innocent people being hit over the head with axes, just 'cos they've got brown skin. From anyone else it would sound like the wooden spoon doing 360s, but not from her. From her mouth it's a grim confirmation, nothing more.

There's only Year 9s behind us, who wouldn't say shit to Sherlock, so we don't have to worry for a moment. Moon is the Year 9 idol.

Kooky has yet to enter their vocabulary, but Moon is most definitely it. Seriously, get Moon in a crowd of Year 9s and the waves part. Something to do her with her mentoring a class last September when they were green and cacking it. She's the big sister that everyone needs.

'I'm gonna break out this afternoon,' I go, 'I can't bear it. There's no way I can sit through an afternoon of this.'

'Do what you have to do,' goes Jase vaguely. 'In an ideal world, you'd confront Pearson and give him a good kicking.'

'That sounds like the ideal solution,' goes Moon all sarcastic, a tone we both hate 'cos it makes us both sound like idiots. 'Show that you're not gay by beating someone up.'

'Sounds about right to me,' goes Jase, even more sarcastic than Moon. He's more pissed at her than he is at either me or Pearson. If we're going to get all grown-up about it, you could say that he feels betrayed. Moon's been doing too much of that lately, ignoring any loyalty to her friends in favour of Pearson and his luscious lips; deferring her responsibility.

Moon gets this and avoids eye contact. Looks down at the pizza on the hot plates like it's the most interesting convenience food in the world.

'What choice do I have?' I go. 'If I don't do this, then it's gonna follow me around for ever.'

'Don't be so dramatic,' says Moon lamely.

She knows as well as I do how much worse Pearson can make it for me.

'That wanker needs to say something about me, so that I can get involved,' goes Jase. 'I am itching for a re-match.'

Everyone is fully aware that there's no way he can dive in otherwise. Them's the rules. My name being swilled around, my battle – simple as.

'Where is he anyway? Why hasn't he shown his face?'

'Don't ask me. We don't live together or anything.'

Moon drops the pose and starts to look rattled. It's the tension on my face, and the fact that I'm speaking through gritted teeth. If I relaxed even slightly, I'd be liable to head-butt the pizza woman or start punching the wall. Away from the track, I'm not so good at keeping my cool. The tension gives away everything.

It's an issue that needs addressing. One that can't be met with a blue bracelet.

The tables are taken, so we stand in a corner and eat our pizza. We're not supposed to stand once we've got our food, but we do it anyway. What's the worst they can do, throw us out? One minor victory against a piss-shower of failures keeps us dry for about a second. Jase wants to stage a table takeover but I'm against it. The front tables are full of jocks and their hangers-on, and we'd get slaughtered. I eat my pizza slice in ten seconds.

'This is stupid. I'm gonna go.'

'You can't leave. Year Head will kill you if she sees you on the CCTV.'

'I'm going to the library. No one's gonna bother me there.'

'Don't be too sure,' goes Jase. In his head, everyone is a conspirator. On the table directly ahead are Pearson's two best hangers-on lunching with their hangers-on. They grin at me like their Christmas has come early. I don't leave for the library until I have a second slice of pizza and a drink. I'm no chicken.

Year Head stops me in the corridor. I'm on my own, Moon and Jase staying to confer/get the gossip they wouldn't get with me hanging around like a bad smell. I don't have to turn round to see their expressions: relief that I have finally left them.

'I'm hearing your name mentioned an awful lot this morning Veerapen,' she goes.

'What can I say? I'm a popular boy.'

'Is there anything you'd like to tell me?'

We're standing by her office. Door's open.

'Why don't you come in and we can have a chat?'

Two girls walk past, sports clique wannabees, way below me on the food chain. They exchange a silent conversation as soon as they

see me, like I'm some *X Factor* finalist on my way out. It's humili-
ating. This is why I want to get shot of this school. Losers like this
are no good for my mental health. I want to become a champion,
not a fuck-up.

'I can't. I need to go to the library.'

'Forget the library. Step inside for a minute.'

The air in Year Head's office is incredibly cool. As soon as I sit
down – blue leather seat that looks about a hundred years old – I
feel the pressure lifting. Being here feels solid and reassuring, the
only rational space I've entered all day. Like I've been airlifted from
the big top halfway during a show or something. I'm not a snitch,
but I sometimes appreciate being in the company of grown-ups that
aren't parents or perverts.

'You're not having a good day, by the sounds of it,' she begins.
She's sitting next to me rather than across the desk, the way she does
with girls who get themselves pregnant and are too scared to tell
their mums, so I know that she's expecting me to pour my heart out,
or cry at the very least.

'I've had better. Mrs Harris gave me a B for my History essay,
when it was clearly A-grade calibre. You know, in our parliamentary
discussion last week, she said she didn't agree with coloured people
being MPs? Said it wasn't representative.'

'I'm not talking about your coursework, Veerapen.'

'Or a blatantly racist teacher, by the sounds of it. She was saying
those things to get a rise out of me. Isn't that illegal?'

'Look, I can only help you if you tell me what's going on. I've
had reports of disruptions in all your classes this morning and I
want to get to the bottom of it.'

'Nothing to get to the bottom of. None of this has anything to
do with me. I can't be blamed just because your teachers have no
grasp of discipline.'

'I'm never sure whether I should give you special treatment because
of your circumstances, but I can, if that's what you'd like me to do.'

'You're the Year Head. You should know what to do.'

'You pushed your History teacher, Veerapen.'

'Like I said, she gave me a B. I wasn't particularly happy about it.'

'Do you think pushing a teacher is acceptable behaviour?'

'It's not as if she listens to what I've got to say. And there wasn't push, just so you know. I brushed past her to get to my seat.'

'I think we both know that it was more than that.'

'She was trying to get me to sit at the front and I wasn't even doing anything. It was everyone else who wouldn't stop talking. She's got it in for me, like I have to be made an example or something.'

'She must have asked you to move desks for a reason.'

'I was telling Lizzie Jennings to shut up, that's all.'

'I heard you were telling her more than that.'

'I told her to shut her fat fucking mouth. That what you wanted to hear?'

This is the only the second time I've ever been in Year Head's office, the first being when I cut Pearson's head open. From the outside, when you walk along the path to the science labs and peer in, it looks huge. So misleading. When you're actually in there, it's as poky as hell and nowhere near as plush as the blue curtains and leather seating suggest. A cupboard with a desk and a couple of Matisse prints ripped from a magazine sellotaped onto the wall (his flowers, not the naked women. We have them at home, that's how I know.) Her desk is covered with paper and books, but all school stuff, nothing personal aside from today's copy of *The Guardian*, a bunch of pickled daffs in a vase that is algae-heavy, and a burnt CD that starts with a 'C' – could be either Coldplay or classical. No family pictures like you'd imagine a woman her age to have. Not sure if that's because she likes to keep her life outside the school just that, or if, as everyone in our year likes to believe, that she's a possible lesbian.

I know that if I breathe right and relax, I'd be able to see things more clearly. Focus on the goals. But it's too tempting to stay wrapped up in my rage, too easy. Everyone's always saying how much better it is to keep on the right side of things; what they don't mention is how hard it is to bring yourself out of that state just so you can behave correctly. It's harder than just flicking a switch. I'm a mass of fine electrical wires, powered to cooking point, brain preparing to sizzle.

She asks me again if there's something I'd like to tell her. That ordinarily an assault on a teacher, no matter how small, can result in immediate suspension, but that under the circumstances my behaviour this morning would be overlooked. But – and there was a big but – I had to open up and tell her what was going on. She's hearing the stories but doesn't know who's behind them; the gossip has gone way beyond its remit at this point. She also wants to know if there's any truth in them, because the seriousness of the allegations makes it something she cannot ignore.

'There isn't anything to ignore,' I tell her. 'Sour grapes 'cos the running's going good. No one seems to like it when the Paki gets the spotlight.'

'Veerapen, don't talk like that. Never talk about yourself in that way.'

She obviously hasn't seen any hip hop videos made in the last ten years.

Also, I can't respect anyone who's only learned to pronounce my name properly in the last six weeks. Year Head's stumbling over a few basic syllables makes Brendan's efforts sound natural.

I'm only getting her riled up because I don't want her to start some discussion about how a kid may get confusing feelings about members of the same sex as he moves into adolescence. I'm fifteen, I don't need those kind of lectures. Especially from a woman who's a lesbian on the quiet. Make a sentence with these words: calling, pot, kettle. Why are adults all such hypocrites?

Mum had a similar conversation with me a few months ago after some twat I didn't even know called out a name while we were queuing at the car park machine in the Bentalls Centre. Walked right up to my face and said it. I didn't get out of that chat as easily. I had to swallow my smirks and pretend to open up, something that I won't be doing again.

We sit in silence for what feels like an hour. I concentrate on Jase's blood stain, which still hasn't been cleaned from the carpet.

'You'd better get going or you'll be late for registration,' she says finally.

Knowing that it's safe to look up, I see she's out of her seat and pointing to the clock.

'I'm going to ask your teachers to keep a close eye on you this afternoon, and if there's any more trouble you must come and let me know.'

'OK,' I go, not 'cos I've got any intention of blabbing or sharing any information with her. Not 'cos I want to let someone who isn't a family member know how I am falling out of my depth into something that feels frightening and uncontrollable, but 'cos it's the easiest thing to say.

'OK. Most definitely. Fo' shizzle m'nizzle.'

I slip into the library on the way back to class and check my emails. Figure I can scrounge a couple of extra minutes and blame it on Year Head. There are two. One sent bulk to the whole of our year, the other one comes up as private. Both JPEGS. The bulk: one with me and Casey with my tits out down the track. Doesn't bother me as much as it should. They're already talking about it, this isn't gonna change that. It's only when I think of Moon that I get the hard knot in my stomach that threatens to turn me inside out. Knowing that, quite willingly, she felt that she had to pass that evidence on, and to him. In the glare of the second JPEG, my own worries are nothing, they don't even compare. Possibly why I got it privately. Pearson has guts, but not that much guts. A picture scanned from the local paper archives, of Jason's dead sister being carried into the ambulance. She's already in the bag, but that doesn't make any difference. I know what I'm looking at. Sick bastard.

Send him a txt to wash over the sick feeling: his dad on the floor in the street with the toe of my trainers in his face. It ends now.

64

Gwyn takes me for lunch at the Italian place. It's expensive, so no one there knows us. She walks with me extra slowly 'cos the band-aged leg has got infected and is hurting like hell. I'm saying nothing about transference either.

She doesn't tell me how much she likes me, only that she saw me snogging Peter Platinum, the runner who's all eyes and teeth, after that race meet in Guildford. She'd come to pick us up from the station, and saw how I was straggling behind, waiting for my oppor-tunity to get my three seconds of tongue whilst the others were getting their shit together. If I tell her that was the first time I'd ever touched a guy's lips, she wouldn't believe it. And he was the one who'd made the moves. The way he'd been checking me out in the changing rooms. One of those times when you think, fuck it. Let him have what he wants. I know he's an old ugly fucker, but there's no other candidates round here. I don't even like the guy. I just wanted to know what it would be like.

'But how come Moon never knew about it? I would have seen from her face, if she did.'

'Because I knew how obsessed with her you are . . . were. How obsessed with her you *were*. How you tried so hard for her to think that you were perfect. That's the reason she was into Pearson, in case you didn't get it – 'cos he's riddled with imperfections. You try too hard to conceal yours.'

'Are you really that easy talking about Pearson like this?'

She's ordered a half bottle of wine for herself, and because they're new and foreign, the staff let it go. She polishes it off almost in one.

'Not really. But as long as he gets what's coming to him, I'll just about be OK.'

'Which is?'

'Nothing less than a long and painful stretch. He killed my sister. He needs locking up.'

65

The first time I see Pearson is at next lesson, English, but Mrs Doe runs her class like a concentration camp, so you can't make the slightest attempt at desk-to-desk conversation unless you want to get killed. We both sit in the centre: me far right by the window, him far left nearest the door. Three desks between us. I have my registration in this room, so haven't moved an inch since I got here. He makes class by the skin of his teeth as usual, so there's no opportunity to exchange pleasantries, which is a big shame. I'm so angry, I'm ready to pull his teeth out.

We spend forty minutes detachedly discussing some book that no one's interested in. Mrs Doe is usually good at reading the code amongst the kids, but she's too busy terrorising us to pick up on our simmering. Also, she was probably late from having a last-minute fag in the language lab with Mrs Fletcher, and so didn't get her ear pulled by Year Head about putting me into witness protection.

I write Jase a note and slip it to him via Chinese Peter.

We all talk about this Rob Fleming guy and his record shop like he's under the microscope, like none of us have ever fucked-up in our lives. Like, ever. And Pearson is the most scathing of the lot. And because he's talking so much, because he's actually read the book for a change, Mrs Doe is nodding her head excitedly and lapping it up. It's enough to make you sick.

'It's not like real life. Who buys records any more?'

'You're such an expert on real life,' goes Jase. 'You're a regular documentary-maker.'

'And he moans all the way through. He's such a loser.'

'Stop interrupting, Jason. Daniel's making an interesting point here. Don't stop, Daniel, please carry on. What makes, him moaning d'you think?'

'A bad technique with women. Those lists. They're not even interesting.'

No one's laughing. Mrs Doe's not picking up on anything. Eyes too blurry with the *joy of teaching*. Focusing on Pearson like he's her private student or something.

'How about this, Daniel. Here's a man whose life is littered with so many disappointments that he's become paralysed with fear. That if he makes a mistake, any happiness with the girl of his dreams will disappear. Do you think his moaning is more or less understandable in this context?'

I'm looking at Chinese Peter, but he's ignoring me. The note is under his book and isn't moving from there, not whilst Mrs Doe is in the vicinity.

'He goes on about lists all the time because it's the only thing he gets right,' I pipe up, making as much noise as possible. 'Makes him feel good about himself.'

'He's hiding,' Pearson barks back, eyes locked. 'My parents taught me to have a low opinion of anyone who hides away from their problems. People like that deserve a slap.'

The only sound in the room comes from Jase scraping his chair back. Note received. He's two seats away from Pearson and could have him eating parquet in a minute. The temperature shifts. The atmosphere becomes thicker and gets caught in my throat. Everyone in class is less interested in Mrs Doe and her legendary temper, and more intrigued by the current exchange of opinion. They all know that we won't be talking about soppy books for much longer.

It's not nails down the blackboard, but it comes close: Jase still seated and pushing his chair slowly back. A plan formulating behind those pinched eyes.

'No one's interested in this book, miss. Why can't we read that one on The Krays, like the other class?'

Pearson continues to lecture but, like the rest of the room, has his eyes on the chair legs as they move closer to the desk behind. Jase is no longer holding his text open at the page we are supposed to be examining. His fist is wrapped around his pen, nib out. Even Lizzie Jennings, who's supposed to hate him after he dumped her outside Tesco, is fixed on his every move.

'I would hardly call The Krays literature,' goes Mrs Doe, who, with her sixth sense that all of the older teachers have when they sniff an ounce of trouble, moves to a space behind our row of desks, at a point equidistant between the two of us.

She stands legs apart, arms behind her back like a high-kicking FBI chick who kills truculent boys with her bare hands. This would be funny if she wasn't nearly sixty and so sharp-tongued.

'Has anyone else got any thoughts they'd like to share? We can talk about any book you like, so long as it's fiction.'

Only me and Pearson raise our hands.

He's up on his feet. I wasn't ready. For once I was actually thinking about the book. The sound of more chairs sliding back, a symphony of screech as everyone prepares themselves for what they think will come next.

It's all very quick. Mrs Doe doesn't get a chance to move out of her FBI-agent-on-alert position. Everything that happens is down to Jase.

In years to come, if we are all still alive and haven't been fried in the electric chair, Jase's dive will become legendary: a sudden leap downwards that most goalies would kill for. It helps that his arms are so long and rubbery, shooting past the statue that is Mrs Doe, and reaching for Pearson's legs.

Both of them are on the floor. Jason on top of Pearson and going for his throat. Pearson struggling to break free, his hands uselessly flattened under him. He wriggles like a half-alive fish in the fryer and makes use of his legs instead, giving one high kick after another.

Most get Jason in the back. Only one manages to hit the target and get him in the head. Gives Jase a hint. He stops strangling Pearson and starts bashing his head against the floor instead.

Mrs Doe is getting her hands dirty during all of this. She doesn't quite step between the boys, but does a job in trying to get Jase off Pearson. She looks like she'd like to slide between them and act as a buffer, if only she wasn't wearing a skirt. She stands to the right, closest to the boys' heads, and pulls at Jase's shoulder, hefty pulls that wouldn't look out of place on a farm, country wife pulling calf out of a ditch, that kind of thing. She gets Jase up a couple of times, but isn't able to see it through. As soon as he senses her tiring, which comes after each great heave, he dives back downwards, the full weight of his body falling back on Pearson. His arms still locked around the bastard's neck means that Pearson is granted a similar window.

Everyone by this point is up on their feet, including me. With Mrs Doe taking the head, I stand at their feet as they flip back and forth, feeling useless and not relieved. It should have been me choking the breath out of Pearson, not Jase. It should have been my call. Pearson continues to twist around, making it hard for Jase to maintain a firm grip, but seeing his face contorted like a fucker, childbirth sounds replacing all the words of earlier, cheeks puffed out with the sheer exertion it takes simply trying to breathe, I still wished it was my hands round his throat. As it was, the way they were thrashing about, I couldn't get involved without looking like Jase's boyfriend, even if you counted all the stuff that had happened earlier. I'm useless. A spare part that's good for nothing.

I do something with the legs, push them about a bit, so that it looks like I'm doing something. If you were standing over me, I'd look real busy the way I rolled my sleeves up and got my hands dirty. You wouldn't guess that my heart wasn't in it.

'Pull him towards you! See if you can make a gap!' shouts Mrs Doe, pointing at Jase with her spare arm. She thinks I'm trying to break them up. I take everything back about the sixth-sense stuff. She's thick.

She yells something else a couple of times, but I can't hear her over the noise from the rest of the class, who are now circling us and screaming all kinds of stuff. No one names names, in case it implicates them later on, but reading between the lines it's mostly shit about Pearson asking for it. Aside from the predictable stoner stuff mouthed by the pretty girls who wished they were at a school where they had cheerleaders, there isn't a bad word to be said about Jase. He's safe, totally.

I'm still pissing about with the lower half, unable to get a punch in, especially now Mrs Doe has christened me her special envoy. I don't feel angry now either, for some reason. Being the gooseberry fighter seems to have drained it out of me. Either that, or any feeling I have is being transferred over to a now-colourless Pearson.

The bell goes, five minutes early. Everyone stops a second, including Jase and Pearson. He loosens his grip on his neck and lets Pearson get some breaths in. The way Pearson gulps for air so noisily, like he's either going to cry or be sick, is so undignified. It makes me embarrassed for him. The bell rings too loud and too long to be a lesson bell. We all stand like statues, not sure of what we're hearing. Fire practise? At a time like this?

Mrs Doe regains her scary element and howls at everyone to clear the room.

'Get out! Get out!' she shouts, like she's just found her husband boffing the neighbour or something.

Jase and Pearson are already up on their feet. They're not stupid. They want to kick the shit out of each other, but neither wants to fry to a crisp unnecessarily. Also, a persistent fire bell gets us all off the hook. Mrs Doe is too busy counting heads and shooing us out to do anything else.

66

We do the sensible thing and hide in the second-floor loos: me, Jase, and a now-breathing Pearson. Moon, who's been txted, is already waiting for us. It's times like this that you need some privacy to handle your business.

67

Gwyn corners me when I'm taking out the bins.

'I don't want you getting any ideas, but I want to make a go of it, us being friends. I don't care what anyone will think. Life's too short.'

'You don't know how happy that makes me,' I go, hugging her in the middle of the drive, not caring whether my mum or her mum sees us.

'This doesn't have anything to do with you telling me about Moon in those last moments. That'll come when you're ready. For now, let's just enjoy things.'

She moves her mouth to my cheek, but I keep her in the hug. Grateful, uncertain. Looks more convincing this way.

I tell her again how happy this makes me, but not how good it will make me look if anyone starts to dig too deep into what I did and didn't do when Pearson had his hand on the knife.

68

There's a whole load of things we shouldn't have done:
- Jason shouldn't have left to retrieve his iPod
- We shouldn't have given up on words
- Moon shouldn't have come between me and Pearson
- Pearson shouldn't have been tooled up
- I shouldn't have gone for Pearson's wrist once he'd got the knife out, and started twisting it
- Pearson shouldn't have kept hold of the knife
- I shouldn't have kept twisting his lower arm, and pushing, slamming his back against the sink
- Pearson shouldn't have kept hold of the knife
- Moon shouldn't have tried to prise us apart, not while I still had a hand on his arm
- Pearson shouldn't have been tooled up
- Moon shouldn't have spoken when she did
- I shouldn't have still been twisting Pearson's arm
- Pearson shouldn't have lunged towards me
- Moon shouldn't have been wedged between us
- Moon shouldn't have been caught in the stomach
- Not cut. Plunged. Sounding like a potato falling into a sack
- Moon shouldn't have looked at me like that. That's all I've got to say about it
- We shouldn't have frozen. We could have saved Moon otherwise
- The toilets shouldn't have been the most silent room in the school. One of us should have done something
- I shouldn't have run to the far corner like some coward
- Pearson shouldn't have had his hand still on the knife

– Moon shouldn't have just stood there. She should have run towards me for help

– Pearson shouldn't have taken the knife out

– Moon shouldn't be losing this amount of blood. It's like someone's dipped her shirt in red ink

– I shouldn't have stood in the corner like a dirty peeping tom. I should have tried to do something

– Pearson shouldn't still have the knife in his hand, not when Year Head comes in

– Jason shouldn't have followed her back in

– Year Head shouldn't have screamed. It sent Pearson further into shock

– Jason shouldn't have screamed. It woke me up and I saw how far Moon was gone

– Year Head shouldn't have tried to give First Aid. It was way too late for that, you can't just scoop the lost blood back into a person. All it did was ensure she'd have a messed up mind for years to come

– Jason shouldn't have been packed off to call for assistance. If he'd have seen more, I might have been able to open up to him

– Moon shouldn't have stayed so silent

– Pearson shouldn't have lost the use of his mouth

– I shouldn't have regained the use of mine. Made sure I got my story straight

69

Mike takes me out when Mum isn't around. Eases me back into the outside world. Going to the Oaks on Epsom Downs, where he gives me a tenner to bet with and I lose the lot. Letting me get away with some very illegal Mercedes-driving on the lanes around Dorking. He takes things slowly. Doesn't pretend to be a dad. Acts like he might actually be interested in me; that I might be worth knowing. Having Mike around makes me less afraid – about a lot of things.

'Want to try flying a plane? There's an airfield about an hour away I could take you to, if you like.'

'You'd let me fly a plane?'

'There's training to do first, fella. You've got a couple of years making-do with the simulator before we can let you go charging around. But . . .'

'No worries. I'll ask Mum when I'm eighteen.'

'You give up too easy, V! We can't call ourselves an action team unless we get you up in a plane! I'll take you up this afternoon. So you can get a feel for it.'

'You'd do that?'

'Course! And when you need your form signing, come to me. I'll still be around.'

A week later at paintballing, he throws himself in front of me to avoid getting hit by his goon friends. He gets caught on the shoulder, the force sending him headlong into my sternum. He holds the pain in his jaw, his priority being a pat on the shoulder to see if I'm OK, and then a push towards the nearest tree before I make a big deal about it.

Once we got the hang of the paintguns, we're heroic on the field. Kings of stealth. Moving in sync like a boyband. He's all signs and no sound. I'm his mirror. By the time our session's over, I've all these endorphins flooding out of me. Makes me feel like doing a victory lap.

On the way back to the car, I get tangled whilst trying to pull myself out of the boilersuit. Mike paid the guy so that we could keep ours – I wanted to show Mum what multi-coloured war wounds look like. My protective vest is an over-the-head number. I get it stuck around my ears like a five-year-old. Mike stops me almost ripping my chain off in my hurry.

'St Christopher? That's a blast from the past.'

'You got one too?'

'Got it when I was confirmed. Never wear it, though. What's with yours?'

'Just an old present. Reminds me of the time when I got it.'

'Birthday?'

'Nah. Just reminds me of good intentions. Not always best received.'

'Now you're talking my language! Did you know your mum's on another food fad? She almost bit my head off when I gave her breakfast in bed.'

'What was it? Bacon?'

'No. Toast.'

When I'm older, I'll have a laugh thinking about how I was such an eejit.

Mike doesn't bring up the subject of school. He's not like that. He isn't nosy. Somehow that makes me want to tell him everything. There's two weeks left 'til the holidays. Mum says there's no point in going back before then. But this morning I woke up and find myself txting Jase. Like it's the most natural thing in the world. Seeing if he'll meet me at the shops. Safe, he txts back.

Everyone needs to pack up their kid gloves. I'm ready.

Acknowledgements

Thanks to the following for all their hard work and belief: Mark Stanton at Jenny Brown Associates, Jamie Byng, Kate Weinberg, Francis Bickmore, and everyone at Canongate. Shout-outs to Shoshanna, Jersey Girl and Suzie F for sound advice on things spiritual and athletic.

H / The Stiletto / Ruben – for saving my bacon.

Neely – coolest sister ever.

Love to family and friends, without whom . . .

THE RAW SHARK TEXTS

Steven Hall

Eric Sanderson wakes up in a place he doesn't recognise. All he can recall are memories of Clio, a perfect love now gone. When he starts receiving letters signed 'With regret and also hope, The First Eric Sanderson', he embarks on a search to recover everything he has lost. *The Raw Shark Texts* is a heartbreaking love story, a brain-warping thriller and a one-way trip into the dangerous waters of the mind.

'Fast, sexy, intriguing, intelligent — a cult waiting to happen.' Toby Litt

£7.99
ISBN 978 1 84767 024 3

FRESH

Mark McNay

Winner of the Arts Foundation New Fiction Award

Sean's days are of a kind. The factory. The chickens . . . And his dreams of escape. But today, his brother Archie gets out of jail. Which would be great if Archie weren't a little loose in the head. And if Sean didn't still owe him a grand. This white-knuckle ride brings to life one unforgettable day. Mark McNay's debut marks the arrival of a major new talent. *(And you'll never buy supermarket chicken again.)*

'Funny, moving, gripping, magical and tragic.' Niall Griffiths

£10.99
ISBN 978 1 84195 929 0

BORN FREE

Laura Hird

Shortlisted for the Whitbread First Novel Award

Punchy, sharp-witted and above all acutely observed, *Born Free* tells the story of an ordinary family who are all trying to escape from something . . . and each other. The voices of Jake, Joni, Angie and Vic reveal a hellish cocktail of adolescent and mid-life crises, savage sibling rivalry, a marriage gone cold — and naturally, the unbridgeable gap between generations. It's a story of everyday life.

'Desperately readable, blackly comic and painful, a delight born of dysfunction.' *The Times*

£7.99
ISBN 978 1 84195 048 8